SEVEN
DAYS

Alex Lake is a British novelist who was born in the North West of England. *After Anna*, the author's first novel written under this pseudonym, was a No.1 bestselling ebook sensation and a *USA Today* bestseller. The author now lives in the North East of the US.

🐦 @AlexLakeAuthor

Also by Alex Lake

After Anna
Killing Kate
Copycat
The Last Lie

SEVEN DAYS

ALEX LAKE

HarperCollins*Publishers*

HarperCollins*Publishers* Ltd
1 London Bridge Street,
London SE1 9GF

www.harpercollins.co.uk

First published by HarperCollins*Publishers* 2019

19 20 21 22 LSC 10 9 8 7 6 5 4 3 2 1

Copyright © Alex Lake 2019

Alex Lake asserts the moral right to
be identified as the author of this work

A catalogue record for this book is available from the British Library

ISBN: 978-0-00-835896-9

This novel is entirely a work of fiction.
The names, characters and incidents portrayed in it are
the work of the author's imagination. Any resemblance to
actual persons, living or dead, events or localities is
entirely coincidental.

Set in Sabon LT Std 10.5pt/13.5 pt
by Palimpsest Book Production Limited, Falkirk, Stirlingshire

Printed and bound in the United States of America by LSC Communications

For more information visit: www.harpercollins.co.uk/green

To Norman: we miss you.
Rest in peace, old friend.

Saturday, 16 June 2018

Seven Days to Go

Suddenly it was so close.

Max's birthday – his third birthday, the one that counted – was right below the date she had just crossed out.

S	Su	M	Tu	W	Th	F
						~~1~~
~~2~~	~~3~~	~~4~~	~~5~~	~~6~~	~~7~~	~~8~~
~~9~~	~~10~~	~~11~~	~~12~~	~~13~~	~~14~~	~~15~~
~~16~~	17	18	19	20	21	22
23	24	25	26	27	28	29
30						

Which meant it was one week until the twenty-third of June.

Seven days away. That was all. Seven more days until it happened. She had been trying to ignore it, but seeing it there, the very next Saturday, made that impossible.

It was a wonder she had the calendar at all. She had started keeping it on the fifth day after she had been locked in this basement. If she hadn't, there was no doubt she would have completely lost track of how long she'd been held captive. There had been times – terrible, terrible times – when she had been unable to record the passing days and weeks as accurately as she would have liked. But as it was, she knew more or less how much time had passed, how many years – eleven, soon to be twelve – since she had seen her parents and brother and older cousin, Anne, who she had been on the way to meet when she made the mistake of speaking to the man in the car that slowed to a stop next to her.

When she'd started the calendar, she'd had no idea that more than a decade later she would still be using it. She'd expected – foolishly, as it turned out – to be back with her family and friends well before this much time had gone by, although even after five days she was starting to understand that this might be something that lasted longer than she could have ever anticipated. She was glad she had the calendar though, glad she had asked for some paper and a pencil – the pencil was a short, yellow one from Ikea, she recalled – and sketched out a calendar in tiny figures on one side. It was her only link to the outside world. Even though it was not totally accurate, on the days she thought were the birthdays and anniversaries of her friends and relatives, she imagined them having parties and opening presents, and in doing so, she felt, in a way, that she was with them.

Since Max was born, the calendar had assumed a new importance; she'd become obsessed with ensuring it was accurate. Her son – named after the boy in *Where the Wild Things Are*, because the storybook Max was able to escape his room through a magic door and travel to the island where the Wild Things lived, and freedom was something she longed for her little boy to experience – had been born on 23 June 2015. And ever since that day she'd had one dread eye on his third birthday.

2

On the day her first son, Seb, turned three, the door to the basement had opened and he – the man whose name she still did not know and whom she thought of only as 'the man' – had come in. Unsmiling, as usual, but with a nervousness which was new.

He pointed at her son. At his son.

Give him to me, he said.

Why? she replied.

Just give him to me.

No.

I want to show him the world. I'll bring him back later.

She refused again.

It's his birthday. I'll get him ice cream. Take him to a park. Think of what you're denying him.

She knew it was close to his birthday. At that point, the calendar was missing a few days here and there, but back then she hadn't thought it mattered.

And it would be nice for him to have a treat. So she agreed.

It was the last time she saw her firstborn. The next time the man came to the room he was alone.

She asked for Seb hundreds – thousands, maybe – of times, but he just shook his head, refusing to say where her boy was. Once, he told her, *Don't worry, he's safe*, but she didn't believe it. If a three-year-old boy had suddenly appeared in his life, people would have asked where the child came from, who the mother was. There was no way he wanted those questions, so she thought she knew what had happened.

The man had made the problem disappear.

He'd taken her little boy and killed him, then disposed of his body somewhere it would never be found.

Beside herself with grief, she'd lost weight – a lot of weight, enough that her skin grew loose and she could almost see the shape of the bones in her arms and legs – but it didn't stop the man coming to the basement and gesturing to the

3

bed in the corner with that curt little nod of his, then waiting for her to lie down and undress before he lay on top of her and did what he did while she closed her eyes and waited for it to be over and for him to be back upstairs in his house where she didn't have to look at him.

And, of course, the thing she had feared most came to pass. Another child. She tried to stop it. Tried to starve the baby to death inside her, but all that happened was she grew thinner and thinner herself until the man figured out what was going on and forced her to eat. Why, she didn't know. Why he wanted the baby to be born was a mystery to her, but then most of what he did was a mystery to her. How could you understand a man who locked a fifteen-year-old girl in a basement for years, then stole her son? Why even try?

And then the new baby was born. A boy again. Pink and beautiful and red-haired. She hadn't wanted him, but now he was there she loved him uncontrollably. Leo, she called him. Leo the lion, with his mane of red hair.

He was different to Seb. Smaller. More watchful. Quicker. By the time he was two he could talk, whole sentences. At two and a half he could read the alphabet. She had taught him by writing out tiny letters on a scrap of paper.

At three he was gone. On his birthday, the man came. He pointed at Leo.

Give him to me, he said.

No, she replied. *Not this time.*

Yes, he said, in his heavy, slow voice. *Yes.*

This time she fought, but it was no use. It had never been any use, not since the first time she had tried and he had taught her – in the most awful, awful way – never to try again. But she had. She had held Leo to her chest, but the man hit her and forced her on to her back and held his forearm against her throat then prised her arms apart until he had Leo and she was unconscious. The last thing she saw before she passed out was her beautiful boy wriggling from his arms and running away.

But there was only one place for Leo to go, and he went there.

Through the open door and up the stairs, to the place the man lived.

The next time she saw him she didn't bother asking where Leo was. There was no point.

And then, as though the universe was punishing her, the cycle repeated itself. The door opening. The nod at the bed. The disgusting act.

Then the missed period and the cramps and the feeling of being bloated and uncomfortable. And nine months later, another baby.

Another boy.

Max, after the boy in *Where the Wild Things Are*.

Max, the curly-haired, ever-smiling, bright-eyed button of joy who she loved with an intensity that surpassed anything she had felt before, even with Seb and Leo, if only because since the day he had arrived she had known she would only have three years with him, three short years into which she had to cram a lifetime of love.

Max, who would turn three on Saturday, 23 June.

She looked at him, sleeping on the mattress they shared, spread-eagled on his back, mouth slightly open and she shook her head.

It couldn't happen again. It couldn't.

But it would. She was powerless. The man would come and open the door and take Max from her, whatever she did. And even if she stopped him somehow, it would only be a temporary respite. He would put sleeping pills in her food or knock her unconscious and take her little boy.

She couldn't fight him every day of Max's life.

And so she had seven days left. Seven days with her son. Seven days until he was ripped from her arms.
Or seven days to find a way to save him.

Twelve Years Earlier,
7 July 2006

1

Maggie pulled on the baby-blue Doc Martens her boyfriend, Kevin, had bought her for her fifteenth birthday. She'd had mixed emotions when she unwrapped the present a week before; she really, really wanted the boots, but they were expensive, and although Kevin was sweet and she was very fond of him, she already knew he wasn't the one – she couldn't see him as the first person she'd have sex with. What they had wasn't special enough, at least not to her, and she'd decided she was going to break up with him. Knowing that, accepting the boots didn't seem fair. She'd seen it on her mum's face, too. When Maggie pulled the boots from the box, her mum had glanced at her, her forehead creased in a frown.

For a moment, Maggie had considered refusing, but that would have been even more awkward. She'd have had to explain why, and she wasn't quite ready for that, wasn't quite ready to break his heart, not on her birthday.

Besides, they really were *amazing* boots.

She stood up and looked in the hallway mirror. She pulled her hair – recently dyed jet black from her natural copper-tinged brown – into a ponytail, considered it, then let it fall loose around her neck. She could never make up her mind what was better. It was long and thick, and wearing it down showed it off. It meant more care though, or at least a more expensive haircut, and she didn't feel like asking her parents for money. Though they both worked, things were tight – they didn't talk about it in front of her and James, her little brother, but she picked up on comments they made about being careful buying groceries and saw how her dad only put in ten pounds' worth of petrol at a time.

Anyway, that didn't matter at the moment. She was going to see Anne, her nineteen-year-old cousin, to get some advice on what to do about Kevin. She grabbed her backpack and walked down the hall.

'Maggie!'

It was her dad. She paused at the front door. He was probably going to tell her to tidy her room or ask if she'd done her homework. If she left immediately, all he would hear was the door closing. When she got home she could say she hadn't heard him.

She gripped the handle. Behind her, the door to the living room opened.

'Maggie.' Her dad was standing there, a piece of paper in his hand. 'Before you go, we need to talk.'

She rolled her eyes. She knew it was immature, and she hated it – she wasn't a little girl any more, she had grown-up decisions to make about things like Kevin, and when it was right to have sex with someone, which was one of the things she was going to ask Anne about – but somehow her parents always brought out her childish side. She hated it, but she simply couldn't help it.

Ironically, on the way home from Gran's the other day, her mum had admitted, *You know, Mags, I'm forty-one years old, but I still feel like a naughty teenager when I'm talking to your gran.*

So maybe it would always be this way.

'What is it, Dad? I'm late.'

'Oh,' he said. 'You're late? I've never known you to worry about that before, but I'm glad you've finally seen the value in punctuality. Let's hope this new approach lasts until Monday morning when it's time to leave for school.'

'Very funny, Dad.' It actually *was* quite funny. Her friends all thought her dad was hilarious, but she wasn't going to tell him that. 'You do know that sarcasm is the lowest form of wit, don't you?'

'I've heard that,' he said. 'And I'm sorry to cause you distress by violating your new-found sense of punctuality by making you even later, but we need to discuss *this*.' He shook the piece of paper. 'It's the phone bill, in case you were wondering.'

The phone bill. Of all things, *that* was what he wanted to talk about?

'Do we have to do it now, Dad? Can't it wait? It's only a phone bill.'

'Only a phone bill for one hundred and' – he peered at the total – 'seventy-six pounds, and nineteen pence.'

'So?' Maggie said. 'I didn't make all the calls.'

'No,' he said. 'Not all of them. But the majority.'

'There's no *way* I made the majority of calls,' Maggie replied. 'James is always on the phone.'

'That's probably how it appears to you. In the few gaps you leave each evening, he manages to squeeze in and grab a few minutes before you wrestle the phone back from him. But I think it's fair to say you're the primary phone user in this house.'

There was a long pause, which Maggie filled by shaking her head, the slowness of the shake indicating the depth of her disbelief.

'That is *so* unfair,' she said.

'Really?' Her dad smiled. It was a smile she hated, smug and pleased with himself. 'One of the things you should know about phone bills is that they are itemized,' he said. 'Every call. Number and duration.' He tapped the phone bill. 'Take this number, called on the seventh of April at seven minutes past five for sixty-one minutes. And again that same evening, at eight twenty-two, this time for ninety-six minutes. It appears the following day, then the day after that, then there's a break for a day, and then it appears again – every evening until the twenty-fourth of April.' He read out the number. 'Do you recognize it?'

'You know I do,' Maggie said. It was Chrissie, one of her best friends. Chrissie had moved to Nottingham – which made it a long-distance call from Stockton Heath – and was having trouble settling in. 'Chrissie needs me, Dad.'

'Then perhaps *she* should call *you*.'

'Her parents won't let her! They put a pin code on the phone.'

'Look,' her dad said, 'I understand you want—'

'Need,' Maggie said.

'Need to talk to your friends. But it costs a lot of money. And apart from anything else, what if someone needs to call us? The phone's always engaged.'

'It wouldn't be if you bought me a mobile,' Maggie said. 'Then you wouldn't have to worry about your precious phone being tied up.'

'I'm not sure that would save any money,' he replied. 'Mobiles are more expensive than land lines. And we talked about it. You can get a phone when you're sixteen.'

'My friends all have mobile phones!' she said. 'It's not fair!'

'When you're sixteen,' her dad said. 'Or when you can pay for it yourself.'

'Fine,' Maggie said. This was *so* annoying. 'Whatever.'

'Maggie,' her dad said. 'I know it's important to you to talk to your friends, and I know this is your house too, but you have to be prepared to compromise. I think maybe one and a half hours a night should be the maximum you spend on the phone. I don't think I'm being unreasonable.'

'Sure. Can we talk about it later, Dad? I need to leave.'

'You want a lift?'

Maggie considered it for a second, then shook her head. 'I can walk. I'm only going to Anne's.'

'OK,' he said. 'Are you back for dinner?'

'Yeah. See you then.'

'See you too, Fruitcake. Love you.'

Fruitcake. He'd called her that since she was a little girl. She kind of hated it, but she also knew that one day there'd be a last time he called her Fruitcake.

And she wasn't sure she was ready for that day just yet.

2

Maggie's Cousin Anne lived on the other side of the village. It was a short walk – no more than half a mile – which she had made many times. The road outside her house led to the village centre, but she turned off it after about a hundred yards and walked along a quiet residential street towards a small park. It was a short cut, of sorts, but the main reason she wanted to go through the park was so she could smoke a cigarette. A stream bordered one edge of the park; it was slow moving and full of litter and nobody – no adults, at least – ever bothered with it. It was the perfect place to hide while you smoked.

It was Kevin who had got her started; the first few times she'd coughed and spluttered and wondered how anyone got addicted to something so disgusting, but after a while she'd grown to quite enjoy it. There was something about the ritual that appealed to her – the flare of the match, the crackle of the paper when it lit, the rush of the nicotine – although what she really enjoyed was the feeling that she was doing something her parents didn't know about. Something grown-up.

She felt in her bag for the cigarettes and matches and smiled as her fingers closed around them. She took one out and held it in her hand, unlit. She'd share one with Anne later. Anne smoked, too; she didn't know yet that her younger cousin had taken it up. Maggie was looking forward to telling her.

She was also looking forward to what Anne had to say about Kevin. He was going to be devastated, Maggie already knew that. They'd been together nearly six months, and, a few weeks back he'd said how it seemed like a month or two, max.

Maybe that's what it'll be like for us, he said. *The years will fly by.*

Years? It was then that Maggie realized they were not in the same place when it came to their relationship. For her, it had been a bit of fun that had lasted six months because Kevin made it work. For him, it was something a lot more significant.

Have you ever thought about taking . . . she said, and hesitated, *about like, maybe taking a break?*

They were lying on her couch and he tensed.

What do you mean? Do you want to take a break?

No, she said. *I was wondering if you want to. If you've had enough of me. I don't want to. Of course not.*

He relaxed, a little.

No, he said. *I've never thought about that. The opposite, in fact. You know I love you, Maggie.*

He had started telling her all the time that he loved her. She found it very irritating. She felt she had to reply in kind.

I know, she said. *I know you do.*

Do you love me?

You don't need to ask, Maggie said. All of a sudden she didn't want to say it. Before, it had felt like an imposition; now it felt like a lie.

Do you? he said. *Do you love me, Mags?*

He'd also started calling her Mags. That was what her

13

dad called her, when he wasn't calling her Fruitcake. It wasn't for Kevin.

Maybe for someone else, later, but not for Kevin.

Mags? he said. *What's wrong?*

She pushed him away and stood up. *Nothing. I'm getting my period. I'm going to get some water.*

That had been his reaction to a vague question about taking a break. She dreaded to think what it would be when she told him she wanted to break up. Anne would have some advice.

The realization that a car had pulled up beside her broke her reverie. She started, and dropped her cigarette. She crushed it under her foot, in case it was someone who knew her parents, although if it was, it was probably too late. They'd have seen it in her hand as they stopped next to her.

The car was dark blue and nondescript. A Ford or something. Maybe a Volkswagen. Nothing too fancy, either way. She didn't recognize it, thankfully. She glanced inside. There was a man behind the wheel, a road atlas in his hands. He was reaching for some glasses and peering at the page. He turned to look at her and smiled. He was about fifty and reminded her of a geography teacher.

No one she knew. She took her foot off the cigarette. No need to worry about that now.

The man looked at the panel by the gearstick and selected a button, his gestures very deliberate, as though new to the technology and needing to think about what he was doing. The passenger-side window rolled down.

'Sorry,' he said. He had a quiet, soft voice and a worried expression. She felt a little sorry for him. 'I'm a bit lost, I'm afraid. Do you know where Ackers Lane is? Is it near here?'

It was on the other side of the park, but to get there by car you had to go through the village.

'You'll have to turn around,' Maggie said. 'When you get

to the main road, turn right, and then right again at the traffic lights. I think it's second – or maybe third – left after that. Ackers Lane is about half a mile down there.'

'What's the name of the road I turn into?' he said.

'I'm not sure,' Maggie replied.

'And you said it's second left?'

'Maybe third.'

'OK,' the man said. 'Thank you.' He paused. 'Sorry to bother you. It's a friend of my mother's. She's very frail and she had a fall. I need to get to her as soon as I can.'

'That's fine,' Maggie said. 'No problem. And good luck.'

The man shook his head. 'Dash it,' he said. 'I'm so sorry. I can't quite remember what you said. Was it left on the main road?'

'Right,' Maggie said. 'Then right again at the lights.'

'I thought it was second left? Or third?'

'That's after you go right at the lights.' It was obvious from the man's blank expression that he wasn't following her. 'Look,' she said. 'It's easy. Let's start again.'

He held up the road atlas. 'Would you mind showing me on the map?'

'Of course,' Maggie said. 'Pass it over.'

The man unbuckled and twisted in his chair so he could pass the atlas over the passenger seat. She noticed that he held it in his right hand, which was weird, since his left hand was closer to her.

His left hand which, with a sudden, unexpected speed, snaked out and grabbed her wrist and yanked her towards the window.

Then he dropped the atlas, and she saw the syringe in his hand, and felt the prick of the needle in her arm. She just had time to read the front page of the atlas and think it was odd that he had a map of Cornwall when he was in Stockton Heath, and then everything went dark.

15

3

Her first thought was that she had a hangover. She recognized the sensation – throbbing temples, dry mouth, disorientation – from the time that she and Chrissie had drunk a bottle of cheap white cider in the park, and then, somehow, made their way to Chrissie's house and passed out in her bedroom. Maggie had woken when it was still dark out and thought *What happened?* before the memories of the cider and the park and the two boys that had bought it for them came slowly back.

This was different, though. This time the memories that surfaced were not of cider and boys and the park.

They were of a car, and a man asking for directions and a syringe.

Holy shit.

Her eyes flew open.

She was looking at a low ceiling, covered in some kind of dark carpet tile.

A ceiling she did not recognize.

The dryness in her mouth intensified and her stomach tightened. Her pulse sped up and pounded in her neck. She sat up too quickly and felt suddenly dizzy; for a moment she thought she was going to pass out, but then her head cleared and she saw where she was.

She was on a narrow, thin mattress in a room lit by a dim lamp on a table by the bed. The room was small; the ends of the mattress were against the walls. There was an area about twice the size of the mattress covered in a brown carpet. In one corner were two blue, plastic buckets, a pink bowl with a jug inside it, and a tall wooden, barrel.

What the fuck were they *there for*? Maggie stared at them, aware that, in the back of her mind, she knew exactly what they were. She just didn't want to face it.

They were the toilet, sink and bath.

She looked away. In the other corner was a door. Beside it was a box that looked like it contained a towel and possibly some clothes.

And that was it. Other than that, the room was empty.

It was also windowless, which explained the dank, musty smell.

Maggie folded her arms protectively. She was still clothed, still wearing the grey jeans and Gap hoodie she'd left the house in.

But there was something missing. She glanced at her feet. Her blue Doc Martens had been removed.

Which meant someone – the man – had touched her while she was unconscious.

Her stomach heaved and she tasted bile in her mouth. She fought the urge to be sick, but she retched again and realized she was not going to be able to stop it. She staggered to the pink bowl and leaned over it and threw up, over and over, until her stomach was empty.

Then she sat back on the mattress. The room was silent and empty, unchanged apart from the sour smell of vomit that cut through the stale air.

'Hello?' she said. 'Hello?'

17

The words seemed to vanish, swallowed up by the walls. There were no echoes, no reverberations, no indications that the sound of her voice had left the room.

She looked at the door and got to her feet. There was some explanation for this. Maybe she'd fallen ill, or been hit by a car and the man who looked like her geography teacher had brought her here to keep her safe, unaware of her name or address. He was probably upstairs – she was sure the room was underground – waiting for her to wake up so he could take her home.

If that was the case – and it had to be, it simply had to be, because the alternative was too awful to contemplate, which was why she was ignoring it and pretending that there was an innocent explanation here – if that *was* the case then the door would be unlocked and would open when she tried it and she would walk up the stairs and in an hour or so she'd be at home with her mum and dad, sitting with them on the sofa and never, never leaving them again.

She took the few steps – three, she counted – to the door and reached out. The silver metal handle was cold.

And it did not move. She tried it a few times, each time with more and more force, but it was pointless.

She was in a locked room.

The thought did not quite register.

She was in a locked room.

She was – the word forced itself into her consciousness for the first time – a prisoner.

She reached in her pocket for her cigarettes. She had a sudden need for the rush of nicotine, of something familiar.

They were gone.

She sat heavily on the mattress. Despite the carpet, the floor was cold on her feet and she looked for her boots, but they were gone. Clearly the man did not think she would have much use for them here.

18

Her boots had been taken off and the door was locked and there was a bucket for a toilet and a bowl for a sink and a barrel for a bath, which meant that the man who looked like her geography teacher – the man who had, she now understood, kidnapped her – intended to keep her here for a very long time.

Forever, she thought. *He wants me here forever. He can't let me go because then I'd tell people what he did and he'd be in trouble. So he has to keep me here.*

She pulled her knees up and hugged them to her chest. She looked around the room, taking in the brown carpet that covered the floor and ran up the walls and over the ceiling, the locked door and the lumpy mattress lit by the weak yellow light pooling out from the one lamp by the bed.

And she understood something else.

He had prepared the room for this purpose. He had a plan.

And she was now part of it.

Sunday, 17 June 2018

Six Days to Go

1

She crossed off another day.

S	Su	M	Tu	W	Th	F
						~~1~~
~~2~~	~~3~~	~~4~~	~~5~~	6	~~7~~	~~8~~
~~9~~	~~10~~	~~11~~	~~12~~	~~13~~	~~14~~	~~15~~
~~16~~	~~17~~	18	19	20	21	22
23	24	25	26	27	28	29
30						

Six days to go until his birthday. She watched him stack his Duplo blocks into a tower, then knock it down, giggle, and build it again. God, his world was so small.

A low ceiling, four carpeted walls – she hated that carpet, *hated* its dust and smell and drab brown colour, and she had vowed that when she was out of here she was going to have a house with clean, wooden floors in every room – the sink-bowl and toilet-bucket and barrel-bath and a door he had never been through.

That was it. That was Max's world. He didn't even understand what the door was for. As far as he knew, it was for the man to come in and out of. He had no idea he could use it, had no experience of all the things that were out there.

No experience of fields and ponds and schools and roads and houses and shops. All he had was what she had told him. She'd asked for books and photos but the man had told her there was no point. He was too young to understand.

And he'll be gone when he's three.

The man hadn't said that, but he didn't need to. It was implicit in his refusal. He rarely gave her anything. It was only after weeks of begging when Seb was born that he'd brought a box of Lego, the large ones for little kids. Duplo, they were called. There weren't many, but Max – as Seb had – loved them. He played with them for hours, arranging them into towers and arches and walls. Once he had made a rectangle filled with odd-shaped objects and Maggie had asked him what it was.

Our house, he replied. *Look. That's the bath. That's you and me. That's the bed.*

She had to bite back the tears. Other kids were building space rockets or gardens or trains. Max was building the only thing he knew.

This shitty prison.

And so she took him places in his imagination, described the blue of the sea by pointing to his blue socks, but told him the sea was a different blue, a brilliant blue, a beautiful shining blue, words that he didn't understand but which reminded her of the world out there, of what she too was missing. She explained the coolness of the breeze by moistening his forehead and blowing on it, and the warmth of the sun by rubbing her hands until they were hot and placing them on his chest. All of it was a pale imitation of the real thing, but it was all she had.

She didn't stop there; she told stories of magical palaces and boats and rivers where Max and she had wild adventures. Along the way they met heroic people with the names Grandpa Martin and Grandma Sandra and Uncle James and Aunty Anne and Chrissie and Fern. She told him how Chrissie was brave and loyal but could be grumpy and Fern was funny and clever but left things wherever she went. She told him how Uncle James was kind of grumpy but sweet and well-meaning, and how Aunty Anne was wise and Grandpa and Grandma were kind and loving, and how they loved him in particular. The stories ended with huge parties where there was every kind of food and all the toys a boy could wish for. She wondered what Max thought chocolate and jelly beans and burgers and milkshakes tasted like. She wondered whether he would ever find out.

She sat on the mattress and watched him play with the Duplo. Behind him, by the door, were two plates. Max had left half of the mashed potato and baked beans the man had brought; Maggie had barely touched hers.

'OK, Max,' she said. 'Time for our exercises.'

She was worried he didn't get enough activity – of course he didn't, living in a cell – so for the last year or so she had been doing exercises with him. They began with jogging on the spot – he found that amusing – and then they dropped to the floor and did press-ups and sit-ups. Max's press-ups mainly consisted of him raising his bottom in the air and then collapsing to the floor, but it was something. Maggie had found that, as the months went by, she could do more and more of them; now it was no trouble to do fifty at a stretch. She also did tricep dips and planks; she could hold the plank for over four minutes.

Maggie took off her T-shirt and shorts – it was always

23

uncomfortably hot in the room, the air still and cloying; the only time there was any fresh air was when the man came and cooler air gusted in through the open door – and knelt on the floor. She dropped into the press-up position and did twenty press-ups, then held herself on her elbows.

'OK, Max,' she said. 'Come and join me.'

Max toddled over. He was in a pair of dirty underpants – she tried to keep them clean, but it was hard with only soap and cold water – and lay on his belly next to her. On the back of the underpants was a Superman logo she'd drawn once, after telling him the story of how Superman had come from the planet Krypton to save people on Earth from their own folly. As she recounted the story she had been gripped by a powerful feeling that Superman would burst into the room and rescue them at any moment. He hadn't, but for days she had been left with a vague sensation of hope.

Max levered himself up into the plank position. He was still some way off a four-minute plank. Once he had managed about twenty seconds, but this time it was closer to four seconds before his buttocks started to quiver with the effort. After a few more seconds his hips slowly lowered to the carpet.

'Watch, Mummy,' he said, looking up at her. 'Watch what I can do.'

He started to wiggle his legs and arms and shake his head from side to side.

'Wow,' she said. She paused while she searched for an appropriate description of his gyrations. 'You're break-dancing!'

'No,' he said. 'I'm being a *snake*. A snake doing yoga.'

'Oh,' she said. 'Of course.' For a while they'd done some stretches she remembered from PE and she'd told him they were doing yoga, and it had obviously stuck with him.

He wiggled around for a while, a look of triumph on his

24

face, then stood up and ran to Maggie. He jumped on her back and pressed his cheek to her skin.

'OK,' he said. 'Ride the horsey!'

Maggie twisted and bucked in an attempt to throw him off. It was a game they had played since he was very small. She had done it with Seb and Leo, but they had not enjoyed it nearly as much as Max. He shrieked with pleasure, laughing uncontrollably. It was a strange thing; despite the circumstances, he was a very happy child. Of course, he had no sense that he was missing out on anything, because he knew no different. In some ways it was the perfect set-up for a toddler: unfettered access to his mum and a guarantee of her undivided attention. Nonetheless, Seb and Leo had not been as happy as Max was. Seb was quiet, and prone to outbursts of crying. He'd been like that ever since he was born, sleeping fitfully and whimpering in his crib during the day. Leo was more like Max, but had a wild temper. From time to time, and without apparent reason, he would have screaming fits during which he was totally unreachable. He would hit her, and, if she tried to hold him, claw at her cheeks.

She had put it down to living in a tiny room, but then Max came along, and she wondered whether it was simply the way Seb and Leo were. Nature, not nurture. After all, if it was all down to circumstances, they should all have been the same – this was the perfect way to test. In normal life there were other things that could influence a child's development, but not here. This was like a cruel experiment designed to examine how three children in the exact same environment turned out differently.

And Max, unlike the brothers he would never meet, was as happy as they came. Perhaps Seb and Leo got it from their dad – she hated even thinking of him as their father, but it was true, at least biologically – and Max took after someone else. He certainly had a look of her brother, the same fair

25

hair and innocent, questioning blue eyes, the same goofy smile and easy laugh.

That was one of the things she regretted most, when she looked at her third son: that he would never meet his uncle, and that her brother, who had been a constant, daily irritation through her unfairly truncated teenage years, would never get to be the mentor to his nephew that he would, in her imagination, have become.

James would have loved him. He would have loved all three of her sons, with the same fierce, painful love that she did.

But Max was the only one she had left. He was the only one James would ever be able to love, and all she wanted in the entire universe was to save him so he could meet his uncle and have the life he deserved.

And she was going to.

Somehow.

2

When she had successfully bucked him off her back enough times to satisfy him, Maggie sat cross-legged on the floor. Max was on her lap, his legs around her waist. She had her hands on his hips; he was holding her forearms, running his fingers over the soft, fair hairs that grew there. They were new sometime in the last ten years; she didn't know when they had started to grow, but she had not had them when she was fifteen.

A lot else had changed, too. Some of it – the hair on her forearms, the ache in her knees – were the result of time passing. Other stuff – the sallow skin, persistent cough, acne on her forehead – were from the lack of light and movement and good food. Others still – the heavier breasts, wider hips – were from the pregnancies.

It was one of the strangest features of her imprisonment. Around her, nothing had changed. Her life was frozen. She had not finished school – not even got her GCSEs – not gone to university, not got a job and a house and a car and a husband. All those things were impossibly distant for her, the achievements and waypoints of the life she had been denied.

And yet she was getting older. She had grown up, become

a woman, both mentally and physically. Her life was moving along, slipping away. Ten years from now her metabolism would be slowing down; ten years later she'd be going through menopause.

And the man was getting older, too. He was – what, fifty-five? – when he took her, so he was in his late sixties now. He seemed healthy enough, but in another decade or two? He could become ill, or slip and fall, and then what? By the time they got to her and Max they might have starved.

If Max was still here then. It might be another two-year-old, unknowingly awaiting removal as soon as his third birthday arrived.

Max leaned forward, resting his face against her chest. He had always loved the feel of bare skin; often in the morning he would lie awake on top of her, his torso pressed to hers. She wondered why it felt so good to him. Perhaps he was listening to the sounds of her body, sounds he remembered in some dim way from his time in her womb.

'Mummy,' he said. 'Can I have a story?'

Maggie kissed his head. The soft curls of his hair brushed her cheek.

'Of course,' she said. 'About Superman? Since you're wearing your Superman undies?'

He shook his head. His eyes were closing. 'About the light beam,' he said.

'Ah,' Maggie replied. 'The beam of light. Our magical beam of light. Our *beautiful* beam of light. Is that the story you want?'

Max nodded. 'Yes.'

'Then you can have it.' She paused, wondering where to start. A few months back she had started telling him a story about a beam of light that had a special property: you could ride on it and it could take you, in an instant, to places far, far away. They had ridden it to visit kangaroos in the

Australian outback and beaches on the Australian coast, to experience snow-capped mountains and winter storms in Antarctica, to shop in frantic markets in Thailand where you could buy anything you wanted, to marvel at giant skyscrapers in America and to stare in awe at ancient civilizations hidden in deep jungles. They had gone to meet Harry Potter at Hogwarts, and to stroke Aslan in Narnia and to ride with the hobbits and elves of Middle Earth. Maggie saw no reason to exclude those places – some of the most magical of her childhood – from the adventures.

Today, she decided, they were going into the cosmos.

'So,' she said. 'The beam of light—'

'Mummy,' he said, suddenly. 'Am I a beautiful boy?'

'Yes,' Maggie replied. 'Of course. That's why I tell you so often.'

'You're a beautiful mummy,' he said.

Maggie blinked, tears springing to her eyes. All parents probably marvelled at the things their children picked up, the words they came back from nursery or kindergarten or school with, the games they learned from their friends, the interests they developed out in the world. Max did not have any of those things, but even he made connections on his own. She had never asked him to call her beautiful, never explained why that would be a nice thing to do, but, somehow, his infant brain had understood that this person who loved him and who he loved used a word to describe him and so it would be nice to use it about them.

It showed that all her stories were working.

'Close your eyes,' she murmured, holding him against her and speaking into his hair. 'Here comes the beam of light.'

He snuggled closer to her. 'I don't see it,' he said.

'That's because it's invisible,' she replied. 'But it's here.' She made a small jumping motion. 'We're on board,' she said. 'Hold on tight!'

She pursed her lips and made the noise of rushing air.

'Oh my,' she said. 'We're going very high. I can see the clouds already. Everything's so small down below.' She paused. 'I think, Max – I think we're going into space.'

His eyes blinked open. 'Space?' he said. 'Is space scary?'

'No,' Maggie replied. 'It's beautiful. And so quiet. Look – there's the Earth, below us. You can see the oceans and the continents. You remember Australia – there it is. And over there' – she pointed to the door, watching as Max's gaze followed her finger – 'there's the moon.'

It was incredible to see how easily he slipped into make-believe. In his mind, the room really was transformed into space, although exactly what he thought space was she had no idea. She remembered doing the same in her own childhood. She had gone through a spell when she was obsessed with some He-Man and She-Ra dolls her dad had bought for her. She had played with them for hours, inventing all kinds of scenarios and stories in which they were rescued from danger or won battles or made and broke friendships. She had really believed in them.

And for Max the moon and stars and Narnia were just as real as anything else. As far as he was concerned, Warrington Town Centre was as remote and exotic as the moon. They both existed only in his mind.

'Look,' she said. 'There's the man in the moon.'

'Who's he?'

'He lives on the moon. You can see his face on a dark night.'

Max looked at her. 'Can I see it tonight?'

Maggie tried to smile. 'You have to be outside.'

'Oh,' Max said. 'Outside.'

Outside was a place Max had heard of, but never been. For him it was a bit like space, or Hogwarts, or Narnia.

'We can see him in our imagination, though,' Maggie said. 'There he is!'

'What's he doing?' Max asked.

'He's digging up some moon rocks to eat,' Maggie said.

'He eats rocks?'

'The moon is made of green cheese. That's what he eats.'

'Where's his mummy?' Max asked.

Maggie's answer caught in her throat. He hadn't asked *where are his friends* or *where is his brother*, but *where's his mummy*. It was an unwelcome reminder of the smallness of his life.

'She's at his moon house,' Maggie said. 'She loves him very much.'

'I love you very much,' Max said, his eyes nearly closed. 'And I want to go back to the moon.'

He was starting to fall asleep, his body relaxing. Maggie kissed him on the forehead as his breathing deepened.

'I love you too,' she whispered. 'More than you will ever know.'

3

Maggie was nearly asleep when she heard him coming. She always knew he was on his way; there was a kind of scraping noise, like rock or steel grinding, which she assumed was a door of some kind hiding the entrance to the stairs that led to the room.

She had imagined it many times since the first time she had heard it. Was it a manhole cover in the corner of his garage? Or a heavy stone in his garden? Or a thick wooden cover hidden at the back of a wardrobe? She had no idea; all she knew was that, twenty or so seconds after she heard the noise it made when he moved it, the door to the room would open, and he would be there.

He came every morning, with breakfast, and every afternoon with dinner. It was how she knew the days were passing for her calendar.

And sometimes he came at night. It was when he brought things she needed. Fresh clothes. Cleaning supplies. A new toothbrush.

And when he wore the blue bathrobe. He never took it off. He just undid the belt and let it fall apart and then made her lie face down while he did what he did.

After he'd raped her he would often stare at her, silent and impassive. She had the impression he was waiting for her to say something, but she never had anything to say. All she wanted was for him to leave her alone.

Now, though, three or four days could go by without him showing up at night. She suspected that, as he grew older, he was losing interest in sex.

It was, other than Max, the only bright spot in her dismal world.

He was coming tonight, though.

The door handle turned and, with a click of the lock, it opened. He stepped inside, his bare shins sticking out from under the bathrobe, the ankles mottled and dark.

He locked the door, the key – as always – suspended on a chain around his wrist.

He was tall, certainly taller than her father, who was six foot one, which put him at what – six three? Six four? – and he wore thick-rimmed, old-fashioned glasses. The lenses were always perfectly polished, and she had a recurring image of him sitting in a floral-patterned armchair, news on the radio, his glasses in one hand and a cloth in the other. When he wasn't in his bathrobe, he dressed in shapeless grey trousers and white or blue short-sleeved shirts, which, although clean, were faded and shabby, and carried a musty odour, as though they had been left in the wardrobe too long.

He looked at her, his gaze resting on her face, before moving down over her breasts and then legs. It was an appraising look, like the look a farmer might give a cow.

He nodded at the mattress where Max was sleeping. 'Move the child.'

She picked up Max and laid him on the carpet next to the barrel-bath. She put a pillow under his head and stood up.

The man put his hands on her shoulders and turned her away from him, then pushed her face down on to the mattress. He tugged at her shorts and underwear, then waited as she pulled them down. She heard the noise of tearing as he opened a condom packet – he always used one when the boys were alive, only getting rid of them when she was childless, for reasons she had never understood – and then she felt his weight on her back.

She closed her eyes and thought of the light beam. Of the Man in the Moon. Of Australian beaches she had only seen on soap operas.

There had been a time, early on, when he had tried to kiss her before he raped her. He'd had a strange look on his face, a kind of nervous yearning, which had hardened into his usual scowl when she turned her head away.

He had not tried again.

It had confused her, at first, but afterwards she had understood what had happened. He wanted a relationship. He wanted her to *enjoy* it, as though they were girlfriend and boyfriend. Wife and husband.

The idea sickened her. The idea *terrified* her. It showed her just how delusional he was.

When it was over, he stood up. She turned to look at him. He gestured to the plates, and she scrambled to pick them up. She walked to him and put them in his outstretched hands. Up close his skin was sallow, his face badly shaved. His eyes were sunken and red-rimmed and he looked tired.

He looked ill.

Maggie had a sudden sense that things had changed, that she – and Max – were becoming a burden to him. Maybe he no longer wanted her there. Maybe he would welcome the chance to be rid of them. After all, he was getting older, and he must be wondering what to do with them.

Hope surged in her. There was – perhaps – a crack in

34

the wall. She could offer him a way out. Make it easy for him.

This was it. This was her chance.

'Can I ask you something?' she said.

The man looked at her. After a few moments he nodded.

'Why don't—' now she was saying it, it seemed absurd, the right words hard to find – 'would you consider – is there any chance – would you – would you let us go?'

There was a long silence. The man blinked, almost as if he had not understood the question. Maggie carried on.

'I wouldn't say anything,' she said. 'I wouldn't tell a soul, I promise. You could drop us off hundreds of miles from here and I'd tell people I didn't know where we'd been. I'd say I had no memory, and Max is too young to say anything. I don't want to get you in trouble. I don't hate you. I just want us to be free. It would work, it really would.'

He stared at her, motionless.

'And then you'd be rid of us,' she said. 'You wouldn't have to be back and forth all the time, bringing food, worrying how we were. You could get on with your life, and we would never mention you. I mean, I don't even know your name!'

He tilted his head, and for a moment she thought she saw a softening in his expression, and she was sure he was going to say yes, he was actually going to say yes.

And then he spoke.

'No,' he said, his voice low and toneless. 'That's impossible.'

'It's not! It's easy! All you'd have to do is take us somewhere far away and leave us—'

'That can't happen.'

'It can,' Maggie said. 'Of course it can, and you were thinking about it. I saw you. You were considering it. Please. Please. It's a good idea. Please.'

He shook his head. 'No. I can't.'

'Why? Why not?'

He pointed at Max. 'Because of him.'

'Max?' Maggie said. 'He's still a baby! He has no idea who you are. How can it be because of him? He won't say anything!'

'He doesn't need to. He's my son.'

Maggie felt a growing confusion. Was he saying that he felt some paternal instinct towards Max? That keeping him here was some weird parenting method, and that he didn't want to be apart from him?

'You can see him whenever you want,' she said. 'I prom—'

'That's not it,' he said. 'He has my DNA.'

'I don't understand,' Maggie said. 'I don't see how that's a problem.'

'They'll look at his DNA and it will lead them to me. They have my DNA in their system. They take it for *anything*. So the answer is no.'

'They can't do that! It's not possible!'

'Maybe not. But it might be possible, and that's enough. I can't take that risk.'

'Then I won't let them have Max's DNA. I'm his mum. I can stop them taking it.'

'They will anyway.' He shook his head. 'It's not going to happen.'

Maggie watched him walk across the room, his thick ankles clicking above his slippers. He took the key from the chain around his wrist and unlocked the door, and then he was gone.

Maggie sank on to the bed. Tears welled up; for a moment she'd believed that the end of this nightmare had come, but, like every other hope she'd had for the last decade it had come to nothing.

She looked at the calendar.

S	Su	M	Tu	W	Th	F
						~~1~~
~~2~~	~~3~~	~~4~~	~~5~~	~~6~~	~~7~~	~~8~~
~~9~~	~~10~~	~~11~~	~~12~~	~~13~~	~~14~~	~~15~~
~~16~~	~~17~~	18	19	20	21	22
23	24	25	26	27	28	29
30						

Sunday was over. Tomorrow was Monday. Five days until he took Max. She had to find a way to save her son. She had to.

But she had had to for a long time, and there was no reason to believe that in the next five days she would be any more successful.

Twelve Years Earlier, 7 July 2006: Evening

1

Martin Cooper held the phone to his ear and dialled his niece's mobile. He read the time on the display: 18.17. Maggie had said she would be back for dinner but she had not showed up. He wasn't too concerned – she was fifteen and could stay out past dinner if she wanted to, but he would have liked her to let him know, which was why he was calling Anne. It would be an opportunity to remind his teenage daughter that it would be polite to tell the people who were cooking a meal for you that you wouldn't be coming.

Anne's voice came on the line. 'Hey.'

'Anne. This is Uncle Martin.'

'Oh,' Anne said. 'Hi. How are you?'

'I'm good. Could I have a chat to Maggie?'

'Maggie? She's not here.'

Martin felt himself become more alert. 'I thought she was with you?'

'I haven't seen her. She said she might come over, but she didn't show up.'

Martin frowned. 'That's what she told me, too. Do you know where she went?'

'Probably to see Kevin. Or maybe Fern.' Anne paused, then

said, with a laugh. 'You should get her a mobile phone, Uncle Martin, then you could call her anytime you wanted.'

For a second, Martin thought this was staged. He had a mental image of Maggie telling Anne she'd stay out until her dad called and asked where she was, so Anne could make the point that it was time to get her a phone of her own. Then Maggie would come on the line and say, *See, Dad? I need a mobile phone.* She may be right; perhaps it was time. At fifteen, she was out on her own a lot more. He and Sandra had agreed that she could have one when she turned sixteen, but perhaps they would have to bring it forward. It was such an expense, though, and then James – still only fourteen – would demand one too.

She did not come on the line, though. Anne's voice returned instead:

'If I hear from her, I'll tell her you're looking for her,' she said.

'Thanks, Anne,' Martin said. 'Call me the minute you hear, would you?'

He hung up, then called Kevin's home number. As the phone rang he felt a mounting sense of worry. He dismissed it; it was not that late, and there was almost certainly nothing wrong.

But still. You never knew.

Kevin's dad, Brendan, answered.

'Hi, Bren,' Martin said. 'I was wondering whether Maggie's with you?'

'Nope,' Brendan replied. 'Not seen her. Let me grab Kev. See if he knows.'

A few moments later, Kevin came on the line. 'Hi, Mr Cooper,' he said. 'Are you looking for Mags?'

'Yes. Have you seen her?'

'She was out in town this morning with Fern. Me and Mark met her at McDonald's. We were going to hang out tonight. She said she'd call when she was home and I could come and watch a film.'

'She's not back yet. You haven't seen her since this morning?'

'She said she was going to Anne's this afternoon.' Kevin hesitated. 'At least, I think she did.'

'She told me that, too,' Martin replied. 'But Anne hasn't seen her.'

'Maybe Anne wasn't there when Mags showed up,' Kevin said. 'She would have gone to Fern's.'

'Thanks. I'll try her there.'

Martin hung up, then selected Fern from speed-dial. She had a place on it, unlike Kevin, which he had heard Kevin ask Maggie about. He'd sounded a little desperate, and Maggie had sounded a little exasperated. He wasn't sure how much longer their relationship would last. He'd be sorry to see Kevin go; he was solid and unthreatening, and Martin preferred that to some nineteen-year-old thug with a driving licence and a car that struggled through its MOT every year.

Fern answered. She had no more information than Kevin; she had seen Maggie that morning and thought she was planning to go to Anne's. She ended the call by offering to call around and see if anyone knew anything.

Martin was about to say, *No, don't worry, I'm sure she'll show up*, but he caught himself.

'Yes,' he said. 'That would be very helpful.'

2

Martin turned the gas hob on and put a pan of water on it. He stirred the Bolognese sauce. As the water began to bubble he heard the front door open.

Here she is, he thought, and walked out of the kitchen and into the hall.

It was Sandra and James. James was in his football kit, his bag over his shoulder. He slung it on to the stairs.

'Don't leave that blocking the stairs,' Sandra said. 'Go and put it away. And tidy your room while you're up there.' She looked at Martin and shook her head. 'He's a savage,' she said.

Martin didn't answer. She frowned. 'Everything OK?'

Martin had a tense, almost nauseous, feeling in his stomach. Even though there was probably a simple explanation, he couldn't avoid thinking the worst. He knew he was unnecessarily anxious, what his mum had called a 'worry-wart'; whenever Sandra was out at night he couldn't go to sleep until she was home, visions of car crashes or worse swimming in his head – but knowing he worried too much didn't help. He was not the kind of father or husband or son who could relax and wait for news to come under the assumption it would be good. For him, no news was always *bad* news.

'I thought you were Maggie,' he said. 'She's not back yet. I called Anne and a couple of others. No one's seen her.'

Sandra stared at him. For a moment there was worry in her eyes, but then she smiled. Unlike him, Sandra assumed that things were generally OK. 'She's a fifteen-year-old girl,' she said. 'She's probably with a different friend. Or at the cinema.'

'She should have told us.'

'Yes, she should. But she didn't. She's not a little girl any more, Martin.'

'I know.' He took a deep breath. 'I still worry though.'

'I know you do. It's one of your more attractive traits.'

'It might be time to get her a phone,' he said. 'Then this won't happen again.'

'That's probably why she's stayed out,' Sandra replied. 'So she finally gets the white whale, the elusive mobile phone.'

'Not fair!' The call came from the top of the stairs. 'If she gets a phone, I want one!'

'You're fourteen,' Martin replied. 'Not a chance. And wash your hands before dinner. It's nearly ready.'

3

He didn't eat dinner; he couldn't. His stomach was tight and clenched and the spaghetti bolognese on his plate looked totally unappetizing.

James nodded at his plate. 'Can I have that?'

Evidently his son was not feeling the same way. Martin passed it over and stood up. He looked at the clock over the sideboard. It was nearly seven p.m. Maggie had never stayed out this late without letting them know; she always told them when she was going to be out, and where she was going to be.

Not this time. Maybe it had slipped her mind, but he didn't think so. She was somewhere, and someone knew where that was.

He went to the phone in the hall and called Kevin.

'Have you seen her?' he asked, when Kevin picked up.

'No. I was waiting for her to call. About coming over.'

'Any ideas where she might be?'

'No,' he said. He sounded as worried as Martin, although Martin suspected it was for different reasons. Kevin was no doubt worried she was with another boy.

He hung up and called Anne again. It sounded like she was in the pub.

44

'Any sign of Maggie?' he said.

'No.' Anne said something to someone and the noise of the pub died down. 'Sorry about that – I've come outside,' she said. 'I couldn't hear in there. Is everything OK, Uncle Martin?'

'Maggie still hasn't turned up.'

'God,' Anne said. 'I hope she's OK. I'll ask around, shall I?'

'Please. Call if you hear anything.'

He tried more of her friends. Everyone he could think of. Chrissie – in Nottingham, but still possibly in possession of some useful information – Jeffrey, Oscar, Fern, Meg, Jessie. They always knew what the rest of them were up to.

Except now. None of them knew anything.

He stood with the receiver in his hand. If she wasn't with a friend, then where was she? Images of bodies in ditches or on hospital trolleys came unbidden. He forced them away. That wasn't it. There was another explanation, a reason she had said she was going to Anne's and then not shown up, a reason she had not told anyone where she was.

And he thought he might know what it was. Maybe Kevin's fears were justified.

She had a new boyfriend. Probably older, probably unsuitable – which was why she hadn't told him and Sandra. And she didn't want Kevin to find out, which was why she hadn't told her friends.

Apart from Chrissie. She told Chrissie *everything*.

He dialled Chrissie's number again.

'Sorry to call again, Chrissie,' he said. 'There's one other thing I wanted to ask you.'

'That's OK, Mr Cooper. Whatever you want.'

'I know you said you don't know where Maggie is, but is there anything I should know? Maybe she told you something and asked you not to tell me and her mum, but if she did, now is a good time to say so.'

45

'No,' Chrissie said. 'There's nothing.'

'Are you sure, Chrissie? Maybe a new boyfriend she wants to keep secret?'

'I promise, Mr Cooper,' Chrissie said. 'I promise there's nothing.'

She sounded – as far as he could tell – as though she was telling the truth.

'OK,' he said. 'If anything comes to mind, or if you hear from her, call me. Anytime.'

4

She did not call back. No one did. By ten p.m., Sandra was as worried as him.

They sat at the kitchen table. Sandra had a mug of tea; Martin still couldn't stomach anything. He was sure, now, that something was seriously wrong.

'Where the fucking hell is she?' he said. He rarely swore; even now the words felt out of place in his mouth. 'I don't understand what she's playing at.'

'Me neither,' Sandra said. 'But when she does get home she's going to be in so much trouble she won't know which way is up for a month. She can't do this kind of thing.'

'What if something's happened to her?' Martin said. 'I can't stop picturing—'

'She's fine,' Sandra said. 'Don't think like that. I did this kind of thing when I was her age. It doesn't make it any better, but this is what teenage girls do. She'll be in the park, drinking and smoking. Or with another boy. She's fifteen.'

'I didn't do this,' Martin said. 'I think there's a problem, Sandy, I really do.'

'You were a good boy,' Sandra replied. 'That's why I

married you. It looks like she has some of me in her. That's all it is.'

'Maybe,' Martin said. 'Maybe.'

5

At eleven, Martin walked out to his car. He couldn't stay in the house, waiting, doing nothing, any longer. He had to go and find his little girl.

He decided to start at the park. He pulled up at the entrance and walked through the gates. From somewhere in the darkness he heard talking, and saw the red glow of cigarette tips. He headed towards them.

It was a group of four or five teenagers, boys and girls, all a year or two older than Maggie. They were smoking, bottles dangling from their hands.

'Excuse me,' he said.

They turned to look at him, their voices falling silent.

'Yeah?' one of the boys said. 'What?'

'I was wondering if you'd seen my daughter?'

'Maybe,' the boy replied. 'Who is she?'

'Maggie. Maggie Cooper.'

The name drew blank looks.

'I haven't,' the boy said. 'I don't know her. Any of youse seen her?'

One of the girls stepped forward. She looked younger than

the others. 'I know Maggie,' she said. Her voice was slurred. 'We have English together.'

'Have you seen her?'

The girl shook her head. 'No. I mean, I seen her at school, but not out.'

'Do you know where she might be? Are there other places kids hang out?'

The girl looked at her friends and shrugged. 'In town, maybe. Some kids go to the pubs.'

'She's a bit young for that.'

One of the boys laughed. 'Yeah, mate. They let anyone in, especially girls. They want them in.'

Martin didn't ask for what. He didn't need to.

'Which pub is most likely?' he said.

'Could be any.' The boy sniffed. 'You'll have to try them all.'

'OK,' Martin said. 'Thanks.'

'Is she OK?' the girl asked.

For a moment, Martin didn't reply. 'I hope so,' he said, eventually. 'I hope so.'

In the car he checked his phone. There were no missed calls, no text messages from Sandra announcing Maggie's' return.

It was 23.34. Nearly midnight.

He'd had enough. The best case was she was outside a pub or waiting for a taxi or with some older boyfriend. The worst case was unthinkable.

It was time to call the police.

Twelve Years Earlier, 7 July 2006: Evening

1

Maggie sat on the bed, legs crossed, arms folded, her fingers stroking the smooth skin of her forearm. The light next to the bed was switched on; she had turned it off but there was no other source of light in the room and the darkness was absolute. There was sweat on her back and forehead; although it was not warm in the room she had, for what felt like an age, screamed and shouted and thrown herself against the door in a desperate – and useless – attempt to find a way out.

She was calmer now, but the panic was there, just under the surface.

Because she knew now there was no way out of the room.

There was *no way* out of the room.

There was no way out of the room.

And there was no one answering her cries. Was that his plan? To starve her to death in here? No – it couldn't be. There had to be more to it than that.

The man who looked like a geography teacher – she didn't know why she chose geography, it could have been one of many subjects, but that was the one that had come to her – had done this for a reason. He'd gone to too much effort for it to be otherwise.

Now she was calmer, the room was silent. It was a kind of silence she had never experienced before. At home, even in the dead of night, there were sounds: plumbing gurgling, floorboards creaking, cars passing by.

But in here: nothing. It felt heavy and dead.

Total, deafening silence.

The smell of vomit.

And then she heard a noise. It came from somewhere behind the door. It was a kind of scraping, like a stone being moved or the brakes of a large truck being hit hard.

A door of some kind being opened, maybe.

She held her breath. The scraping noise stopped, then came again.

The stone being put back. The door being closed.

And then a footstep, right outside the door to the room.

And then the handle turning.

2

At first she didn't recognize him.

She'd been expecting a man in grey trousers and a scruffy shirt, but he was wearing a blue towelling bathrobe. It had a faded insignia on it – some kind of animal – and was tied tight at the waist. He was wearing socks with snowflakes on them – given, perhaps, by a grandchild – and a pair of dark green slippers.

He was tall and heavily built, but looked soft, his muscles slack and fleshy. There was a sheen to the skin on his face that made him look almost like he was made of wax.

In his hands he held a tray. There was a plate of food and a glass of milk on it. He put it on the floor, then locked the door with a key he kept on a chain around his wrist. She made a note of that.

'Here,' he said. 'Something to eat.'

His voice was halting, the words coming in bursts. *Something* – pause – *to eat*. It was as though he didn't get much practice speaking.

Maggie looked at the plate. There were some kind of fried potatoes and a few stalks of boiled broccoli, along with some fish fingers. Fish fingers! How old did he think she was? Six?

'I'm not hungry,' she said. 'I want to go home.'

He stared at her for a while, his mouth settling into a look of resigned disappointment.

'I thought you might say that,' he replied. 'That's not going to' – another pause, followed by a rush of words – 'be possible, I'm afraid.' He smiled, his gums pink and fleshy. 'Sorry, my darling.'

Maggie's skin prickled. 'You can't keep me here,' she said. 'Let me go.'

He shook his head.

She clenched her fists. 'Let me go!' she shouted. 'You have to let me go!'

'I don't have to do anything,' he said. 'Not any more. Not now.'

'My mum will find me,' Maggie said. 'My mum and dad will come and find me so you might as well let me leave now. If you let me go I won't tell anyone what you did.'

'I'm touched by your faith in your parents,' the man said. 'But I don't think you're right. There's no way she will be able to find you here. No one will. I've put a lot of thought – and effort – into this.' He made a sweeping gesture, indicating the room around them. 'It's totally hidden. I made sure of that.'

He spoke in a serious, quiet voice. Maggie fought the urge to scream.

'What do you want?' Maggie said. 'What do you want from me?'

'I don't want anything from you,' the man replied. 'What would I want *from* you? I want to *help* you.'

'Help me?' Maggie shook her head. 'This isn't helping me,' she said. 'This is the opposite of helping me.'

'No,' the man said. 'You say that because you don't understand. This is what you need. I'm giving you what you need.'

His pink, gummy smile came again. He looked at her, his

eyes lidded. He was trying to be seductive, she realized. She shuddered.

The panic came closer to the surface. Her vision blurred. She took a deep breath. It was a struggle to retain what little control of herself she had left.

'You're right,' she said. 'I don't understand. How is this what I need?'

'Because this will keep you safe,' the man said. 'That's all I want. To keep you safe.'

It was the worst possible situation. He thought he was doing the right thing, and people who thought that were nearly impossible to convince they were wrong, especially when they were crazy.

She didn't know much – where she was, who he was, what his plans were – but she knew one thing. She knew she was in a lot of trouble.

'Why me?' she said. 'Why do you care about me being safe?'

The man frowned. His expression darkened, his mouth flattening into an angry line. 'Isn't it obvious?' he said.

It was far from obvious, but Maggie nodded. 'Kind of,' she said. 'But not completely.'

The man raised his eyebrows and tilted his head, as though explaining something extremely simple to someone who should not need it explaining.

'Well,' he said. 'Why would anyone do all this?' Again, he gestured at the room. 'I mean, there's only one reason to go to all this trouble for someone, isn't there?'

'I suppose so,' Maggie said. 'It's because . . .' she paused, leaving the question hanging.

The man laughed. 'I can't believe I have to tell you!' he said. 'You really don't know, do you?'

Maggie shook her head. 'No,' she said. 'I don't. I'm sorry.'

'Don't be sorry,' he said. 'Everything's going to be OK, for the same reason that I built all of this.' He smiled. 'It's because I *love* you, dummy. Why else would it be?'

Maggie stared at him.

'You don't – you can't love me. You don't even know me!'

The man giggled. 'Come on now, Fruitcake, of course I do!'

Fruitcake? Had he called her *Fruitcake*? That was impossible. Only her dad called her that.

'Who told you about Fruitcake?' she whispered. 'How do you know that?'

'I know *everything* about you,' he said. 'I've been watching you for years. And now you're mine.' He smiled. 'Safe and sound and all mine, forever and ever.'

Maggie felt bile rise in her throat. She leaned forward and retched, vomit splattering the carpet by the side of the bed. The man tutted. His expression had hardened, the anger back.

'I'm sorry you did that,' he said. 'What a mess you made.' He shook his head. 'I'll bring you something to clean it up with tomorrow, but tonight, to remind you not to do it again, you can live with it.'

Maggie didn't care. The room already smelled of vomit. She'd rip up a corner of carpet or pull the mattress over it and cover it somehow.

'Fine,' she said, looking up at him through narrowed eyes. Part of her knew antagonizing him was a bad idea, but she didn't care. She was angry. 'Leave it. If it means you go away then that's fine by me.'

His expression hardened further. 'I am trying,' he said, slowly. 'To *help* you. To *take care* of you. Have you any idea what could happen to you out there? Here you're safe. *Protected.* Sheltered. Out there' – he shook his head – 'you could be ruined.' He reached into the pocket of his robe and took out the packet of Marlboro Lights she had bought a few days back. 'These, for example. It's unbecoming for a young lady to smoke this filth. I can't allow that. I *have* to help you. Don't you see?'

Maggie ignored the question. 'Leave me alone,' she said. Her voice rose to a scream. 'Just fucking fuck off!'

He flinched. 'Don't swear,' he muttered. 'I don't like it. Good girls don't swear. And you're a good girl, which is why you're here.'

'Fuck, fuck, fuck, fuck!' Maggie screamed. 'Fucking fuck off, you fucking bastard!'

He rubbed his cheek and temple. His left foot tapped on the floor. 'I can't,' he began, 'I can't believe you're doing this. This is *awful*, it's' – he puffed his cheeks out, his eyes twitching in agitation. 'It's simply *not acceptable*.' The last words came out as a shout, and he glared at her, his body now still again. 'Stop it. Stop it *now*. You're ruining everything.'

'I don't care.'

'You will,' he said. 'I didn't want to do this today. Not the first time we met. But I think I *have* to. I think I have to teach you a lesson. This really isn't what I wanted, I'd like you to know that. But you leave me with no choice. This is *your* fault.'

His right hand went to the blue belt of his bathrobe. He undid the belt and the bathrobe opened. Underneath he was wearing a white T-shirt and pale blue Y-fronts. They were tented at the front. He gripped the cloth. 'This is your doing, Fruitcake,' he mumbled.

'No,' she said. 'Please, no.'

'You brought this on yourself,' he said. His face was now fixed, a hungry, wild look in his eyes; he seemed almost like a different person. 'Lie down. On your front.'

Maggie shook her head. 'No. I'll do what you want. I won't swear. I'll be good, I promise.'

'This is what I want,' he said, and took a step towards

57

her. She shrank back, her shoulders pressing into the wall. He reached out, and grabbed her arm. He twisted it, forcing her on to her front. He lay on her, heavy, his breath hot against the back of her neck.

She tried to pull away from him but it was impossible. He was too strong. He forced her legs apart with his knee.

When he was finished, he grunted and stood up. She lay face down, her eyes closed.

'I love you,' he said. 'I love you, Fruitcake.'

Monday, 18 June 2018

Five Days to Go

1

She was woken up by Max climbing on to her. They slept together, but most nights he rolled off the mattress on to the floor. Wherever he slept, though, he almost invariably woke before her and climbed on top of her. The lamp was on low. She didn't like to sleep with it on, but hated the darkness when it was off, so she had begged the man to buy her a dimmer switch – she had told him exactly what to buy – and installed it herself. He had watched, his eyes narrow with confusion that she knew how. It was one of the many things he didn't know about her. She was not what he thought she was, not a helpless child in need of rescue, and she was glad to have the light to remind her of who she had been, of the girl who had been taught electrics and plumbing and car maintenance by her father.

Now she was awake she turned it up full. Max climbed off her and she watched as he emptied the box of Duplo on to the floor. He arranged them into some kind of square. Maggie propped herself up on her elbow.

'What you making, bub?' she said.

He glanced up at her.

'Light beam,' he said. 'So we can go somewhere.'

If only it was so easy, she thought.

'Great,' she replied. 'I can't wait. Where should we go first?'

'I think to the moon,' he said. 'To see the man. And his mum.'

'OK,' Maggie said. 'The moon it is. You work on the light beam and I'll get some fuel.'

By the bath there were two boxes. One contained Max's clothes, and the other contained hers – over the years, the man had brought her some jeans and T-shirts, as well as underwear. She had no bras – the elastic on the one she had been wearing when he took her had worn out, and he had never replaced it. She supposed it would have been odd for a man of his age to buy bras. Children's clothes or nappies were one thing – he might have grandkids – but not bras. He probably could have done it without being noticed, but she had learned that the man was super careful.

She took out a pair of dark blue jeans. They were high-waisted and shapeless and the kind of thing her mum would have considered out of date but the ones she had been wearing needed to be washed. She would leave them by the door and the man would return them in a day or two.

As she pulled them on the button came off. She picked it up; it was cheap, the front metal but the back made of plastic. She reached to the back of the shelf for her sewing kit. It wasn't much; just a spool of cotton thread and one needle, but it was enough for the infrequent repairs she needed to do. She had convinced the man to get it for her a few years back; at first he had refused, but he seemed to like the idea that she could use it to reduce the number of clothes he had to buy, and so, one day, the spool and the needle had been left on the tray.

That was all she had. Other than the bucket, bowl, and mattress, all he had brought her were some clothes, the Duplo

Lego, and the sewing kit. No knives and forks, no shoelaces, no blunt objects. It was wise of him. The last thing he needed was for her to have a weapon of any kind. There were times – many of them – when she would have used it.

There wasn't much you could do with a needle and thread and some Lego, though. She'd thought about it often enough.

She'd thought about everything. Tried some things; in the first few weeks she was here she had attacked him when he opened the door, clawing at his face with her nails, feeling the skin break and blood flow.

But he was a man and bigger than her and stronger and he threw her across the room then advanced on her, his face puce with anger, his cheeks lined with scratches. He screamed at her and for a moment she thought he was going to kill her – he could, no one knew she was here – but then he breathed deeply and turned around and walked out.

And a few minutes later the lamp went off.

The only light source was gone. She had assumed that the only switch was the one on the wall, but it turned out she was wrong. The man had one on the outside, or maybe he'd turned off the trip switch. Her dad – an electrician – had showed her how they worked a few years back, explained how they kept the electrical system safe. Since she was young he had included her in his work, and, when she was fourteen he had let her change the light fitting in her bedroom from a simple overhead fitting to an angled downlighter.

So she knew a bit about electrical work, but it didn't help her. The room was in darkness.

And it stayed that way for a *long* time. Days, maybe. She lost track of time, became disorientated, screamed until she couldn't hear herself. She lay on her bed shaking, visions swimming through the dark.

It was a terrible few days. To this day she didn't know how long it had lasted. She had it marked as three on her calendar, but it could have been one, or seven. She'd see what the real date was when she got out of here and find out how many days had gone missing.

If she got out of here.

Eventually the light had fizzed back on. The man appeared in the doorway minutes later.

Don't do that again, he said. *Or it will be twice as long.*

She had tried again, though, and the memory of the punishment after that attempt still made her blood run cold. It had been worse than darkness, even darkness for twice as long.

Much worse.

She picked up the jeans and the needle and thread and began to sew the button back on. The plastic hoop at the back of the button had cracked and was going to fall off again soon, so she wrapped the cotton thread tightly around the plastic to secure it before sewing the button into place. She felt jaded, foggy, like she'd barely slept. It was the lingering effect of the disappointment the night before. For a moment she'd been sure the man was going to agree to let them leave – she'd seen it in his face, a tiredness at having to keep them there and a desire to embrace her suggestion and let them go – but then he had said no.

They have my DNA.

Which meant what, exactly? What little she knew about DNA had come from watching television shows in which cops used it to catch criminals and daytime chat-show hosts used it to prove paternity. Was that what he was afraid of? That the cops would take Max's DNA and match it to his? But how would they even know?

There was only one way. They had his, in some database, and that meant he had done something – or been a suspect for something – like this before.

Her hands stopped moving, the needle part way through the waistband of the jeans. Was she not the first to be down here? She looked around the room, picturing another mother sitting on the bed, her child playing on the floor. It was hard to imagine someone else in here. She associated it so much with her and Seb and Leo and Max.

And he'd said, years ago, when she was first here, that he'd built it for her.

So maybe he had done something else, committed some other crime, and, when he was caught, had decided to make sure he could never be caught again.

By building this hidden room that no one could ever find.

And keeping her here forever. If she hadn't known it before she did now – this was forever.

She had to do something, and soon. She looked at Max, her son who would be three in five days.

Five days.

She had to do something *now*. And she had – she thought – the first glimmerings of an idea.

'So,' Max said, oblivious to the tragedy of his surroundings and the fact that, in five days, even this would be taken from him. 'Are you ready to come on the light beam, Mummy?'

'Yes,' she said. 'I am.'

But her mind was elsewhere. It was on what she was going to do.

2

The man stood in the door, a tray in his hand. When he was leaving food or water or cleaning supplies he never came into the room. He put them on the carpet, picked up anything Maggie had left for him – nappies, plates, cleaning supplies – and left. It was only when he was in his blue bathrobe that he locked the door behind him, secured the key on a chain around his wrist, and entered the room properly.

It was the morning, so there was no bathrobe. He lowered the tray to the floor and stood up. There were two paper plates, each covered with creased tinfoil. He liked the tinfoil to be folded and placed back on the tray; Maggie assumed he re-used it.

He was that kind of person. Neat, particular, fastidious. She pictured his house as a museum, the rooms fixed and unchanging, almost unlived in, with patterned wallpaper on the walls and lace curtains filtering the daylight. It was a sham, a face to the world. His life was down here.

The thought made her shudder.

When he walked out she noticed a stiffness in the way he moved. She'd seen brown spots on his hands, the skin loose and sallow. He was still strong but there was a growing unsteadiness in him. He was getting older.

Weaker. More vulnerable. One day she would be able to overpower him.

Today, maybe.

Today she might get out of here. She pictured the newspapers: *MISSING GIRL FOUND DECADES LATER*. She'd be reunited with her parents. In her mind they were the same as when she had been abducted, but, like the man, they'd be older too. Fifty-three now. She tried to imagine what they looked like. Would Dad be bald? Mum grey? Were they still together?

Still alive?

And James would be twenty-six. He might have kids. She wondered what music he listened to, what books he read, what job he did. He'd have cast his first vote, lost his virginity, gone to university, all of it a mystery to her. She didn't even know who the prime minister was. Was it still Blair? Surely not. Probably someone from a whole new generation of politicians. Maybe the country was at war; maybe it had adopted the euro. She knew nothing.

She closed her eyes. She'd missed so much. It was weird, though: without the man there'd have been no Seb, Leo or Max, and she couldn't imagine life without them. Especially without Max.

She looked at him. He was sleeping on the mattress, his mouth parted. She picked up the calendar, took her pencil and crossed out another day.

S	Su	M	Tu	W	Th	F
						~~1~~
~~2~~	~~3~~	~~4~~	~~5~~	~~6~~	~~7~~	~~8~~
~~9~~	~~10~~	~~11~~	~~12~~	~~13~~	~~14~~	~~15~~
~~16~~	~~17~~	~~18~~	19	20	21	22
23	24	25	26	27	28	29
30						

The sight and smell of the breakfast made her feel sick.

But she couldn't have eaten anyway. She was too on edge. Because today she was going to get out of here.

She pushed the breakfast away.

3

She had a plan. It was simple, but she thought it could work.

When he came, she would attack him.

Which was a start, but it still wouldn't be enough. She'd learned that the hard way before. He was older now, though, and weaker; she was strong from the press-ups and planks and other exercises. It would be different.

Even so, she was still five-three and about eight and a half stone, and he was six-foot-three and probably sixteen stone. She knew from the times he had lain on top of her how heavy that was, and how hard it was to move that kind of weight.

She'd get only one chance to hit him and it would have to work, or he'd overpower her and take Max anyway and repeat the awful, awful punishment he had meted out last time.

So that one hit had to work. She had to maximize its effect. And for that she needed one more element, an element she thought she might have figured out.

4

The man opened the door. He was holding a tray, and he locked the door, his attention on the key.

When he turned to Maggie, he frowned.

'What?' he said. 'What are you doing?'

Maggie was sitting on the mattress. She smiled at him. Max was sleeping on the floor, his head on a pillow; it had been a struggle to get him to go to sleep.

She stood up. The man's gaze moved up and down her body.

Her *naked* body.

'Put the tray down,' she said, in the closest approximation she could manage of a sultry tone. 'I've been thinking about you.'

The man's eyes narrowed in suspicion but she could see the sudden flare of desire in them.

Desire for sex, yes, but more for love.

He bent at the waist and placed the tray on the ground and she launched herself at him, hitting him hard in the small of his back. He fell forward and there was a thud as his head hit the wall. The tray fell to the floor, the plate and cup clattering together before settling on to the carpet. She grabbed for the key, but he twisted his hand away and rolled on to his back, staring at her, his breathing heavy. Blood beaded on his forehead. He put his finger to it, and examined his blood.

'You fool,' he said. 'You stupid fool. You really think that is enough to hurt me?'

He levered himself up on to his elbows then stood up. Maggie took a step backwards. It was over, already. Her plan had failed miserably. And now he was going to punish her.

At least Max was still asleep. He was a good sleeper, so she doubted he'd wake up. She was glad; he didn't need to see this.

He grabbed her upper arm and shoved her, hard. The gasp she made as her back hit the wall and the air left her lungs reminded her of his strength, of the strength she had thought – ridiculously – she could overpower.

And now, the payback.

'What are you going to do to me?' she said.

The man contemplated her.

'Fruitcake,' he said. 'My little Fruitcake. I understand why you did that. I'm not inhuman. I know how hard what's to come will be for you. But it's for the best. I can't leave him with you. If I do, we won't be able to be together.'

Maggie didn't reply. She couldn't. The fear of what he was going to do to Max and her anger at her failure to save him were too great.

'So I won't do anything to you, this time.' His expression hardened. 'But don't do it again, Fruitcake. This is your one free pass, OK?'

She nodded.

He smiled.

'Love you,' he said, and unlocked the door.

Twelve Years Earlier,
9 July 2006

1

Martin Cooper opened his eyes. He looked at his watch; it was almost four thirty in the morning, which meant he'd been asleep for around two hours.

That was all he was going to get.

It had been two nights. He rubbed his eyes. They felt raw. The night Maggie disappeared he hadn't slept at all and, with tonight's two restless hours, he could feel the exhaustion building up. It made no difference, though. There was no way he would be able to sleep again.

And he didn't want to. He wanted to find his daughter.

He got out of bed and crossed the landing to her room. He opened the door and looked inside, half-expecting, half-hoping, to see a shape in her bed, sleeping off the effects of wherever she'd been.

It was empty.

On his way back from the park the night she disappeared he'd called the police and reported she was missing.

We'll put out an alert, the officer he spoke to said, *but she's probably with a friend. More than likely she'll turn up in the morning*.

Except he'd spoken to all her friends and she wasn't with

them, and they didn't know of anyone else she would have been with, any boy or man she'd mentioned.

So he and Sandra and James and his brother, Tony, and his friend from work, Reid, and Freddie, his neighbour, had spent the day looking for her. Between them they'd gone to every pub in Warrington and Manchester and Liverpool and Wigan and St Helens and anywhere else they could think of, and shown them a photo of Maggie.

None of them remembered seeing her. Quite a few said they couldn't be sure.

Busy night, mate. Lots of people in here. Have you tried the cops?

He had. They hadn't done much. They were looking for her, but they still thought she'd show up.

He'd lost track of the number of times he'd heard someone say *most of the time teenagers do.*

Most of the time wasn't good enough. And Martin knew his little girl. She hadn't gone off with a new boyfriend, enjoying herself while her parents worried. Some teenagers would – and maybe they were the ones that showed up – but not Mags. Not his Fruitcake.

If she was missing there was a reason, and he needed to find her.

He hadn't, though. He came home, eventually, at one a.m., flat and exhausted and terrified. He'd slept, for those two hours.

And now he was awake. He didn't know when he would ever be able to sleep again.

2

Next to him, Sandra rolled on to her side. Her breathing quickened and she sighed.

'Are you awake?' he said.

'Yes. I barely slept.'

'Me neither.' He looked at his watch again. 'It's four thirty-seven.'

Their bedroom door opened slowly. James stood in the frame. 'I couldn't sleep,' he said. 'I was waiting for you to wake up.'

'You should have come in,' Martin said. He felt a surge of love for his son. 'Anytime you need me, I'm here.'

'It's early.'

'It doesn't matter.'

'Dad,' James said. 'Can we go and look for her?'

Martin replaced the nozzle in the petrol pump and walked across the garage forecourt to pay. The car had been full the day before, but he had driven every street and park and country road for miles around. Martin had marked the ones they had driven on a map with a fluorescent marker and there were very few left. He had driven slowly, James looking out of one side, him looking out of the other. At every open pub or newsagent or café or clothes shop or place that looked like it might have attracted a fifteen-year-old they had stopped and shown photos of Maggie.

No one had seen her.

He scanned the shop as he entered, in case Maggie was inside buying chewing gum or a magazine or a packet of cigarettes. He hoped she was. He hoped he found his fifteen-year-old daughter buying cigarettes, because then he would know she was safe.

Because then he would have her back, and he could sleep and eat and breathe and live again.

He handed his card to the shop assistant.

'Number six,' he said. As she rang it up, he put the photos of Maggie – one a close-up of her face taken a couple of weeks ago, the other her school portrait – on the counter.

'You haven't seen this girl, have you?' he asked.

The woman – about his age and with a pinched, smoker's face – gave him a suspicious look.

'No,' she said. 'She missing?'

'Yes. She's my daughter.'

The looked softened into one of sympathy.

'Oh. How long's she been gone?'

'Two nights.'

Just saying it made him feel sick with worry. It had a similar effect on the woman.

'Two nights is two nights too long,' she said. 'Hold on. I'll be right back.'

She picked up the photos and walked through a door into an office. A few minutes later she came back holding a sheaf of paper.

'Photocopies,' she said. 'I can hand them out, see if anyone recognizes her. Give me your number and I'll make sure we let you know.'

Martin wrote down his phone number, in part glad of the help, and in part terrified.

Because it suddenly felt all the more real.

3

They got home at nine. There was a car parked in the driveway next to Sandra's red Ford Focus. A dark blue Honda Civic with a large dent in the boot. Martin stiffened.

'Who the hell's that?' he said. He pulled up at the side of the road and opened the car door. 'Let's go and see.'

James followed him into the house. He had large dark circles under his eyes and a drawn look. Martin put his arm around him and kissed his forehead. It was oily; his son was giving off a pungent, hormonal smell.

'It'll be OK,' Martin said. 'Really, it will.'

He was trying his best, but he wasn't sure he was able to sound like he really believed his own words.

In the living room, Sandra was perched on the edge of the sofa. She had a mug of tea in her hands. A woman with short, dark hair was sitting in the armchair opposite her.

'Hi,' she said. She didn't need to ask if he had found Maggie. She gestured at the woman.

'This is Detective Inspector . . .' her voice tailed off.

'Wynne,' the woman said. 'DI Jane Wynne.' She looked at Martin, her face still and expressionless. There was a questioning, intelligent look in her eyes. 'I'm here about Margaret.'

'Maggie,' Martin said, reflexively. 'We call her Maggie.'

Wynne nodded. 'Maggie,' she said. 'You reported her missing two nights ago, around midnight.' She paused, her expression carefully neutral. 'Even though most of these cases resolve quite quickly, we do feel that this case requires more attention.'

Martin steadied himself against the back of the sofa. Although he wanted all the help they could get with finding Maggie, these were not words he wanted to hear.

'Why?' he said. 'Why does it require more attention?'

'It's a combination of things,' Wynne said. 'Maggie has no history of this kind of behaviour. You reported that none of her friends have seen her. She's fifteen. And then there's the amount of time that has passed. Although many teenagers go missing, it's been two nights. And that is a concern.'

'You think something bad has happened?' Sandra said, in a low voice.

Wynne glanced at James. 'I think it's a possibility,' she said. 'If she was away for one night, that would be pretty normal for a teenager. Drink too much, fall asleep somewhere, come home the next day, fearing punishment. All pretty standard. But two nights is different.'

'So what happens next?' Martin said.

'We contact the press,' Wynne said. 'Get her photo out there. You take me through the last few days, I interview her friends, look at phone records, see what might be of interest, whether there are any leads. We assemble some officers to follow those leads.' She rubbed her eye. 'And then we do whatever we can to find your daughter.'

4

Martin stood in his daughter's room. It was a curious mixture of childlike and grown-up; on her desk were some earrings and a CD by an artist he had never heard of and a book of short stories by Kate Chopin, yet by her pillow there was the blue bear – Rudi – he had bought her when she was six and he and Sandra were trying to stop her climbing into their bed every night.

He'll keep you safe, he said. *You can cuddle Rudi.*

It had worked, after a while. When she came into their room he let her settle then carried her back to her bed. If she stirred, he put Rudi in her arms and she went back to sleep.

Wynne had looked around the room, searching for anything that might give a clue to where she was. She didn't find anything – Martin wasn't sure what she would have found: drugs, maybe, or someone's name or address – but whatever she had been looking for, she had left empty-handed. Likewise Maggie's emails. Sandra knew her password and Martin had agreed to let Wynne look at her account. There was nothing that hinted at where she might be.

He sat on the edge of her bed. Wynne had talked about

a press conference, an appeal on television to anyone who might have information important to the investigation.

You'd be surprised what they throw up, she said. *People's memories get jogged about something they saw, they call it in, it turns out to be valuable.*

It hadn't reassured him. In fact, it had had the opposite effect.

It brought home that this was not simply a teenage girl doing something irresponsible.

This was an *investigation*, a news story. It was not going away. He picked up Rudi and rubbed the soft, threadbare patch over his right eye. He held him to his face and the smell of his daughter enveloped him.

For the first time he wondered whether he would ever smell that smell again, and he started to cry.

Twelve Years Earlier, 9 July 2006

1

DI Wynne sipped her coffee. It was milky and sweet. She didn't like it that way, but Detective Superintendent Marie Ryan – a couple of ranks above her and not known for her frivolity – had handed it to her and she didn't want to say anything.

'So,' Ryan said. 'You're working on the missing girl? You don't think she's gone off with a boy? Escaping to the big city.'

'I don't think so,' Wynne replied. 'She doesn't seem the type.'

'There is no type,' Ryan said. 'At least not in my experience.'

'I know. But I think there's more to this than a runaway teenager.'

'OK. It's your case. What do you think happened?'

'I think someone took her,' Wynne said. '*Could* be random. Rape, maybe. Or murder. Or both. But I think she was taken.'

'If she was, you want to hope she's dead,' DSI Ryan said. 'Because the alternatives are not pretty.'

Wynne nodded. This was the reason she'd come to talk to Ryan. She was an expert in the kinds of criminal gangs who trafficked young girls. Boys, too, sometimes.

'What are the alternatives?' Wynne said.

'Forced prostitution. If it's that, she could be anywhere in the world by now. Those people know how to move their victims around quickly. Or pornography. The really vile kind. Snuff movies, rape movies. Live shows on the internet where the punters tell the gang what they want them to do.' Ryan caught Wynne's gaze. 'I've seen some bad things, Detective Inspector. People mutilated. Killed even. All so some bastard can get an erection. You want to hope she's not caught up in that.'

'Do you know anyone who might be able to tell us if she is? A grass?'

Ryan shook her head. 'No. It's a closed world. Some of the gang bosses might know something, but even they keep away from this stuff. And they won't talk to us anyway.'

'Who would be most likely to know something?'

Ryan looked at Wynne, her head tilted. 'They won't tell you anything. You're police. The enemy.'

'I can try.'

'It's your investigation.' Ryan lifted her mug to her lips. 'One name springs to mind. He might know how to find out what's out there. If there's a new video, or live event or whatever they do.'

'Who is it?'

'Mullins. Mike Mullins.'

Wynne nodded. It was a familiar name. 'I've heard of him. Manchester?'

'That's him.'

'Thank you, Detective Superintendent,' Wynne said.

Ryan took a deep breath. 'Be careful,' she said. 'Be very careful.'

2

She had brought a uniformed officer, Mark Edwards, a tall man in his twenties. She didn't think there'd be any trouble, but the presence of a uniform added a certain formality that could be useful.

It also drew attention, which Wynne knew would piss Mike Mullins off. He had bought a large house on a tree-lined street in Lymm, a wealthy commuter village which was home to doctors and lawyers and accountants as well as a handful of gangsters who wanted their kids to go to good schools and have respectable friends, and he would not want his neighbours seeing the police show up.

She didn't care. She was glad to remind him how he had got hold of the money he'd bought his newfound respectability with. She parked by one of the trees – she didn't know which type of trees they were, only that she couldn't afford to live on a street with trees like them – and got out of the car.

An electronically controlled gate blocked the long driveway leading to his house, but, as she and PC Edwards approached it there was a click and it swung open.

The gravel crunched underfoot as they walked up to the large, black front door. Wynne rang the bell.

No one came.

'Bastard's in,' Edwards said, gesturing to a red Range Rover parked next to a Bentley. 'He's messing with us.'

Wynne nodded. 'Let's go,' she said. 'Time's a-wasting.'

She turned and started to walk back down the drive. The gate swung shut. Behind her, she heard the sound of the front door opening.

'So,' a voice said. 'To what do I owe this pleasure?'

Mike Mullins sat in an armchair facing them, his legs crossed. He was wearing tan brogues, green cords and an expensive-looking V-neck sweater over a pale blue shirt. He could have been a banker at his golf club. He probably had similarly well-developed moral principles.

'I've never met you,' he said, little more than a hint of a Manchester accent left in his voice. 'Although I've met quite a few of your colleagues over the years. Which one sent you?'

'Ryan,' Wynne said.

'I remember her. A superintendent now, correct?'

'Correct.'

'She deserves it.' He shook his head. 'Incorruptible, and I tried. Most of your lot have a price, higher or lower, but not her.'

'I'm glad to hear it.'

'Not that I'd say if I *had* bought her,' Mullins said. 'That would be stupid, right?' He leaned forward. 'And if there's one thing I'm not, Detective Inspector Wynne, it's *stupid*.' He sat back again. 'Now we've got that out of the way, what can I do for you?'

Wynne was impressed he had remembered her name. She had only mentioned it once. 'I need help. Information, if you have it.'

'And why would I help you?'

'Because I've done my research.'

84

He stared at her. His eyes were dark. 'What does that mean?'

Wynne held his gaze. 'It means I know you have a fifteen-year-old daughter. Amanda goes to Withington Girls' School.'

His eyes narrowed. 'What the fuck are you saying? Is this some kind of threat?' He pointed at Wynne, his finger stabbing the air. 'Because if it is, and you bring my daughter into this, I will destroy you, understand? Do you under—'

PC Edwards got to his feet. 'Watch it,' he said. 'Be careful, Mr Mullins.'

'Shut your mouth, Plod,' Mullins said. 'This is between me and her.'

'Your daughter is of no interest to me,' Wynne said. 'Other than the fact you have one. And she's fifteen.'

'Go on.'

'A fifteen-year-old girl has gone missing,' Wynne said. 'And we have reason to believe she has been abducted. It's possible it was opportunistic and she has been killed, but I don't think so.'

'What do you think?' Mullins said.

'That she's being forced into prostitution or pornography or something similar.'

'And you think *I* might be involved in it?'

'No,' Wynne said. 'But you might know someone who is.'

Mullins shook his head. 'No. I don't. I know those people exist, but I have nothing to do with them. They're filth.'

'I'm glad you're so principled,' Wynne said. 'But I'm sure there's something you could tell me.'

Mullins laughed. 'It's not principle,' he said. 'It's lack of information. The scum who peddle that kind of shit keep themselves to themselves. It's a very secretive world, Detective Inspector. It has to be. If people like me found out who they were, we'd take care of them. For good. We're not as squeamish as you.'

Wynne felt her hopes deflate. She'd been right that Mullins

would find it disgusting, but she was wrong that he would have anything he could tell her.

'But you would inform us if you heard anything?' she said.

He studied her. 'Yes,' he said. 'I would. Just this once, I would.'

She stood up.

'Thank you,' she said.

3

DI Wynne knocked on the door of a semi-detached house on a quiet street about a mile from the Coopers' house, in the village of Stockton Heath. It was a lively place, prosperous and growing, populated with a mixture of long-established inhabitants and more recently arrived commuters.

In Wynne's experience, the arrival of new people changed the character of places like Stockton Heath: they were less embedded in the life of the village, less likely to call on their neighbours. Once, everyone would have known everyone's business in the village. Now, people kept themselves to themselves.

She looked to her right. There was a large bay window. The curtains were open, but there was a blind drawn halfway down. Through the gap she could see a floral couch and a large television. To the left was a garage; it was closed, and no car was in the driveway.

She rang the doorbell again.

PC Edwards nodded at the side of the house. 'Want me to take a look around the back?'

'Give it another minute,' she said. A few seconds later, she heard footsteps, then the sound of a chain being put in place. The door opened the length of the chain.

'Yes?' a man's voice said. 'How can I help you?'

Wynne gestured to Edwards to step back so that he would be visible to anyone looking through the side window. She wanted the occupant to see that it was the police.

'We'd like to talk to you, Mr Best,' Wynne said. 'There's something you might be able to help us with.'

'What's it about?'

'It's an ongoing inquiry.'

'I've done nothing,' Best replied.

'I only want to talk to you.'

'I have nothing to say. And you're not coming in without a warrant. You can't, and you know it.'

Wynne was expecting his answer. People like Best knew the system. They knew their rights, and they claimed them at every turn.

At least, they thought they knew the system. The system had some tricks of its own, and Wynne was not above using them, especially with people like Best.

Especially when something so important was on the line.

'OK,' she said. 'You're right. We can't come in. We'll go.' She turned to PC Edwards. 'But we might need to come back. My colleague thinks he may have heard a noise from inside this abode. Sounds like possible domestic violence. And it wouldn't be the first time there's been a complaint about this address.' She rubbed her forefinger on her lips, as though thinking. 'And that *would* be grounds for a warrant, I'm pretty sure of it.'

She leaned forward and put her face near the gap between the door and the frame. She spoke in a stage whisper. 'I don't want my colleague to hear this,' she said. 'He's young and I wouldn't want to shock him. But when he and his buddies turn up with that warrant they'll turn this place upside down. Rip up your mattresses, smash your cupboards, take a shit on your bathroom floor, dig into your computer. And they'll

88

find something, won't they, Best? Because people like you always have something. Kiddie porn, stolen knickers, evidence of hours spent in chatrooms pretending to be the same age as the people you're talking to. We'll find it, Best. We'll find it and then we'll use it to unravel your life and lock you up for as long as we see fit.'

She stopped then stepped back.

'So, Mr Best,' she said. 'If you aren't going to let us in, we'll be on our way. But we'll see you soon.'

The door closed, and there was a click as the chain was undone.

4

Wynne stood in the hallway. To the right was the room with the bay window. At the far end was a door open on to a kitchen. A pale green carpet covered the floor and ran up the stairs to her left. There was a faint smell of disinfectant.

She recognized it from the last time she'd been here. The neighbours had called in a domestic dispute. She'd been in uniform then, and had come in to find Best's wife, Carol, hiding in the upstairs bathroom. Her nose was broken and she had a contusion on the back of her head. Best was gone; another unit picked him up on the M56 heading towards Manchester.

He said he'd had an argument with his wife and was going for a drive to clear his head. Carol Best had a different explanation. She said he'd gone to destroy the photos they'd been arguing about.

Photos of school girls that he'd taken with a long lens camera and collected in an album, which he had hidden at the back of a cupboard where they kept the computer manuals. She had found it when the computer failed to start and she called customer support. She couldn't follow their instructions, so they suggested she find the manual and look through it.

She found more than the manual, and, when she confronted her husband with the album, he went crazy and said he was going to kill her.

He didn't; she managed to get away and lock herself in the bathroom. Best left the house, taking the photo album – and any negatives, Wynne checked the house for them – with him. He'd developed them himself, so there was no other record of them.

Despite the darkroom he had, he denied the photos had ever existed, claiming Carol had invented them to cover up an affair she had been having, which was the real cause of their argument. He had confronted her with it, and she had attacked him. He had hit her in self-defence – and he apologized for it, he really felt truly sorry, he'd not meant to hurt her – and then fled the house, worried about the police.

In the end, she declined to press charges in exchange, Wynne suspected, for a quick and generous divorce and the chance to get as far away from Best as quickly as possible.

Wynne, though, asked around, and heard from more than one teenager – boys and girls – that they had seen him at the window with his camera.

He's a creepy fucker, one girl said. *Always lookin' at you.*

That in itself wasn't a crime, but Wynne hadn't forgotten it.

And now a fifteen-year-old girl was missing and she was going to look Best in the eye and ask him if he knew anything about it.

Maybe Mike Mullins knew nothing about the people who sold this stuff, but he was different to Best. The people who sold it needed Best. He was a consumer. And consumers of any commodity made it their business to know how to get hold of it. There were hidden networks, and she would have bet that Best knew all about them.

Best nodded towards the kitchen. Wynne and Edwards

followed him through the door. He and Edwards sat down. Wynne stayed on her feet.

'So,' she said. 'How've you been?'

'Fine. This isn't a social call, I take it?'

'No,' she said. 'It isn't.'

'Then what is it?'

'Any ideas?' Wynne asked.

'None.'

'A girl has gone missing. She's fifteen. Local.'

Best shrugged. 'Nothing to do with me.'

'You sure about that?' Wynne stared at him. His demeanour was unassuming, meek, broken by life, but the look in his eyes belied it. They were cold and unflinching. He was, she saw, a dangerous man.

'Hundred per cent,' he said. He crossed his arms. He was wearing a white shirt and grey trousers. Behind him by the sink was a plate with some boiled vegetables and fish fingers on it.

'Early for dinner,' Wynne said.

'I eat when I want. I'm hungry now.'

'For fish fingers?'

'I like them.'

'Aren't they kids' food?' Wynne said.

Best sighed. 'They're easy to cook, and I'm not fussy.'

Wynne placed a photo of Maggie on the table.

'Recognize this girl?' he said.

'No. Never seen her before in my life.'

'You sure? You sure she's not the kind of girl you might have taken an interest in?'

Best's eyes narrowed. 'That is a *vile* allegation, and it is totally unfounded. What my wife – ex-wife, thankfully – accused me of is disgusting, and I would never do anything like that.' He pointed at Wynne. 'And you need to understand that.'

92

He picked up the photo and passed it to Wynne.

'We both know that's not true,' Wynne said. 'Which is why we're here. Since we are, you mind if we have a look around? Still got that darkroom?'

Best nodded. 'It's upstairs. And look all you want. There's nothing to find.'

'We'll take a look anyway,' Wynne said. She was unnerved by his confidence. He certainly didn't seem at all perturbed by the prospect of his house being searched. Perhaps there *was* nothing.

Or perhaps it was just well hidden. 'We'll start upstairs,' she said.

She and Edwards walked out of the kitchen and up the staircase. There were four doors, three closed – bedrooms, she assumed – and one ajar. She could see a sink in the gap.

She gestured to Edwards to go into the furthest room. She took the nearest.

It was the darkroom. There was a table with pans of liquid on it, and a rack on to which Best had pegged photos. A duck on a pond, a view of a woodland, a boat going past a swing bridge.

'Those will be ruined now,' Best said.

'You'll live.'

'I have the negatives. I can make more.'

Wynne backed out of the room. She opened another door. A guest bedroom, by the look of it. A single bed that had not been slept in, a bookcase, and a wardrobe. She looked around, glancing under the bed, then opened the wardrobe. There were a few old suits hanging in it, dust on the shoulders. On the floor was a ukulele, the strings broken. Other than that it was empty.

She went on to the landing. Edwards was standing at the top of the stairs. He shook his head, then gestured to the ceiling. 'I'll check the attic,' he said.

'I can get you a stepladder, if you'd like,' Best said.

Edwards shook his head. 'No need.' He went into the master bedroom and came out with a chair. 'I can use this.'

He stood on the chair and opened the hatch, then pulled himself through it. A light went on, then Wynne heard his muffled voice.

'It's empty.'

They went back downstairs and into the kitchen. Edwards opened the back door. The garden was small, surrounded by a high fence. There was a patio and a fish pond and a messy, overgrown lawn. At the far end was a shed. Wynne walked slowly to it, looking for places – maybe a corner cut off behind the fence – where something – some*one* – could be hidden.

There was nothing. Nothing in the shed, either. Just some old tools and a push mower.

'Let's check the garage,' she said.

It was a one-car garage, Best's blue Ford Focus taking up most of the space. Wynne and Edwards entered through the kitchen; there was a door to the garden on the far side.

She tried the car door. It was unlocked and she pulled the lever that opened the boot.

It – and the garage – was empty.

When they had finished, she went back to the kitchen. Best was drinking a cup of tea. The plate was in front of him, empty. There was a smear of ketchup on the edge.

'Find what you were looking for?' he said.

Wynne didn't reply. Next to her, Edwards tensed.

'I didn't think you would,' Best said. 'I tried to tell you, but some people won't be told.'

'Don't take the piss, mate,' Edwards said. 'I get a bit twitchy when people take the piss.'

Best held up his hands. 'Look,' he said. 'I'm sorry. But you come into my house and go through my belongings for no

94

reason, so don't be surprised when I'm a little miffed. I don't know the girl and I don't know where she is. Whatever's happened to her, it's nothing to do with me.'

Wynne ignored him. 'Where were you on Friday around four p.m.?' she said.

'Shopping,' he said. 'I went to Morrisons to get my weekly shop and then came home. I do it the same time every Saturday. You can check my credit card bill. The transactions will all be there. A neighbour probably saw me come home. You can ask them.'

He wasn't lying, Wynne could tell. But that didn't mean he was telling her everything.

'Have you heard anything?' she said.

'About what?'

'About a missing girl. Or about new material that might be available. Photos. Videos.'

'Of course not,' he said. 'If there was such a thing, what makes you think I would have heard about it?'

Wynne looked at him and smiled. It was not a warm smile. It was not meant to be.

'Listen,' she said, in a low voice. 'If you *have* done anything then one day I'll get you. And I'll do whatever it takes to make sure you end up on the worst wing of the worst prison in the country, and I'll make sure that the other inmates know all about you. They'll be thrilled. It's boring inside and they love something to do. But' – she held her hands up in a gesture of friendship – 'if you tell me about the videos and photos and I find Maggie Cooper, I'll make sure that doesn't happen. I'll be your friend, and someday soon you're going to need all the friends you can get.'

Best stood up. He walked to the kettle and flicked it on, then put a teabag in a mug. When the water was boiling he poured it on to the teabag, and turned to look at Wynne.

'Thank you for your advice, Detective Inspector Wynne,'

he said. 'But I've done nothing.' He smiled, and his smile too was lacking any warmth. 'If anything comes to mind, I'll let you know. Now, please leave.'

Twelve Years Earlier,
9 July 2006: Evening

1

Maggie was hungry. She hadn't eaten any of the food the man – she still didn't know his name – had brought, in part as a protest but mainly because of a constant low-level nausea. She'd drunk some of the orange cordial, but that was it. Now, though, her hunger was becoming insistent. Her body needed what it needed, despite what was happening.

She was hoping the man would be back soon with something to eat.

She sat on the bed and stared at the door to the room. She'd examined it not long after moving in, wondering if it was like the doors in her house, in which case it might be possible to kick a hole in one of the panels.

But the man had clearly thought of that. It was made of metal, and, from the dull thud it made when she hit it, thick metal. There was no way of getting out through it.

There was no way of getting out at all.

The walls and floor – she had banged on the carpet – were concrete, or maybe stone. Even if she had a tool, a knife or a fork, there was no way she would be able to get through it. Besides, if she could make a hole, the man would see it as soon as it reached any size.

She was trapped. Well and truly trapped.

And no one knew where she was. If they did – if someone had seen the man pick her up – they would have come to rescue her by now. The fact they hadn't meant that they weren't coming at all.

She could be here for a long time.

She could be here *forever*.

And when she thought about it like that, she was overtaken by a panic that left her curled into a ball on the bed, trembling, her eyes wide open and her mind blank with fear.

When she wasn't consumed by panic she was thinking about her parents and brother and friends and what they were going through. She could picture them all: James would be quiet and withdrawn, keeping his feelings to himself. He'd always been like that; often he would be worried about something at school or with his friends and he would deny there was a problem over and over, until eventually he would come to Maggie's room and lie next to her and tell her what had happened.

She was the only person who could calm him down. And now she was gone.

Mum would be angry and tearful and fierce, and Dad; well, she worried about him the most. Mum loved her and James with total devotion, but Dad's love went further. He depended on them. His kids were what gave his life meaning. His own father had died when he was young and his mum had not seemed to cope very well. Maggie didn't know exactly what had happened, because he never talked about it, but she didn't think he had had a particularly happy childhood, and he had made up his mind to make sure the same didn't happen to his kids. He was never too busy for them, never had anything to do which was more important than whatever it was they wanted from him. All her life he had been there for her, calm and patient and reliable and loving. If she was interested in something, he explained it; if she wanted to help him wire plugs or change the oil in the car or put up shelves, he told her how and put the tools in her hands and watched as she did it. And he kept her safe, always.

She had no idea how he would cope with her disappearance.

That was what made her angriest about the man who had taken her. He didn't care what he did to her family, didn't care whether they became depressed or split up or committed suicide. All he cared about was getting what he wanted.

Which was her, in a cage.

She hated him for that. Not for wanting her, but for his selfishness and what it was doing to the people she loved.

And now, on top of it all, she was hungry. She was going to have to take food from him.

She heard the scraping noise. Her heart rate sped up; she felt the first fluttering of panic, a tightness in her chest. She sat up on the bed. Seconds later, the door opened.

The man stepped inside.

He was not holding a tray. He did not have food or water.

He looked tired and irritable.

'Well,' he said. 'I've had quite the afternoon, Fruitcake.'

Maggie looked behind him, wondering whether he had brought a tray and put it down and she had somehow missed it.

He followed her gaze, frowning.

'What is it?' he said.

She didn't answer. He looked at her, his expression at first questioning and then, slowly, understanding.

'Ah,' he said. 'You want something to eat. Well, I'm afraid that's impossible.' He scratched his nose, then inserted his finger into a nostril. 'I *did* make something, but I had to eat it.'

She closed her eyes. She didn't want to hear this. If there

was no food she wanted him to leave. Then there was no chance of him doing what he'd done the night before.

'Do you want to know why I had to eat it?'

Maggie shook her head.

'Don't be like that! It's interesting!'

Maggie shuffled backwards on the mattress until her back was against the wall. She hugged her knees to her chest.

He folded his arms. 'The police came. They were looking for you.'

She blinked, looking at him.

'Don't get your hopes up, though. They didn't have a warrant, and they have no reason to suspect me, other than the fact they always suspect me. They don't like me, you see. I let them have a look around so that they'd go away. I knew there was no chance they would find this place!'

He bounced up and down on his heels. 'That's when I ate the food. I'd made it for you just before they arrived. They saw it and I didn't want them wondering who it was for. So while they were banging around looking in cupboards and under beds – as if I'd be so stupid as to hide anything valuable in such an obvious place – I ate it. As though it was mine all along.'

He shrugged.

'And so no food until tomorrow.'

'Why,' Maggie said, in a whisper, 'why do they not like you?'

He shook his head ruefully. 'My wife,' he said. 'Ex-wife, that is, found some photographs I'd taken. She couldn't understand that they were harmless and innocent and she made a big fuss, and then the police came and she told them – can you believe that? She told them – about the photos and I had to destroy them.'

'What kind of photos?'

'Nothing, really! Photos of people. Girls, mainly. On the

way to and from school. She said it was disgusting that I took them, but she was wrong.' He leaned forward, his eyes bright. 'They were *beautiful*. Not obscene. Not disgusting. They were works of art. And they were harmless. The girls didn't even know I'd taken them.' He sighed. 'But it worked out well. It was serendipitous. You know what that means? It comes from the Three Princes of Serendip and it means lucky. Fortuitous. I'll tell you all about it some day. Anyway, it was serendipitous because it meant I had to re-start my collection and that meant I found *you*.'

Maggie was glad she hadn't eaten. If she had, she would have thrown it up.

'I saw you soon afterwards and I realized immediately you were special. You were the one I had to have. It had all happened for a reason: to lead me to you. There was something about you. A light you gave off. I could see you were kind and sweet and loving and I decided at that moment that I had to have you. I had to pluck you from the cruel and corrupting world you were in and keep you safe. You don't think so now, but in time you'll appreciate what I'm doing for you.'

'Please,' Maggie said. 'Leave me alone.'

'Then I discovered who you actually were. It was perfect. I couldn't *believe* who you were.'

'What do you mean?' Maggie said. 'Who am I?'

'That's for later,' he said. 'It took me a long time to get you. Every week I drove near your house, waiting for a chance to talk to you. And it finally came.'

He took a step towards her.

'And now you're finally here. Home.'

'This is not my home,' Maggie said. 'This will never be my home. This is a *prison*.'

'I'm sorry you feel that way,' the man said. 'But you'll change your mind, eventually. And I'm in no hurry. I have all the time in the world.'

He undid the belt on his blue bathrobe and walked across the room. Maggie pulled her knees tighter to her chest. 'No,' she said, her breathing shallow, the panic in full flow. 'No. Please. No.'

He frowned. 'OK,' he said. 'For you, Fruitcake, anything. But there is one thing I want.' He bent down and pressed his lips to her forehead. 'I just want a kiss from my little girl.'

She closed her eyes. The man said it again.

'Give me a kiss. Then I'll go away.'

It was awful, but it was better than the alternative. She turned her head and kissed him. His lips were warm and wet. His tongue stabbed into her mouth and she fought not to gag. The kiss only lasted a few seconds but it felt like a lifetime.

'Good night, my darling,' he said.

She waited until the door closed and she heard the scraping sound before she opened her eyes.

And then she started to sob.

Tuesday, 19 June 2018

Four Days to Go

1

She was already awake when Max rolled on to her chest and pressed his cheek to hers. Sleep had been impossible, her mind replaying her useless escape attempt.

Reminding her that her last chance was gone. The man would be on alert now, watching for anything out of the ordinary.

Behind it all was fury. She was furious with herself for her pathetic, stupid attempt. How could she have thought that would be enough? Had she really believed he had aged that much?

His words echoed in her head. *You really think that is enough to hurt me?*

He'd also called her a fool. He was right. She *was* a fool. A fool who had wasted her son's last chance at a life.

She picked up her calendar.

S	Su	M	Tu	W	Th	F
						~~1~~
~~2~~	~~3~~	~~4~~	~~5~~	6	~~7~~	~~8~~
~~9~~	~~10~~	~~11~~	~~12~~	~~13~~	~~14~~	~~15~~
~~16~~	~~17~~	~~18~~	~~19~~	20	21	22
23	24	25	26	27	28	29
30						

It was Tuesday. Tuesday of the last week she would have with Max. Tuesday of the last week of his life.

She blinked, and looked at her son. He was smiling in his half-sleep.

She listened for the man. He normally came soon after they woke and Maggie put the lights on. Maggie assumed it was the morning out there, and the man came at the same time every day, but it was possible he had a camera in the room and knew when she had woken. She had looked for one and hadn't found anything, but maybe it was too well hidden. She didn't really care.

All she cared about now was the calendar.

She lay on the mattress, listening for him. There was no sound of scraping. No footsteps outside the door. No handle turning.

Nothing but the low hum of the electric bulb in the lamp and the soft breathing of her son next to her.

Maybe he wasn't coming today. Maybe there was no food after what she had done. She didn't care. What was hunger in the midst of all the rest of it?

Max, as he was every morning, was full of energy and plans for the day as soon as he woke up.

'OK, Mummy,' he said, arranging his Duplo on the floor in front of him. 'Let's make a city. And then we can go to the moon on the light beam.'

'What a fun idea,' Maggie said. It was hard to keep her tone light and a smile on her lips. It was important, though, and she had discovered that if she kept her eyes locked on his she could almost forget what was coming.

Almost. It was as though there was a shadow at the corner of her vision that she could never quite escape.

But Max didn't need to know that. She didn't want to ruin his day – his last days – with the knowledge of how few of them there were. Besides, what would she tell him? That he had two siblings, eleven and seven, who may or may not have been killed by the man who brought them food? That he was next? That the world they visited in the stories his mum told him was real, and she had been stolen from it? Even if she did he would not be able to understand it.

No: better to pretend everything was OK. Better to keep the looming darkness as far from him as possible.

She knelt next to him, and reached for a red block. She was about to hand it to him and suggest he use it as the base for a tower when she was hit by a vision of Max screaming, his face twisted in an uncomprehending grimace as the man dragged him from her arms and from the room leaving her sobbing on the bed, her heart torn into pieces, wondering how – if – she would survive.

And then it shifted from a vision to a memory, first of Seb and then of Leo, her lost boys, her stolen chicks, the babies she had been unable to save.

The babies who had come before Max. The babies whose fate he was now facing.

She gasped, and turned from Max. She gripped her knees

and squeezed and tried to bring herself back to some semblance of control, her breathing fast and shallow.

'Mummy?' Max said, his eyes narrow with concern. 'MUMMY! Stop it, Mummy!'

Maggie blinked, staring at the wall and taking deep breaths, her heart gradually slowing.

'It's OK,' she said. 'I'm OK, darling. I had a – I just had some wind.'

Max was still, a Duplo brick in each hand, his eyes fixed on her. She – somehow – smiled and then scooped him up in her arms and pressed her face to his neck and kissed him and inhaled the smell of him and felt the panic starting all over again.

She closed her eyes and forced herself to think about something, anything, other than the man and Saturday and Max's third birthday, and, slowly, she calmed down.

'Mummy,' Max said. 'I think it's time for exercises.'

'Yes,' Maggie said. 'I think that sounds like a great idea. How about some running?'

Max nodded. The room was barely big enough for him to run in; Maggie was limited to jogging on the spot, which was, even when you were locked in a room with nothing to do, incredibly boring. She'd thought running on a treadmill was bad, but it had nothing on jogging for half an hour and not moving an inch. She could make it more interesting by throwing in some lunges and jumps and crouches, but it was a marginal improvement.

Other things held more appeal. She had become obsessed for a while with doing the perfect press-up: hands exactly shoulder-width apart, eyes slightly forward, back and legs a table, then a slow descent until her chest pressed to the floor followed by a clean, explosive return to the start, arms straight, elbows locked.

There was something satisfying about repeating it over

and over, focusing on each small detail until the sweat was dripping off her nose, her body quivering, nearly unable to carry on, slowly adding more and more press-ups to the total she was capable of. She enjoyed the firmness in her stomach, the lean muscles in her thighs, the strength in her back and shoulders. If – when – she got out of here she was going to keep doing her exercises with Max.

Apart from running on the spot. She was never doing that again. She would only run in forests and by rivers and in the sunlight and fresh air.

This time, though, she couldn't focus. It seemed pointless. Why bother? It passed the time, but other than that it didn't help. What was the point of keeping in shape? So she could live longer? Prolong the agony of being trapped?

She stopped and sat on her haunches, watching Max run from wall to wall. If he was taken from her she wouldn't be able to go on. All of a sudden it was clear: if he was taken, she would kill herself. One way or another, she would take her own life. Not because she wanted to die; she didn't. She believed she would get out of this, one day, and then she would, somehow, make up for all the years she'd been in here and her life would be full of family and friends and love and affection.

She would kill herself because she couldn't go through it again. Couldn't fall in love with another of her babies knowing that they would be taken from her.

After Max was gone the man would stop using condoms and she would get pregnant again and this sorry cycle would repeat itself. She didn't know why he did it. She asked him, once, but he looked away, suddenly hurt. She thought it might be that he had some twisted fantasy that they could be a family, and, if she was here long enough and had enough children it would somehow come to pass.

It would never come to pass, because this was the last

107

time. Either she saved Max, or she killed herself. She had thought about it before, but she had always pushed the idea away, thinking *maybe, sometime in the future, but not now.* This time was different. She could not repeat the cycle again.

She glanced at the calendar.

Whichever it was, this was the last time.

2

The hours spooled past with no sign of the man. Maggie was beginning to think he really wasn't coming when, Max lying in her arms, she heard the scraping noise. Max was talking to himself; he did it more and more these days, disappearing into a world of his own making. He had nowhere else to go. Other kids might have run to their bedroom, or watched a TV show or played make-believe with a friend. Max had only the inside of his own head.

The door opened. The man stepped inside and closed it behind him. He was holding a tray.

So they would eat – or at least Max would, she wasn't hungry – after all.

There was a bowl and a plate, both covered in foil, and a plastic jug of water.

He set the tray down on the floor.

Before she could stop him, Max jumped off her lap and toddled over to the man. He had never done it before. Ever since he was a baby, Maggie had held him on her lap when the man came. She hadn't said anything to him, hadn't *told* him to be wary of the man, but she hadn't needed to. It was easy enough for him to pick up on his mother's uneasiness.

When Max was awake the man rarely stayed longer than it took to drop off some food and pick up the plates from the day before, and he more or less ignored him. It was only at night, when Max was asleep, that the man stayed longer.

'Hello,' Max said. 'Is this food?'

The man looked at him, a half-smile on his face.

'Yes,' he said. 'It is.'

'I'm hungry,' Max said. Of course he was. He'd had no breakfast. He bent over and pointed to the bowl. 'Is that for me?'

Again, the man smiled. 'Yes,' he said. 'It's for you.'

Maggie watched, tensed on the edge of the bed. This was new. Part of her wanted to snatch Max up, keep him away from any contact with the man.

Part of her wanted it to carry on. He would, she was sure, fall in love with Max given the chance. He was, after all, his father, and there had to be some paternal instinct in there, somewhere. Moreover, there was the change in the man she'd noticed recently, the change that had led her to ask him to let them go.

The change that had led him to smile – half-smile – at Max.

And if he could do that, then . . . then . . .

She held the thought. She couldn't bear the hope.

Max gripped a corner of the foil and pulled it up.

'Mmm,' he said. 'Sausages.' He pulled the rest of the foil off and pointed at some broccoli. He looked at the man sternly. 'I don't like *that* though.'

'I don't suppose you do,' the man said, a playfulness in his voice that Maggie had never heard before. 'But then whoever heard of a little boy who liked vegetables?'

Max pulled the foil off entirely. He crunched it into a ball, listening to the sound it made. He dropped it on the floor, then picked it up and threw it across the room.

110

He laughed, and ran after it.

The man held out his hand to Max. 'Can I have that, please?'

Max frowned. 'I want it.'

The man's smile faded.

'Give it to me,' he said.

Maggie leaned forward. 'Give it to him, Max,' she said.

'But I like it,' Max said. 'I want to play with it.' He looked up at the man. 'Please,' he said. 'Please can I have it?'

There was a long pause, and then the man slowly nodded.

'OK,' he said. 'You can keep it.' He looked at Maggie. 'I'll be back later.' He pointed at the bath. 'With the hose.'

3

Bath day.

Once every three weeks they had a bath. Normally she looked forward to it; it was a rare treat. But today her mind had been on other things.

The bath in the corner had no water source. There was none in the room. All they had were the jugs that the man brought, which they used for drinking and washing and brushing their teeth.

On bath day, he fed in a hose. There was a nozzle on the end; he passed it to Maggie to fill up the bath and when she was done, he took it away. He stood by the door the whole time, unable to close it behind himself because of the hose blocking it.

The bath was an old rain barrel that the man had converted. It wasn't long enough to lie down in, so she and Max had to stand or kneel. Still, it was a luxury, because when he left, the bath was full of hot, clean water and she and Max could sit in it and play and splash and close their eyes and pretend they were in a warm sea somewhere far, far away.

When the water was cold, she would get out and dry Max

and hold him until he fell asleep, which wasn't long because he was exhausted by the novelty and excitement.

Then she would take out the plug and watch the water drain away, knowing that it would be another three weeks until they had another bath day to look forward to.

Because, even though there was no tap, there was a drain. There had to be. Short of removing the water in buckets, there was no other way of getting it out.

The water disappeared down a plug hole and into a pipe that came out of the base of the bath and crossed the two or three feet to the concrete wall. Maggie had tried to figure out where it went – maybe to a drain or a pump or on to some patch of earth floor on the other side of the wall. She had also tried to pull it out, hoping to make a hole in the wall that she could enlarge. But it was stuck fast.

It went somewhere, though, and watching the water drain away tortured her. She always wished that she and Max – or Seb or Leo – could somehow dissolve into the water and escape through the drain.

She heard the scraping sound and waited for the door to open. The man stood there, a hose in his hand. He passed it to her and she squeezed the trigger. Warm water sprayed on to the base of the bath. Max sat on the mattress, playing with the tinfoil ball. The man stared at him, with a look Maggie had not seen before. There was interest, but it was the dispassionate interest of a scientist. Her stomach felt loose and her thighs were weak. She wanted to throw the hose at the man and scream for him to get out, but she didn't. She held the hose over the bath and let it run.

When the bath was full, the man took the hose from her. He looked at the water.

'Have fun,' he said.

4

When the man was gone, Maggie stripped naked and climbed into the bath. The base of the bath was higher than the floor of the room. It had to be – the pipes for the drain needed some space under the plug hole – and it meant she had to bend extra low to pick up Max.

He was standing on the floor, in his underpants and a T-shirt, looking up at her. He gripped the bottom of the T-shirt and pulled it up, exposing the pale, smooth skin of his stomach. His belly button protruded about half an inch; she wondered whether it was because of the way she had cut the umbilical cord when he was born, or whether it would have been like that anyway.

He lifted his hands, stretching the cotton over his face. He wriggled his shoulders, bending at the waist and twisting his arms in a futile attempt to take the T-shirt off. She laughed; watching him try to undress but succeed only in wrapping himself even tighter in his clothes was one of the few sources of amusement she had.

'Mummy,' he said, his voice muffled. 'Can you help me?'

'Of course,' Maggie said. She straightened out the T-shirt

– it was getting tight, he was growing so quickly – and pulled it off in one smooth movement.

He smiled up at her, his face red with the effort, then stepped out of his underpants and held up his arms to be lifted into the water.

As she picked him up she held him against her body. She loved the feeling of his skin against hers; it had been the same with Seb and Leo and it brought back memories of her other sons, of Max's brothers.

It reminded her she had lost them.

And it reminded her she was going to lose Max.

She started to cry. She blinked away the tears. Max didn't need to see her crying. She sank down and dipped her head under the surface, washing her face clean, then sprang out, water dripping from her face, and grinned at him.

'Surprise! It's the bath monster!'

He giggled, and started to splash water at her. 'No! *I'm* the bath monster!'

'You *are*,' Maggie replied. 'You're my little bath monster.'

He splashed her again and she shrieked in mock terror. 'Oh! Stop! Please, Bath Monster, please!'

He erupted in laughter and splashed harder. She remembered doing the same thing with her parents; for a child of Max's age there was something irresistible about splashing or tickling or pushing your parents over. It was a kind of subversion of the natural order, and she remembered finding it delicious.

Max clearly did, too, and she let him throw and kick and push as much water at her as he wanted.

When he had had enough and the water was getting cold, she pulled the plug and climbed out of the bath. She reached for Max.

'No,' he said. 'I want to stay in.'

'OK.' She picked up the towel – the man left one by the door, a thinning, faded-pink scrap – and dried herself. 'Let me know when you're ready.'

She dressed, running her hands over the dark hairs on her thighs and lower legs. It had been a few months since the man brought her a safety razor and she had shaved her legs. She never asked for one, but from time to time he left one, along with a bar of soap, on the food tray.

The first time she had ignored it – God, it seemed so long ago, so much of her life had been spent between these four walls – but the next bath day it was there again.

The man gestured at it as he left the room, then caught her eye. His face was expressionless, but it looked like he was struggling to keep it that way. She got the impression that underneath it was a subdued rage.

He pointed at the light bulb.

Use the razor, he said. *In fact, I'll watch. I shouldn't have left it with you. Never know what you might do. I wasn't thinking.*

And since then, every few bath days, he brought a razor and sat and watched as she spread soap on her legs and shaved them. It would probably be time again quite soon, judging by the hairs that had grown.

She became aware that the room was totally quiet.

She looked up, and her heart stopped.

There was no noise coming from the bath – no splashes, no dripping, no giggles.

No little boy peering over the side.

'Max!' she called. 'Max!'

He was probably fine. The bath was deep, so he could easily be hidden, but it was the lack of noise that worried her, that made her picture his body, face down in the water.

It was funny: losing your child in a supermarket or park or outside school was every parent's worst nightmare. The moment, even if it only lasted for a split-second, when you couldn't see them, was heart-stopping. Even she, trapped in a place where there was nowhere he could have gone, had that feeling. It was something primal, instinctive.

And she was panicking now.

Then there was a noise. A hollow thump, like a bass drum. There was a pause, and then it came again. Maggie breathed out, her lips pursed. He was there. Safe and making noise. She walked over to the bath. Max was sitting on the floor, banging his heel against the wood. The noise reverberated around the room, amplified by the space between the floor and the base of the bath.

Maggie smiled. 'Well, well,' she said. 'Quite the musician, aren't you?'

'Bang!' Max thumped the wood. 'Bang!'

Maggie leaned over and tapped out the knock that everyone learned – *dum dum duh-dum dum* – *dum, dum* – then ruffled his hair.

'Try that.'

Max banged a random series. Maggie did the knock again. He frowned in concentration, then tried to copy her. It wasn't much better, but she clapped her hands together.

'Well done! I think you might be a pop star when you grow up.'

'What's that?' he asked.

'Someone who sings songs.'

'I like singing.'

'Me too. And you never know. Maybe you'll be famous.'

He would be, if he ever got out of here, but not as a pop star. As the boy who had been born in a basement. The problem was he wouldn't get out. In four days he'd be three, and the man would come for him.

There'd be no more baths. No more laughter and splashing. No more anything.

She wanted this moment to never end. She wanted him to stay in the bath, happy and clean and naked and perfect, forever.

Twelve Years Earlier, 29 July 2006

1

Martin stirred milk into his tea and stared out of the kitchen window. It had been three weeks since she had gone. He looked at the orange pill container in his hand. Only a few left.

There should have been more. At a rate of one a day there should have been a *lot* more.

But one a day wasn't enough to quiet the voices in his head. Not nearly enough. Two muted them; three turned them into background noise.

For a while. And then the volume slowly turned up again.

Sometimes the voices blamed him. Told him he was useless. He should have protected her, taken her to Anne's house, made sure she got there safely.

Sometimes it was Sandra's voice saying those things. Even though she'd never said it in real life, she probably thought it. She must do. He did, after all.

Other times it was Maggie's voice. That was when it was the worst. That was when he took more of the pills, took as many as he needed to quiet her voice.

Hi, Dad. Door slamming. *What's for tea? Can I have a lift to Kevin's house?*

Can I have a lift to Anne's house?

And he'd turn and look but she wouldn't be there and it would all come back. The loss, the pain, the terror.

And she would speak again.

Help me, Daddy. Why can't you help me? Why can't you find me? I'm your daughter? Why can't you find me?

And he would clap his hands to his head and try to shake the voices loose but it was impossible. There were reminders of her everywhere. Her bedroom door was closed; Martin didn't want to see inside it, didn't want to be slapped in the face with a reminder of the fact she was gone, but he was anyway, she was everywhere in the house. It wasn't the objects, the photos of her, the shoes she had left on the mat in the hall and her coats in the closet, ready for her return, it wasn't the things themselves which bothered him.

They were just objects. They could be ignored or hidden or put away.

It was the memories that haunted him, and they were *everywhere*.

When he went up the stairs he saw her sitting on the top step, back to the wall, phone to her ear. When he sat in the armchair he saw her lying on the couch, feet dangling over one arm, a hole in the toe of her socks. When he switched on the hallway light he remembered installing the dimmer switch with her, watching as she screwed the wires into place, her tongue between her teeth as she concentrated.

The house was full of her, but she was nowhere to be found.

And so he would take a pill, or two.

Or three.

And now there weren't many left. He'd explain it to Doctor Chalmers. She'd understand. She'd known Maggie since she was a baby; when she'd come to the house to see him and Sandra and given them the prescription she'd been in tears herself.

120

He unscrewed the lid and emptied the contents on to his palm. Three left. He felt a rising panic. He'd call Dr Chalmers later and get some more.

'Hey.'

He turned. Sandra was in the doorway. She was wearing jogging pants and a sweatshirt. Her hair was scraped back in a bun and her face was lean.

Gaunt, nearly. She'd lost weight.

They both had. For the first time in years – decades, maybe – he had a flat stomach.

'Tea?' he said.

She shook her head. 'Have you got any more of those?'

He showed her the pills in his hand. 'This is it.'

'Share?'

He didn't want to. He didn't want to at all, but he nodded and handed her a pill. Her eyes rested on the two he still had in his palm, the two to her one, but she said nothing. He lifted them to his mouth and swallowed, then took a sip of tea.

'You've not got any left?' he said.

She shook her head. 'I thought I had more. But they're gone.'

'OK,' he said. 'We can get more.' He looked at her, his lip quivering. 'When will this get better, Sandy? When will it stop hurting so much?'

'When she's back.'

For a second he didn't reply. When he did, the words were ash in his mouth. 'When she's back.'

2

Martin sat on the couch, staring into space. The cup of tea in his hand was cold. The living room door opened.

'Dad,' James said. 'I'm going out. With Andy.'

Martin swallowed. This was the second time James had gone out alone. It had been hard to let him, when, two days before, his friend Andy had knocked on the door. They had promised to stay together, and so Martin and Sandra – after giving him one of their mobile phones – had agreed.

Be back at six p.m. Promise.

He had promised, and then come home much earlier than six, pale and strained, and gone straight to his room. Martin had followed and found him curled up on his bed.

OK? he asked.

James nodded. He was crying, softly.

I miss her, he said. *I miss her, Dad.*

Martin hugged him. *Me too, son.*

And now he was going out again. Martin didn't know how he could. He hated leaving the house. Outside, he saw her face in the windows of each bus or car or truck that passed him. Every girl of her age that he saw in a crowd was her. Twice, he had glimpsed someone, and, convinced it was Maggie with a different haircut and new clothes, had run after them.

Twice, he had tapped someone on the shoulder and, when they turned to look at him, seen only an expression of alarm on the face of a girl who was not Maggie.

Twice, he had mumbled an apology and shuffled away, pulse racing, breathless, his heart freshly broken.

Twice he had told himself she was not going to be on a bus or walking around the supermarket and he must not approach strangers. Still he saw her everywhere.

But it was never her.

'Is Andy coming here?'

'Yeah. Soon.'

'What time will you be back?'

'Seven. We're seeing a film.'

'Promise?'

'Promise.'

There was a knock on the door.

'That's him,' James said. 'Bye, Dad.'

Martin handed him his mobile phone. 'Call Mum's number or the house phone if you need to. OK?'

'OK.'

'Love you, Jimbo.'

'Love you too, Dad.'

He kissed him on the forehead, and watched him leave the house, praying silently that he would be back safely.

3

Martin looked at the clock on the DVD player: 19:00.

He glanced at Sandra. The minute-counter changed: 19:01.

'He's late,' Martin said.

Sandra looked at him. 'It's one minute past.'

'I was expecting him early.'

Sandra nodded slowly. Her face was expressionless and he was half expecting her to tell him, *Life goes on, don't worry, it's only a minute*, but she covered her eyes and rubbed her temples. When she looked up, her cheeks were wet with tears.

'I know,' she said. 'I've been waiting for him to come home ever since he left. I can't bear the thought of him being away from us, not for even a second. But we can't live like that. *He* can't live like that, trapped in his house by his parents.'

She was right, but Martin couldn't help thinking he'd quite like it if James was trapped in the house. The thought of anything happening to him was unbearable. He knew that he would take his own life if he lost his son; already daily life was a torture of desperation and grief, made all the worse by the hope, the tiny sliver of hope that she would walk in the door any day and apologize and they would hug and kiss her and be angry for a second but too relieved, too happy to really care where she'd been. It was that tiny hope that made it all so hard. He couldn't move on, couldn't give up on someday having her back.

From time to time he had wondered whether it would be better if she had died, if there had been a car crash and they had gone to identify her body. At least that would have been final.

But it wouldn't have been. The hope may have made it all that much more torturous, but it was a price he would pay if it meant he got to see her again.

He tried not to think of the price she might be paying. If she was alive, the best possibility was that she was with a boyfriend, too high to call her parents, or living on the streets, suffering from some kind of amnesia. The other alternatives were far worse: kidnapped and sold as a sex slave, locked in a basement and chained to a bed somewhere.

The thought of that made him wince with a physical pain. She was his little girl. She should be here, where he could protect her.

And now James was late. He picked up Sandra's phone and dialled the number of the phone he had given James.

It went to voicemail.

'James,' he said. 'Phone when you get this.'

'He didn't answer?'

'Voicemail.' He tried to recall when he had last charged the phone he'd given to James. He was pretty sure it had been full when he handed it over, but maybe the battery was faulty. 'Maybe no battery,' he said.

Sandra shook her head. 'Go and look for him,' she said. 'Drive to the cinema and see if he's there. They sometimes play video games afterwards.'

He stood up. 'OK,' he said. 'I'll go.'

'I'll stay here. In case he comes home.'

Martin walked out of the living room. On the way past the phone in the hall he called Andy's house. His mum answered.

'Hi, it's Martin Cooper. I was wondering whether James is with you?'

There was a long, awkward silence. He could almost hear her thinking, *The poor man, worrying about his son. It's no wonder, though.*

'No,' she said. 'I think Andy went to meet him. He said he'd be home soon. He's normally quite punctual.'

'OK. If he does show up, would you call?'

It was light outside, the summer sun still warm and high in the sky. He started the car and wound the window down, driving slowly so he could look at the pedestrians. He felt a sudden weakness in his legs at the memory of doing this three weeks ago, looking for Maggie.

He couldn't believe it was happening again.

It was about a ten-minute drive to the cinema. By the time he got there he was in a full-on panic, heart racing, palms sweating. It was a struggle to stop himself coming to a dead stop in the middle of the road and screaming at the top of his voice. He parked directly outside – if he got a fine he'd just pay it, he didn't care – and went inside.

There was a long queue for tickets. It snaked through a set of ropes; he ignored it and walked to the front, standing behind a middle-aged couple. He looked back at the people who were next in line.

'Sorry,' he said. 'Emergency.'

The man behind the counter tilted his head. 'Yes?' he said.

'Have you seen two boys? About fourteen.'

'It's a cinema, mate. On a Saturday. It's full of teenage kids.'

'I know, but . . .' His voice tailed off. 'It's important.'

The man sighed. 'What do they look like?'

He realized he had not brought a photo. 'One of them – James, my son – is tall. About five ten, skinny. Hair's blond, short on the sides and kind of long on top. Lots of gel. He was wearing a Nirvana T-shirt. His friend is shorter, very blond hair. Bleached, almost.'

'Blond eyebrows?'

'Yes. I think so.'

'Tall?'

Martin nodded. 'Exactly.'

'I think I did see them. A while back. Their film's over now, though. Has been for a while.'

'Do you have CCTV?'

The man frowned. 'Yeah, but I can't let you see it. You'd have to ask the manager. Is everything OK, mate?'

Martin pursed his lips.

'I don't know,' he said.

4

He called Sandra. 'Is he home?'

'No.' She didn't ask whether he had found James. She didn't need to.

'OK,' he said. 'I'm on my way back. And then we're going to find him, one way or another.'

It was eight-thirty when he walked into the house. There had to be something wrong. There was no way James would have been so stupid – not to say insensitive – as to stay out late after what had happened to Maggie.

Sandra was standing in the kitchen, staring out of the window.

'You didn't find him,' she said. 'He's gone.'

Martin's chest constricted. 'No,' he said. 'No. I can't believe this. This cannot be happening. Not again.'

'Call DI Wynne,' she said. 'Let her know.'

Martin scrolled to her number. She picked up on the second ring. There was music playing in the background. Something classical Martin did not recognize.

'This is Martin Cooper,' he said. 'Maggie's dad.'

The music went off.

'Yes,' she replied. 'Is something the matter, Mr Cooper?'

'James is missing,' he said. 'He went out earlier and hasn't come back.'

There was a long silence. 'How long has he been gone?'

'He was due back a couple of hours ago.'

'That's not long for a teenage boy.'

'I know. But with Maggie . . .' Martin's voice tailed off.

'Yes,' DI Wynne said. 'I understand. I'll come to your house. I'll be there as soon as I can.'

As he hung up the doorbell rang. He looked at Sandra. She walked out into the hall and he followed her. He watched as she opened the door.

Her shoulders straightened and her eyes widened, then she opened her arms and half-ran, half-jumped outside. Martin ran to the door.

She was standing on the step, hugging James.

Martin hugged him too. There was a sour smell coming off his son. 'Where've you been?' he said, his relief keeping his anger in check. 'We were so worried.'

Before James could answer a man stepped into view. He was in his fifties, bald and wearing faded chinos and a white shirt.

'Good evening,' he said. 'I take it this is your son?'

'Yes,' Martin said. 'Did you bring him home?'

'I found him and he gave this address.' He gave a tight smile. 'I think he may have been drinking.'

He had. That was the sour smell. Martin would deal with that later. For now, he wanted to get James inside, then call Wynne to tell her not to come after all. Before he could thank the man, Sandra spoke.

'Are you . . .' she said. 'Are you Mr Best?'

5

The man – Best – peered at her through his glasses. 'Sandra?' he said. 'Is that Sandra Ferguson?'

'Cooper, now,' Sandra said. 'But yes.'

'Well, I never. How nice to see you. It's been what? Twenty years?'

'I guess,' Sandra said. 'Although it's hard to believe it's that long. How are you?'

'Good. I'm retired now. How are you?' He hesitated, and took a small step backwards. 'Didn't I hear . . . ?'

'Yes,' Sandra said. 'Our daughter – she – she went missing.'

'Oh dear,' he said. 'How very sad.' He looked at Martin. 'I'm very sorry for you both.'

'Thank you,' Martin said. There was something about the precise, polite formality of the man that he found almost intimidating. It was so practised, so impenetrable. 'I take it you two know each other?'

'We do,' Best said. 'I had the pleasure of teaching your wife. Although that was a long time ago. I was much younger then.'

'We both were,' Sandra said. 'I was Maggie's age. Mr Best taught Maths at St Joe's.'

James was standing between Martin and Sandra. Without warning, he sat heavily on the step. His eyes were bloodshot and unfocused.

'OK,' Martin said. 'We need to get you inside.' He knelt and held James's face in his hands. It was hot and flushed. He kissed his son's forehead. 'Come on, Jimbo. Time for a cup of tea.'

James nodded. 'I'm OK.' His words were slurred and another wave of booze wafted off him.

'I'm not sure about that,' Martin said. He helped James to his feet. 'Where did you find him?'

'I was out for a walk,' Best said. 'And I saw him coming out of the park. He fell into a hedge and was sick. He was with a friend, but the other boy ran off when I came near. Your son was too incapacitated to follow him.'

'And you brought him home?' Martin asked.

'I have some experience with boys of this age,' Best said. 'And they will do this kind of thing. I felt it was for the best that he was not left on the street.'

Sandra smiled at him. 'Thank you,' she said. 'With what happened to Maggie – our daughter – we were going crazy with worry.'

'I can imagine.' Best took a deep breath. 'Well, he's home now. I didn't know you still lived here. Perhaps I'll see you around the village.'

'Yes,' Sandra said. 'That would be lovely.'

'And good luck. I hope your daughter is returned to you soon. I'm sure she will be.'

'Thank you. Goodnight, Mr Best.'

Sandra closed the door. She turned to James and wrapped her arms around him.

'James,' she said. 'I want to be angry at you, but I can't. But don't you ever do that again. I can't go through it. Promise?'

131

James looked at her through bleary eyes. 'Promise,' he mumbled.

Martin slipped an arm around him.

'I'll put him to bed,' he said. 'We can deal with this in the morning.'

6

When James was upstairs – shoes off but still wearing the rest of his clothes – Martin went downstairs. Sandra was on her mobile. He sat next to her on the couch and called DI Wynne.

'No need to come,' Martin said. 'He's here.'

'I'm glad to hear it,' Wynne said.

'Sorry. For wasting your time.'

'That's fine. Totally understandable in the circumstances. Call any time you need.'

Sandra hung up. 'That was Marcia. Andy's mum. Apparently he got home and tried to sneak upstairs without anyone noticing. He was drunk too. She got the story out of him – some older boys bought them some cider or something and they went to drink it in the park.'

'The cinema guy said they were at the film.'

'Sounds like they had the bright idea to get drunk on the way home.'

'I'll talk to him in the morning,' Martin said. 'But honestly, for now I'm just glad he's home.'

'Me too,' Sandra said. She moved closer to him and he

put his arm around her. 'What are we going to do?' she said. 'How are we going to get through this?'

Martin didn't answer for a while.

'I don't know,' he said eventually. 'I really don't know.'

Twelve Years Earlier,
30 July 2006

1

DI Wynne scrolled through her contacts. She hated making this kind of call, hated knowing that the recipient might think she had good news, and would be disappointed when she told them that *no, there were no new leads*.

But she had to call Maggie's parents. She couldn't leave them in the dark; even though she had nothing specific to share, people wanted to be kept in the loop – as far as she could – about the investigation.

And she had nothing. Maggie was either dead, or she had been abducted and was a prisoner somewhere – and it could be anywhere – or she had been trafficked, in which case she could be anywhere in the world, working most likely in the sex trade, watched day and night, with no documents and no money. She'd be given ready access to drugs and alcohol and, when she was no longer of value, she'd be killed and disposed of, dumped in a lake or river, buried in a forest or desert, or thrown into an incinerator. No one would miss her. No one would report her absence to the police, and even if they did, the police wouldn't be able to do anything. They would have no idea who she was.

Martin Cooper answered on the second ring.

'Yes,' he said. 'DI Wynne?'

She was stung by the hope in his voice.

'Just a routine call, I'm afraid,' Wynne said. 'To let you know we are still pursuing all avenues as thoroughly as we can. And to answer any questions you might have.'

'I don't have any.' His voice was flat. 'But thank you for checking in.'

'Not a problem,' Wynne said. 'By the way, is your son OK?'

'More or less,' Martin Cooper said. 'Although I'm not sure OK is the best description. He was very drunk.'

'Perhaps he needed to let off some steam,' Wynne said. 'He's safe, at least.'

'Exactly,' Martin Cooper said. 'And he would have been gone longer but someone found him and brought him home.'

'That's fortunate,' Wynne said. 'Better than having him stagger around the streets. He was lucky to run into someone so responsible. Not everyone is that civic-minded these days, especially when it comes to teenage boys.'

'He was a teacher,' Martin said. 'So he wasn't scared of fourteen-year-old boys. It was an odd coincidence, actually. I knew him. He was Sandra's maths teacher in school. Mr Best.'

Wynne almost missed it. She had not been fully paying attention; she was going out that evening – a rare occurrence – with someone she had met at the gym. Wynne was having a coffee after a spinning class; the woman had been in the class and, afterwards, had sat at her table and pointed at the coffee.

That won't re-hydrate you, she said.

It might give me some energy, Wynne replied, aware that she was still red-faced and sweating, whereas the woman – Nicky, it turned out – was showered and dressed and fully composed.

136

Try one of these. She had a bright green antioxidant fruit shake. *It's a great boost.*

Wynne shook her head. *Coffee, for me,* she said.

Want to meet for one? the woman asked. *Or a real drink?*

And they were meeting tonight.

She paused.

'Best?' she said. 'Late fifties? Balding? Metallic glasses?'

'Yes,' Martin said. 'You know him?'

'I do.'

'Did he teach you?'

He didn't, but Wynne knew she couldn't say how she knew Best. An unproven allegation of interest in underage girls – Wynne happened to believe it, but that was irrelevant – was not something she could share with the general public. It was slander.

It was also a coincidence.

And Wynne did not like coincidences.

'Oh,' she said. 'It's a small town. I've come across him a few times. He seems a pleasant man.' She hesitated. 'I was wondering whether you would be OK with me talking to James? About the night he was brought home?'

'Why?' Martin said. 'What's that got to do with anything?'

'Probably nothing,' Wynne said. 'But it's better to be thorough.'

There was a silence on the line. 'Then feel free,' he said.

137

2

James sat on the couch. His hands were folded in his lap, his fingers moving nervously.

'Am I in trouble?' he said. 'For underage drinking?'

'Not with me,' Wynne replied. 'Although I imagine your mum and dad aren't too pleased.'

He sat back on the couch. 'Then what is it?'

'I want to talk to you about what happened that night. Why don't you take me through it?'

'Is someone else in trouble? For selling us alcohol?'

She shook her head. 'I'm not really interested in that kind of thing. And I can promise you I won't do anything with any information you give me. I want you to speak as freely as possible.'

'OK.' He paused. 'Me and Andy went – we went to see a film. We saw *Pirates of the Caribbean*. Andy had some White Lightning cider and he snuck it in. We drank it and we were pretty loud – laughing, that kind of thing – and the usher kicked us out. So we went to the park, and on the way we bought some Mad Dog—'

'Mad Dog?' Wynne said.

'It's a drink: MD twenty-twenty. We call it Mad Dog. It's cheap.'

'And you drank it in the park?'

He nodded. 'We bought four bottles. I drank a bit more than Andy, I think.'

'And then what?'

'I was sick, and I lay down by the roundabout. Andy said we should go home and after that I don't really remember anything until I woke up at home.'

'And Mr Best?' She leaned forward. 'Do you remember seeing him?'

'No. I think I'd passed out before he showed up.'

'You didn't see him before you passed out? In the park?'

'No. Why would I? Has he done something?'

Wynne shook her head. 'Just checking.' She got to her feet. 'Thank you, James. That was very helpful. I can see myself out.'

3

DI Wynne walked up to Best's front door and rang the door-bell. She stepped back and waited.

It opened a few moments later. Best looked at her. He was dressed in a pair of old jeans with grass stains on the knees and a loose-fitting sweater. He folded his arms.

'Hello,' he said. 'You again. How can I help you this time?'

'I have some questions.'

'I've given you all the information I have.' Best shook his head. 'What's your name again? I've a mind to report you. This is tantamount to police harass—'

Wynne glanced around then shoved him hard in the chest. He stumbled backwards and she stepped into the hall. She shut the front door, her heart beating hard in her chest, and swung her right foot hard into his shin. There was a loud crack. Best bent over, his hand clutching at his damaged leg.

'You shut the fuck up,' she said. 'And listen to me.'

Best looked up at her, his eyes wary.

'What were you doing last night? With Maggie Cooper's brother?'

'Nothing.' He stood up, wincing in pain. 'It was a simple coincidence.' He gestured at the front of the house. 'The park

140

is there. I was walking home and I saw him come out. I didn't know he was related to the Coopers.'

Wynne stared at him. 'I don't believe you,' she said. 'I don't believe a word you say. You're a lying piece of shit.'

He shrugged. 'He was in the park getting drunk. How could I have had anything to do with that? He was drunk on the street outside my house and I was concerned. That's all there is to it, Detective Inspector Wynne.'

It was true: James had confirmed it. But still. Why was he watching? And would he have done the same for another teenager?

'So you took him home?'

'I did. Like I said, I was concerned.'

'Do you make a habit of that? Driving drunk young boys home?'

'No, I don't. This was the first time it has happened.'

'And by coincidence it was the brother of Maggie Cooper.'

'Yes.'

'Whose mother you taught.'

'Yes. I taught a lot of the people in this town.' He sighed. 'I'm afraid you're chasing shadows. I saw a young man in need of help. That's all. I look out for my fellow citizens.'

'Especially the young girls.'

'This again.' He ran his hand over his face and shook his head. 'I told you last time, it's not true. My wife and I had a very messy break-up and she invented the whole thing to discredit me. It was scurrilous nonsense. And it cost me a lot of money in the divorce. She threatened to spread her lies to more people if I didn't give her whatever she wanted.'

'But you paid,' Wynne said. 'Didn't you? You settled with her. Why would you, if it wasn't true?'

'Because people would have believed her. She is a very unpleasant and unstable woman and I was happy to be rid of her.'

Wynne shook her head. 'You're lying to me.'

'I hope you can prove it.'

The problem was, he was right. She was skating on thin ice. She had no right to be here – his wife had dropped the charges against him and they had found no photos at the time. Wynne was sure he had been taking them – and that he continued to do so – but she had no proof. Best was too clever to leave any evidence in the house.

There wasn't much she could do.

Best rubbed his shin. 'This is harassment, and if it continues I will report you to the Police Complaints Commission.'

'No you won't,' Wynne said.

'I will, and you'll be in all kinds of—'

Wynne prodded a finger in his chest.

'Go to the PCC,' she said. 'Go and tell them what I did, and when you do, I'll explain why. There'll be all kinds of attention on you – and I think that's the last thing you want, Best.'

'Look,' he said. 'I understand what you're thinking, and I have every sympathy with you. You think there is a coincidence here – because you believe my wife's accusations you think I may have something to do with the disappearance of this young girl. Then you discover I brought her brother home, and I taught her mother. But there is no coincidence, because those accusations are untrue. I have no . . .' he paused, searching for the right word, '. . . *unnatural* interest in young girls, and I had nothing to do with whatever happened to Maggie Cooper. Once you discount my wife's accusations then you'll see all that happened is I helped out a young man – remember, I was a teacher, so I understand teenagers – who is the son of someone I taught . . . And there are many sons and daughters of people I taught in this town.'

She looked at him, keeping her face expressionless. What he said was perfectly plausible, but only if you accepted that his wife's accusations were false. And Wynne didn't.

142

'Moreover,' Best said. 'If you return here, I will not let you in unless you have the correct legal status, by which I mean a warrant. And then, even if you have one, when you fail to find anything, I will lodge my complaint.' He looked at her. 'I imagine you are quite proud to have achieved your rank, Detective Inspector. No doubt you are considered promising and talented. What you lack is the wisdom to know when you are mistaken – as you are now.'

Wynne put her hands behind her back. She dug her fingernails into her palms. She wanted to grab him by the throat and squeeze the truth out of him. Squeeze the *life* out of him.

But she couldn't. That would end her career.

And there was always the possibility that she was mistaken. All she had to go on was a feeling, and that was not enough, at least not in a court of law.

She turned, and walked to the front door. She closed it behind her and walked away. It was her only option, but she could not shake the feeling that she was making a terrible mistake.

Twelve Years Earlier,
31 July 2006

1

Maggie lay on her side, her knees to her chest. She didn't know what to do, whether to sit or stand or lie down. Even the choice between keeping her eyes open or closed was beyond her: if she opened them, she was reminded of where she was, the horror of her situation. If she closed them, images of the man in his bathrobe came to her.

And it had only got worse.

She had stomach cramps, cramps she recognized. Period cramps. She felt bloated and lethargic and soon she would need a tampon.

There were none, of course. The man had not thought of providing any. She would have to ask him for some, but if the blood came before he did then all she had was the wash-cloth. She would have to use that.

In amongst it all, though, was relief.

She was not pregnant.

He had raped her four times, each time without using a condom. Each time she had wondered if she was pregnant.

So the cramps were welcome. They also meant – she hoped – that he would leave her alone, that there would be some respite from the door opening and him standing there in his blue bathrobe, his thin, hairless ankles above his sandals.

She clutched her stomach and groaned. She always got bad period pains but the cramps were worse than usual this time. She'd have to ask for something to help. Paracetamol, maybe.

Then she heard it. The scraping sound that meant he was on his way. She'd been awake awhile; it was probably lunchtime. He'd bring one of the awful meals he made but she wouldn't eat much of it. She had no appetite. Maybe she'd drink something.

The handle turned and the door opened. The man was standing there holding a tray. He stepped forward and put it down; he was moving awkwardly, like he was in pain. His jeans had grass stains on the knees. She had an image of her and her mum and dad and brother in the garden, mowing the lawn and sunbathing, and a wave of longing washed over her.

'I need something,' she muttered.

'What? Are you ill?' His voice was low, and clipped.

'I have – I have my period.'

He looked at her blankly. 'I see. I hadn't thought of that. What do you need, exactly?'

'Paracetamol,' she said. 'For the pain. And Tampax. I need two types: heavy and regular. Heavy for the first few days.'

'I have ibuprofen,' he said. 'I had to take some myself earlier. I had a bit of a' – he glanced at his shins – 'a run-in with something.'

'That'll be fine. But I need the Tampax more.'

'Where would I get them?' he asked.

'Supermarket. Or chemist.'

He nodded. 'But why would I be buying – those things? It'll look strange.'

'I don't know,' she said. 'But I need them.'

'How soon?'

'Now.'

He looked at the tray. 'Here's your dinner. I'll be back as soon as I can.'

2

Maggie didn't know exactly how long it was before he came back. Hours, certainly, but how many she could not tell. Time was different in here. She had no way of knowing whether it was morning or afternoon or evening. All she had to go on was the man. He came with breakfast, and then he came with dinner.

And sometimes after that, in his bathrobe.

In the mornings she marked her calendar. Another day gone. Over three weeks, now. Over three weeks in here, in this place where there was nothing to do but sit and stare at the walls.

It felt like a different life. A different *world*. She was already finding it hard to picture her family, but she knew one thing.

They would be missing her. More than missing her. They would be torn apart by her loss. By now they would think she was dead, and would be grieving for her. Had they held a memorial service for her? She pictured it, all her friends and family gathered in some room, photos of her playing on a projector.

It was sick. She needed to help them, somehow. Get a message to them to let them know she was still alive. At least if they knew that they would not have to worry she was dead.

But there was no way she could contact them. The room was totally isolated; the only way would be telepathy, and she'd tried that. She'd sat cross-legged on the floor in the middle of the day and closed her eyes and concentrated, hard, on her brother and mother and father, beaming messages to them.

Nothing came back. Was it possible they had felt her presence for a moment? Maybe, but she had no way of knowing.

She wondered how James was taking it. She missed him with an intense, physical ache. Yes, he was annoying – he was a younger brother – but she loved him, and she knew he loved her. *Adored* her, in fact. On her twelfth birthday he had made her a sculpture of a crab out of clay; they had been on holiday to Brittany and eaten crab, which they had all loved, so he had honoured the memory in art. Sculpture, it turned out, was not one of his gifts and she had laughed at it; James had snatched it back, hurt.

Afterwards her mum had taken her aside.

Be kind to him, Mags, she said. *You're his big sister and he looks up to you. He always has. He was an anxious toddler, and often the only way we could calm him down was if you were there. He needs* you. *And he was hoping you'd love that sculpture.*

Her words sank in. Maggie fished the sculpture out of the bin and put it on her shelf. It was still there.

The thought of James looking at it in her empty room made her head swim with nausea.

She yawned and lay on the mattress. How could she be tired? She did nothing but sleep and lie around. She needed to start doing some kind of exercise, if only for something to do.

She heard the scraping noise. The door opened and the man came in. He placed two boxes on the floor.

'Is this what you need?'

He prodded the boxes towards her with his toe and she picked them up.

'Yes,' she said. 'These are fine.'

'I had to go far away to buy them,' he said. 'I didn't want anyone to see me. That's why it took a long time.'

She nodded. She pictured him in a supermarket in some out-of-town retail park, a cap pulled low on his head, buying the tampons in silence then hurrying to his car and driving back on the motorway. For the first time she wondered what would happen to her if something happened to him? What if a truck hit him and he was killed? How long would it be before someone found her? Presumably wherever she was was well hidden, so it could be days. Weeks.

Months.

He nodded at the food he had brought earlier. It was untouched.

'You're not hungry?'

She shook her head.

'You need to eat.'

Maggie looked away. She didn't need a lecture on nutrition from him. 'Like you care,' she said, aware she sounded like a surly teenager.

She wasn't too bothered. She wasn't normally a surly teenager, but she had a pass this time. She had plenty to be surly about.

'Of course I care,' he said.

'No,' Maggie said. 'If you cared about me you wouldn't keep me in here.'

'That's *why* I keep you in here. Don't you see that? I told you. I have to keep you safe.'

'How is this safe?'

'Because it's not out there.' He pointed above his head. 'Out there will corrupt you, Maggie. And you must *not* be corrupted. I can't let that happen to you.'

150

'It won't,' Maggie said. 'I promise. I'm a normal teenager, really.'

'You are *not* a normal teenager. You're special. Like I told you before, I've been following you Maggie, keeping an eye on you until the time came to save you.'

Maggie shrank back on the bed. This was crazy.

'I've been watching over you. Like a guardian angel. Ever since I saw you. You never knew, but I was there.'

'How long,' she said, gesturing around the room, 'how long have you been planning this?'

'The room?' the man said. 'I built this years ago, I knew I'd need it one day – for someone – and I was right. Because you started to go down the wrong path, and I had to step in.'

'What do you mean, the wrong path?' Maggie said, her head spinning. 'I don't understand.'

'That boy,' the man said. 'He was taking you in the wrong direction.'

'Kevin?' Maggie said. 'He was – he was only a friend. I was going to break up with him!'

'He was a dangerous influence,' the man said. 'And he was the first of many. There would have been others, I could tell. You're susceptible to men, Maggie. It runs in your family. I couldn't let it happen again.'

'Again?' Maggie said. 'Kevin was my first boyfriend. There's no again.'

'I'm not talking about you,' the man said. 'I'm talking about your mother.'

151

3

'My mum?' Maggie said. She felt dizzy. She had assumed that the man had seen her alone and taken the opportunity to kidnap her. All the stuff he'd said when she was first here, about rescuing her and keeping her safe, was his way of justifying it.

But now it seemed there was more to the story.

A lot more.

Maggie blinked, trying to focus. 'What has my mum got to do with this?'

'Everything,' the man said. 'I failed her. She, too, was special, but I did not do what I should have done. I wasn't ready. I *won't* make the same mistake again.'

He said it emphatically, as though proud of the strength of his resolve.

'I don't understand,' she said. 'How do you know Mum?'

'I was her teacher,' the man said. 'But not merely any teacher. It was obvious from the start that she was special and I was put there to save her. She stood out from the others. There was something' – he looked up – 'luminous about her. A light from within. I saw it – others didn't, but I did – and I tried to tend it, but I did not see the dangers.

I underestimated them. I thought she would be able to resist temptation, but it turned out she was weak. Delicate. And before I could do anything, I'd lost her.'

This wasn't making any sense. 'What do you mean, "lost her"?' Maggie said.

'She had a boyfriend. Like you.'

'So?' Maggie said. 'That's normal.'

He shook his head. 'No,' he said. 'Once she'd been with him – in *that* way – she was lost to me. I needed her to be perfect.' He wrinkled his nose in disgust. 'She let him do it to her. I don't think she wanted to – she was misguided – but he led her astray. I watched it happen. He ruined her.'

Maggie felt she was losing her grip on the conversation. 'How do you know they weren't just friends?'

'Because they were doing it, Fruitcake. She was letting him. I saw them.'

'You saw them? Where?'

'In his house. His parents were out and I watched them go inside. They closed the curtains in an upstairs window, but they didn't lock the door. I let myself in and heard them. Heard their *grunts*.' He shuddered in disgust. 'I went to look, so I could be sure.' He breathed in deeply. 'And there they were. The door was ajar. I watched them. It was disgusting.'

Maggie closed her eyes as tightly as she could. This man had spied on her mum and her boyfriend, crept into a house and watched them have sex. And now she was in some prison he'd made. This was more fucked up than she had imagined.

He tapped her on the shoulder and she opened her eyes. He leaned forward. 'You are the same, Maggie. You have the same light. And I saw the fate coming to claim you, and I could not let it. Once you were with that boy, I knew I had to save you. And now you are safe. Your light will *never* go out.'

'Me and Kevin are friends,' she said. 'That's all.'

'For now. But he would do the same to you as that animal

153

did to your mother. And I had to keep you safe. Keep your light shining.'

'But I'm trapped,' Maggie said. 'There is no light in here. This is no life.'

The man shook his head. 'This is the *only* life. The only place your light is safe. I won't make the same mistake again, Maggie. I loved your mother. Loved her like no man has ever loved a woman before, and if only she had known it, if only I had been able to tell her, we could have made a beautiful life together. But it was impossible. And even if that boy hadn't ruined her, people' – he spat the word out – 'society, wouldn't allow it. They were blind to the truth. They saw only my age. And it was all ruined. Ruined forever.' He wagged his finger. 'And then you came into my life and I had another chance. And I'm not going to miss it.' He looked around. 'This is the only way. If it wasn't for this, you would not give me a second look. You – like your mother – have been conditioned by society to think of age as an insurmountable obstacle to love. Buy why? In other areas society has moved on. Black people used to be unable to marry white people. Men could not have sex with men. The poor could not marry the rich. But all these things have become acceptable. So why is age still such a problem?'

He tapped his feet on the floor.

'It won't be, eventually. But I cannot wait for that day to come. I love you, Maggie, and this – all this – I did for you. One day you will understand.'

Maggie hugged her knees to her chest and closed her eyes.

'Please,' she said. 'Please go. I need to be alone.'

She heard footsteps, then felt a hand on her shoulder. He kissed her head with his soft, fleshy lips.

'This is the only way we can be together,' he said. 'Goodnight, my love.'

4

One thing was clear now. Among all the uncertainty, all the doubt, one thing was clear.

She had to get out of there.

The man wasn't going to let her go. He wasn't going to relent and start feeling sorry for her. This wasn't some temporary imprisonment that he would end once he had what he wanted.

No, this was for good. This went back to her mum, went back decades. She was important to him in ways she couldn't begin to understand, but she understood what that meant.

It meant that, unless she escaped, she'd be here forever.

And there was no time like the present.

She was awake the entire night, turning over her options.

And there weren't many. She couldn't hide, she had no weapons. Her only advantage was that he wasn't expecting her to fight, which meant she'd have one chance to surprise him and get away.

She pictured his routine when he came into the room. He closed the door, then locked it with a key he kept on a chain around his wrist.

That was the moment. Once the door was locked, she wasn't sure she could get the key off his wrist, but if she could hurt him in the second before he locked the door she could get out.

And maybe lock him in the room, if there was a lock on the outside and she could find some way of locking it.

But she would only have one chance.

She was lying on the mattress, staring at the ceiling, when she heard the scraping sound. She tensed. When the door opened the man needed to see her on the mattress or he would not come in, but then she would be ready.

The lock clicked. The handle turned.

The door cracked open.

'Good morning, Fruitcake.'

The man stood in the door frame, a tray in his hand. He put it on the carpet, his eyes on her. Her stomach tensed. He was going to leave without coming inside.

'Morning,' she said. 'How are you?'

He caught her eye. 'I'm fine – as usual. You're talkative.'

'I was thinking about what you said last night. I think you were right.'

A faint smile touched his lips. 'Right about what?'

'About me being safe. In here.'

'*Exactly.*' The faint smile swelled into a grin. 'I knew you'd start to understand, eventually.'

'I needed time to consider it.' She smiled back. It took a huge effort. 'Tell me more. About how you decided on all of this.'

The man nodded. He gripped the key in his fingers, the chain taut.

'Of course,' he said, a look of something like triumph in his eyes. 'Of course I will, Fruitcake.'

5

He turned, and bent down to put the key in the lock. As soon as his eyes left her, she sprang off the mattress and threw herself across the room.

She hit his back, hard. He was much bigger than her but he was off balance and his head smashed into the door. He twisted away from her and she slammed her knee into his balls. His eyes widened and he puffed out his cheeks, then groaned and clutched his groin. He sank back on to his haunches, his face pale.

Maggie tried the handle.

It turned, and the door opened. Ahead of her wooden stairs led up into blackness.

To a hatch of some kind.

To freedom.

She had done it.

She ran up, her hands over her head, feeling for the way out.

And felt a hand on her ankle, pulling her back. Pulling her back *hard*.

The hand yanked and her foot slipped, and then she was being dragged backwards down the stairs and back into the room.

157

The man threw her on to the mattress. He stood over her, his face purple with pain and rage.

'You lying fucking *bitch*!' he screamed. 'You're not my Fruitcake! You're not my Fruitcake at all!'

He stamped his right foot on the floor.

'I'm going now,' he shouted. 'I'm going before I do something I regret.' He stepped backwards and kicked the tray across the room. 'But I'll be back. You needn't worry about that, Margaret. I'll be back before you know it.'

He walked out and slammed the door.

Seconds later the light went out.

6

It was dark – black, black dark – for a long time. She didn't know how long, exactly. Many hours, certainly. Days, probably.

Long enough to get very, very hungry.

But that was the least of her concerns. It was the thirst that tortured her. It was all she could think of. Her tongue swelled in her mouth and visions of glasses of cold water swam in front of her eyes. She reached for them, her hands groping in the darkness for a drink that did not exist. The only liquid she tasted was the salt tears that ran down her cheeks.

And then she heard the scraping sound. The light came on. She squinted, the brightness hurting her eyes.

The door opened. The man was stood there, something in his hand.

A tray, she thought. *With food and drink.*

But it wasn't a tray.

It was something much worse.

The man locked the door – this time keeping his eyes on her – then put the thing down. It looked like some kind of helmet.

'Please,' she said, her voice a croak. 'I need a drink.'

'You need to be punished,' the man replied, his voice flat. 'That's what you need.'

'What's that?' she said, pointing at the helmet.

'It's a cage.'

She didn't understand. Now her eyes had adjusted she could make out that it was a motorbike helmet.

'It's not a cage,' she said.

'Oh, it is.'

She was puzzled. There was nothing here to put in it. 'What for?'

He looked at her, his head tilted sideways.

'For my pet.' He grinned at her. 'My *other* pet.'

She blinked. 'I don't understand.'

'You will,' he said. 'You will.' He picked up the motorbike helmet and walked towards her. When he got to the mattress he lifted it up and, before she could do anything, he put it over her head. He tightened a strap under her chin, and secured it with a small chain, through which he threaded a padlock.

'There,' he said. 'Fits perfectly.'

It didn't fit perfectly at all. It was way too big. Maggie shook her head; there was plenty of space around her face and between the helmet and her neck.

But not enough to get her head out, not with the strap secured. She tugged at it, but the padlock – clearly his own addition – held fast.

It was uncomfortable, but not *that* bad. She started to relax a little.

Then he turned and walked to the door. He unlocked it and reached on to the stairs. When he came back into the room he was holding a shoebox. He took off the lid and held it up to show Maggie what was inside.

There was a large, white rat. Its pink nose sniffed the air.

160

'No,' Maggie croaked. 'Please, no. I'm sorry.'

'It's a bit late for that,' he said.

He picked up the rat and pulled the chin of the helmet towards him, then put the head of the rat in the gap between her neck and the helmet. She tried to twist away but he grabbed her neck with his free hand, and, seconds later, she felt tiny feet scrabbling on her cheek.

And then a pink nose came into view and she screamed.

'Don't do that,' the man said. 'You'll upset him.' He tilted her chin up so she was looking at him. 'This is James,' he said. 'I thought you'd like the name. And he's *very* hungry.'

7

Sometimes the rat – James, he had called it, and even though she knew he was using her brother's name to punish her she couldn't get the name out of her head – slept, or was still. Sometimes it moved slowly, walking around her head and mouth and lips and nose in steady circles.

Sometimes – and these were the worst – it scuttered around, making sinister, high-pitched noises.

She waited for it to bite her, waited in the darkness for its needle-sharp teeth to pierce her cheek, waited to feel her blood flow as the rat lapped it up.

And when she thought she could bear it no longer, when she thought she was going to lose her mind, the light came on and the door opened and the man came and took the rat and the helmet away.

He stood by the door, his arms folded.

'Don't do that again,' he said. 'Got it, Fruitcake?'

Wednesday, 20 June 2018

Three Days to Go

1

Max sat on the end of the mattress, trying to balance the tinfoil ball on top of a Duplo tower. It was a precarious situation; even if he got it to stick, as soon as he moved, the mattress shifted and the ball fell down.

Every time it fell, Max burst into loud, uncontrollable laughter. Maggie wasn't sure why he found it so funny, but she was glad he took so much joy in it. It wasn't unexpected; Max was one of those people who always saw the light side of everything. Whatever happened, however simple the pleasure, he was almost always happy.

That was how she would remember him. Despite the tininess of his world, the lack of fresh air and friends and sweets and ice cream and all the things a child should have, despite everything he had to put up with, he was happy.

He had a constant smile and bright, inquisitive eyes, and at the slightest provocation – a tickle or a song or a funny face – he would let out an explosive laugh. She could see the man he would have become: charming, engaged and warm. He would listen and smile and laugh and make people feel good about themselves. He made *her* feel good about herself;

if his guffaws were anything to go by, she was the funniest person in the world.

He reminded her of James. He had been prone to fits of giggles; a memory came to her of him, aged about six, clutching his stomach, bent double with laughter at the sight of their dad miming to the song 'Daddy Cool'.

Max would never get the chance to watch her dad miming. In a few short days he would be gone.

She picked up her pencil and the calendar and put a line through the date. More than halfway there. More than halfway through the last week of Max's life.

S	Su	M	Tu	W	Th	F
						~~1~~
~~2~~	~~3~~	~~4~~	~~5~~	6	~~7~~	~~8~~
~~9~~	~~10~~	~~11~~	~~12~~	~~13~~	~~14~~	~~15~~
~~16~~	~~17~~	~~18~~	~~19~~	~~20~~	21	22
23	24	25	26	27	28	29
30						

The image was with her always, now. In her dreams, at night, in her thoughts during the days. All she saw was herself, sprawled in the corner of the room, beaten back and powerless, while the man stood in the doorway, Max in his arms, screaming and looking at her, pleading for him to save her.

Pleas that she could not answer.

And then the door shutting. Max's screams fading. Silence.

And after that? What would happen to Max, to her laughing, gentle, beautiful boy? The same as happened to Seb and Leo, no doubt. She didn't know what that was, exactly, but she was sure it was nothing good.

She'd asked the man where Seb was. He had left her alone for two nights after Seb had been taken, but when he came down, wearing his blue robe tied at the waist, she had fought back the tears and asked him.

Where is he? she said. *I want to see him. Please.*

He shook his head.

That's not possible.

Why not? Is he OK? Please, tell me he's OK.

The man didn't reply. He loosened the belt of his bathrobe and pointed at the bed.

Lie down.

Please. Is he safe?

The man ignored her. *Lie down,* he said again.

I need to know he's not suffering. That's all.

The man nodded. *He's not suffering.*

And that was all he said. Over the weeks she asked for photos, for an item of his clothing, anything, but the man ignored her. Eventually, though, he could not ignore her any more.

Don't ask about him again, he said. *Ever again.*

She carried on. How could she not? He was her son. The next time he came, she badgered him with questions until he turned and left the room.

He never answered. All she had were the man's final words.

He's not suffering.

She had turned the words over in her mind a million times. She always came back to the same two possible interpretations.

Seb was not suffering because he was alive and well and happy somewhere – maybe living in the man's house, or in some foster care – or he was not suffering because he couldn't.

Because he was dead.

And she was pretty sure she knew which one it was. It was inconceivable to her that the man would take the risk

165

of having a three-year-old in his house, or of trying to find a foster home. People would ask questions. Far easier to get rid of Seb. All he had to do was dispose of the body, and that would be simple enough. He could put it anywhere – in a lake or a forest or even in his back garden. No one would report Seb missing, because no one knew he existed.

She watched Max try to balance the tinfoil ball. In three days, that was the fate that awaited him.

She blinked back tears.

Max placed the tinfoil on the top of the tower. It wobbled, then settled on top of the tower.

Max whipped around, his eyes wide in delight.

'Mummy,' he said. 'Look!'

As he spoke, he pointed at the Duplo and the movement unbalanced the ball. It tumbled to the mattress.

Max giggled. 'It fell, Mummy! It fell down!'

She grabbed him in a hug to hide her tears. She didn't want to fill his final days with worry about his mum.

'Yes,' she said. 'It did. Let's build it again and see if we can make it stay on, OK?'

2

Max concentrated on the Duplo tower. She noticed he was holding his tongue between his teeth; that was new. It reminded her of Leo. He had done that.

Probably around this age, too, right at the end of his life. She had known what the man would do, and so when he had come for Leo she had refused to hand him over, holding him on the bed and shaking her head when the man gestured for her to hand him over.

He asked again; she refused again. He clenched his jaw and said, in a tone of forced reasonableness that she recognized, *Give him to me.*

She did not. And for the briefest of moments she thought he might leave, but then, with surprising speed, he marched to her and hit her hard on the head with the base of his hand. She was dizzy and faint, but some instinct made her hold on to Leo.

Then he pinched her nose and covered her mouth with his free hand. Her chest tightened and she started to panic.

The panic grew until she felt her chest was about to explode, and then her vision darkened.

When she came back to consciousness, he was gone.

And so was Leo.

It would be the same this time. She had wasted her chance. She was powerless; he was too strong and now he would be suspicious of her. The only way she could do anything was if she had a weapon, and there was nothing she could use as one. He had designed it that way. All she had were their clothes, two toothbrushes, and her calendar. In terms of furniture there was the mattress, the toilet bucket, the plastic basin and the bath. Next to her bed were a handful of paperback books and the needle and thread she used to mend clothes.

Other than that there was only Max's paltry collection of Duplo bricks.

Oh, and a rolled-up ball of tinfoil. Don't forget that. It was hardly a deadly arsenal she could use to deal a mortal blow to the man.

She heard the scrape. Waited for the knock. Max got up from his Duplo tower and climbed into her lap. The door opened.

The man put a tray down. There were two paper plates and, unusually, four paper cups.

'Breakfast,' he said. 'Toast and jam and water.' He indicated the other cups. 'And orange juice.'

Max laughed. 'Orange juice!' he said. 'It's orange juice!' He slid off her lap and looked at the man. 'Can I try it?'

The man stepped back. 'If your mother says so.'

Maggie paused. Was there some trick? Was it drugged? It was unlikely. If the man wanted to drug them he could put it in their food. He didn't need to waste orange juice. So why deny Max a treat? 'Yes,' she said. 'You can have it.'

Max laughed again and walked over to the tray. He picked up the paper cup and peered into it. He glanced at Maggie, then took a sip. After a pause, he began to drink greedily, until the orange juice was gone.

'Yum,' he said. 'That's good.'

The man smiled at him.

'I'm glad you liked it,' he said.

Max looked at Maggie. He pointed at the other paper cup. 'Can I have this one?'

'I don't know,' Maggie said. 'That's a lot of orange juice. A lot of sugar.'

'I think it's fine,' the man said. 'A special treat.' He grinned. 'After all, it's nearly his birthday.'

3

Maggie flinched at the word.

He had never made a reference to Seb or Leo's birthdays. He had just come and taken them.

This was different. He had given Max orange juice. He had said it was a birthday treat, after a fashion.

She felt dry-mouthed and on edge. Something had changed. Maybe he didn't mind her having her son this time; maybe the day would come and go and nothing would happen.

Maybe he would fall in love with his son and want more for him than this room.

'Do you have anything else in mind? For his birthday?' she asked.

The man shook his head. 'No,' he said. 'Not really.'

'It would be good for him to have some new toys,' she said. 'And some books. He can read, almost. He knows his letters. He's a very bright boy.'

The man did not reply.

'Like his dad,' Maggie said. 'I don't think he gets it from me!'

She happened to think he did get it from her; she had

170

been a straight A student in school, but that wasn't the point. She sensed that the man was softening and she wanted to make him feel some connection with Max.

The man took a step towards the door.

'He won't be getting any toys,' he said. 'There's no point.'

Maggie tensed. 'What do you mean, "there's no point"? It's his birthday.'

'Yes,' the man said. 'His third birthday. I think you know by now what happens when these children' – he waved in Max's direction – 'turn three.'

'What?' Maggie said, her throat tight. 'What happens?'

'You know.'

She did know. But not why. If she knew why, maybe she could reason with him. Find a way to change his mind.

'I do,' Maggie said, the struggle to draw breath making her voice a gasp. 'But why? Tell me. Why is their third birthday so important?'

The man blinked. 'They become people at that age,' he said. 'And then you become too attached. I didn't want to take them earlier because you needed some company.' He smiled, almost proudly, as though he felt he should be praised for having thought of her.

Maggie let out a groan. She couldn't be *more* attached, and the fact that the man didn't see that – couldn't see it – showed how vain her hope that he would feel some tenderness and love for Max had been.

He thought Max was *company*, but he was wrong. Max was a child. He was her son. He was so much more than *company*. He was her flesh and blood, in his face she saw herself and Seb and Leo and her mum and dad and brother.

But the man didn't understand, and he never would. He was not capable of it.

She held out her hands. 'Max,' she said. 'Come here.'

He looked up at her, a piece of toast in each hand, red jam around his mouth.

'Mummy,' he said. 'This is *good*.'

4

The man came that night. He stood in the doorway in his
blue bathrobe, his shins bare, leather sandals on his feet.

He gestured and she moved Max from the mattress to the
floor.

It took a long time. Longer than usual, or maybe it was
the disgust she felt for him that made it seem longer.

That was all that was left now. Disgust. She had gone
through periods of hating him, fearing him, being furious
with him, even pitying him. She'd never liked him or admired
him or wanted to be anywhere near him, but she had, once
or twice, felt sorry for him.

But not now. Now she felt nothing but disgust. Revulsion.
It was the inhumanity he'd displayed, the inability to understand anything about how she must be feeling. He was not
a damaged, broken version of a human being. He was not a
human being at all.

And he would come and take her son, without any remorse.
Then he would keep her here. She would never get out. Never
be free. He would see to that. He would rather she died here
than leave.

And she couldn't do it. Not without Max; maybe not even with him. She couldn't stay here forever.

But there was no way out. None.

Eleven Years Earlier:
Sunday Morning, 1 July 2007

1

Martin Cooper glanced at the clock on the dashboard. 'We're going to be late,' he said. 'It's ten o'clock already.'

James shrugged. 'Not that late. Only a few minutes. And we're nearly there.'

'But still late.' They were *always* late. It drove him mad; it was so easy to be on time. He took a deep breath. He knew his words would go unheard, but if he said them often enough maybe they would sink in. 'You know, all you have to do if you want to be on time is think for a few seconds and make a plan. So, if you know it's a ten-minute drive to your tutor's house then you leave ten minutes before the start time. And if you know it takes twenty minutes to shower and get ready, you start showering and getting ready twenty minutes before that.'

'I had to have a shower, Dad. Or would you prefer me to go there without taking one?'

'That's not what I'm saying. I'm saying you need to take a shower earlier, if you want to be on time.'

'*If* I want to be on time.' James wagged his finger. 'Which I don't. I'm quite happy to be late. I don't exactly want to spend my Sunday morning doing extra maths with a tutor.'

'Maybe,' Martin said. 'But that is how you're spending your Sunday morning, and it's disrespectful to turn up late.'

'I don't see why I have to.'

'You know why.'

'But I don't care about Maths! I don't like it.'

'You still have to pass your GCSE. And get a good grade.' Martin sighed. 'Look. I know it doesn't come easily to you. And you've had a hard year' – that was an understatement; James had effectively missed most of the school year after Maggie disappeared – 'and got behind, which isn't your fault. But whatever the reason, you do need to catch up. And this is the way to do it.'

'But it's so lame.'

'I know. Still, it's only an hour and a half. And then you'll be free. We can go to the game.'

'Can I go to Louise's house?'

'Is she expecting you?'

James nodded. 'I said I'd be there at lunchtime.'

'So you don't want to come to the rugby with me?'

James glanced at him quickly, but it was long enough for Martin to see guilt in his expression.

'I do,' he said. 'But I told Louise . . .'

His voice tailed off; Martin patted him on the knee. 'It's OK, Jimbo. You want to see your girlfriend and not your old man. I understand.' He gave a theatrical sigh. 'I remember when you were a little boy how you used to trail around after me. You were like a second shadow. But now you don't even want to go to watch the rugby with me.'

'Dad!' James said. 'All right! I'll come with you.'

Martin laughed. 'That's OK. I'm only kidding. Go and see Louise. I love you anyway.'

'I love you too.'

They said they loved each other – Sandra, too – often these days. It had started after Maggie vanished; it felt urgent back then, necessary, a way of keeping the bonds between them visible and real. Now it was a habit, and a good one. Less urgent, maybe, but equally important.

At the time Maggie went, Martin had wondered what would happen to them. He had feared that he and Sandra would split up, grow apart, blame each other, and there had been moments when that seemed like it would happen, when they had reached a fork in the road and faced a choice about which way to go. Each time they had stayed together, and now they were closer – as a family and as individuals – than they had ever been.

It had spilled over into a renewed passion in their sex lives as well. Things had been a bit stale after they hit their forties, but now they had started to have more sex and – this was what surprised Martin the most – more adventurous sex.

In fact, since James had been going to maths tutoring, they had been taking advantage of his Sunday morning absences in ways which he would hardly be able to imagine, and which would probably have left him disgusted by what his parents were getting up to when he was out.

It was another reason Martin was annoyed at being late. There was less time for him and Sandra.

He pulled up outside the tutor's house. James opened the car door, then looked at him.

'Is something wrong?'

James raised an eyebrow. 'Money?' he said. 'To pay him? I forgot it last week as well.'

'Oh. Of course.' Martin climbed out. 'I'll give him a cheque.'

They walked up to the front door and rang the bell. After a few seconds Martin heard footsteps and the door opened.

Mr Best, Sandra's old teacher, smiled at him.

'Sorry we're late,' Martin said. 'My son and punctuality seem not to go together very well.'

'That's fine,' Best said. 'Glad you made it. Come in, James.'

177

Martin took out his cheque book and felt in his pockets for a pen. Best reached into the hall and handed one to him.

'Sorry about the cheque. I don't have cash.'

'Thank you.' Best took the cheque. 'I appreciate it.'

'Pleasure.' Martin grabbed his car keys. 'I'll be back in ninety minutes. See you then.'

2

Sandra was watching a politics programme when he came into the living room. She was sitting on the sofa, her legs crossed. It was clearly engrossing; she didn't turn to look at him.

He watched her for a few moments then started to massage her shoulders. With James out of the house, they could do it right here.

Or in the kitchen. Anywhere, really.

She stiffened, and he stopped.

'Is everything OK?'

She turned and looked up at him, her face red and her eyes wet with tears.

He sat opposite her.

'It hit me when you left,' she said, her voice soft. 'I watched you and James go and then I thought, in a week from now she'll have been gone a year. I've known the anniversary is coming up, but all of a sudden it was there. A *year* without our baby girl.'

Martin nodded. 'I know. It's been on my mind too.'

'It doesn't really get better, does it?' Sandra closed her

eyes. 'It fades a bit, becomes part of the background, but when you remember it, it hurts as much as it ever did. I still find it hard to believe she's gone.'

'Sometimes I dream she's home,' Martin said. 'And in my dream I'm so happy. Ecstatic. But then I wake up and remember she's not there. It takes all day to recover.'

'Me too.'

'James as well, probably.'

'How was he?' Sandra asked. 'Do you think he knows it's coming up?'

'I imagine so. I'll talk to him later. Check he's OK. I'm glad he's got Louise.'

'Kind of,' Sandra said. 'I like her – she's a lovely girl – but I can't bear the thought she might hurt him. I want him to be in love and happy, but I don't want him to be vulnerable. And teenage boys in the grip of their first love are the definition of vulnerability.'

'I think we have no choice but to let it go,' Martin said. 'We can't protect him from everything. I will talk to him though, about Maggie and the anniversary.'

'OK.' Sandra looked at him, her expression suddenly serious. After a pause, she spoke. 'Do you think she's alive?'

'You know,' Martin said, slowly, 'I think about that all the time. All the evidence says she isn't. I've read everything, all the statistics about the likelihood of someone turning up alive after one day, two days, a week, a month, and they're pretty clear: she's more than . . .' His voice broke, and he looked away. 'More than likely dead. But some part of me is convinced she isn't.' He looked at his hands. 'But sometimes, when I think of where she might be, I wonder whether she would be better off if she was.'

'Don't say that,' Sandra said. 'If she's alive – wherever she is – that's better than the alternative. Because if she *is* alive, she'll come back to us. One way or another, she'll find a way to come home.'

Martin caught her gaze. 'I hope so,' he said. 'I hope so.'

3

James looked at the equation. Mr Best – he insisted on being called that – had finished explaining how to do it, and for a moment he'd understood, but it was already gone. He shook his head.

'I don't really get it,' he said.

Best was sitting on the other side of the dining room table.

'Let's forget that specific example,' he said. 'And talk about what quadratic equations are used for.'

'OK,' James said.

'Let's say you kick a football. It goes up and forward and then starts to come down until it's still. A quadratic equation can tell you the height of that ball at any time.'

'I don't need it to,' James said. 'I can see the ball.'

'What about a missile? You can't see a missile.'

'I don't want to fire a missile.'

Best smiled. 'Very admirable, but if you did, a quadratic equation would be very useful. It's like probability. Which do you think is more likely to come up in the lottery? Six sequential numbers – like four, five, six, seven, eight, nine, or six unconnected numbers?'

'Unconnected.'

'No,' Best said. 'It's exactly the same.'

'So I should pick sequential numbers if I do the lottery?'

'Pick any numbers you like.'

'What would you do, if you won the lottery?' James said. He was desperate to change the subject.

Best looked up at the ceiling. 'Buy a canal boat,' he said. 'The canal network covers the entire country and you can move about it at your leisure. Undetected.' He smiled, again. 'Anyway, back to quadratic equations.'

James rubbed his eyes. He didn't get it, and he didn't care. He was never going to use it in real life. Best's example was the proof of that: why did he want to fire missiles, or figure out how high a football had gone? All he needed was to get through his Maths GCSE and then forget this bullshit forever.

And then there was Louise. He thought about her *all* the time. When he tried to concentrate, his mind slipped to thinking about her. She went to a different school, so he only saw her on evenings and weekends, but all day long he imagined she was at his school, hovering in the background and watching him tell jokes and play football and hang out with his friends. In lessons he wrote her long letters about how much he liked her – he loved her, but he hadn't told her yet – and describing in great detail all the many qualities she had: kindness, beauty, wisdom.

He felt a bit guilty, truth be told, because before he met her it had been Maggie he imagined watching over him. Now he imagined introducing Louise to Maggie, and Maggie telling him she was amazing and the right girl for him.

At times like that she felt so close to him, even though he knew he'd never see her again, never be anywhere near her.

And in a week it would be a year since she'd gone. He hadn't mentioned it to his parents. They didn't seem to have noticed and he didn't want to upset them.

He pushed his chair back. 'Could I use the toilet?'

Best nodded. 'You know where it is? In the hall.'

James got up and left the dining room. He closed the bathroom door behind him and unzipped his jeans. When he had finished, he washed his hands and went back into the hall.

The kitchen door was ajar. He'd never been in. Other than the bathroom and the dining room, he'd never been in any other parts of Best's house.

He glanced inside.

There was a box to the right of the door. It was unopened, but he recognized the brand name.

Pampers.

Best had a box of Pampers? Weren't they nappies? What did he want nappies for? Maybe he had a new grandkid and was helping out his son or daughter. There were no photos of any kids in the house, though, and he'd never mentioned any.

The dining room door opened. Best stood there.

'Everything OK?' he said.

'Yeah.'

Best looked at the open door. He chuckled.

'Ah. I see. You're wondering why I have nappies. Maybe I have a baby squirrelled away in a hidden basement under my garage, that kind of thing?'

'No,' James said. 'Of course not—'

'It's fine. No baby, I'm afraid. It's a box of old books. They happen to be in a Pampers box.' He closed the kitchen door. 'Anyway. Back to quadratic equations . . .'

4

It had been a while since she had driven past Best's house. There had been no reason to.

Until today. Until the letter had come.

It had arrived at the police station that morning, addressed to her. Three sentences, typed on a piece of A4 paper.

DEAR DETECTIVE INSPECTOR WYNNE:
IT'LL BE A YEAR SOON.

She had known immediately what it was referring to.

Maggie Cooper. It had to be. She'd been taken nearly a year earlier.

Forensics had examined it, but there was nothing useful. Standard ink and paper, LaserJet printer, no fingerprints or DNA. It could have come from anyone. The postmark was Manchester, but that meant nothing. Lots of people lived in, worked in or visited Manchester.

And then the second sentence.

YOU MISSED SOMETHING BACK THEN. THE CLUES WERE THERE. THEY STILL ARE.

And then the finale.

HERE'S TO ANOTHER YEAR. BETTER LUCK NEXT TIME,
DETECTIVE INSPECTOR.
  YOURS SINCERELY,
  ???

It was not unheard of for criminals – particularly serial criminals – to taunt the police like this. They liked to make it personal, which was why it was addressed to her. It made it a game of wits.

Either that, or it was a hoax, some idiot getting a kick out of causing trouble. That wasn't unheard of, either.

She turned into Best's street. She wanted to drive past and take a look, see if it jogged any memories. There was a car parked outside, with a man getting out.

It took her a second or two to recognize him, and another second or two to wonder why he was here, of all places.

She pulled up behind Martin Cooper's car and got out.

'Mr Cooper,' she said. 'Detective Inspector Wynne. I—'

'I remember you.' He didn't seem pleased to see her. She couldn't blame him.

'How are you?' she said.

'Not too bad.' He raised an eyebrow. 'You decided to stop for a chat?'

'No. Not exactly.' She put a hand on her car roof. 'I was wondering what you were doing here. At Best's house.'

'Is there a problem?'

'No. I was wondering. That's all.'

'Well, nothing to wonder about. I'm picking up my son.'

'Your *son*?' Wynne said. 'What's he doing here?'

Martin looked at the front door. It was open and James and Mr Best were standing on the threshold.

'Maths tuition,' he said. 'He was struggling a little and Mr

Best offered to help. He used to teach Sandra.'

'Is everything OK?' Best called out. 'Hello, Detective Inspector. Or is it something else? Maybe you've been promoted?'

'No.' Wynne's skin prickled. She was sure he was mocking her. 'Still the same rank.'

'I'm sure it will come, in time.'

'You know each other?' Martin said.

'Yes,' Best said. 'Our paths have crossed during the course of various civic duties I fulfil. Haven't they, Detective Inspector?'

The implication was obvious: you can't tell them about any unproven – Wynne preferred that to 'false' – allegations. If she did, Wynne had no doubt that a writ for something – defamation or slander – would be coming her way. A writ that would be successful.

'That's right,' she said. 'Well, it's been nice to see you all. Give my regards to your wife.'

She got in the car and started the engine. As she pulled away she could see Best in her rear-view mirror. He was smiling, and she had to fight the urge to go back and wipe the smile from his face once and for all.

Eleven Years Earlier:
Sunday Morning, 1 July 2007:

Maggie

1

Maggie was woken by a cry. It was high and faint and, for a moment, she thought that an animal – a cat, maybe – had broken into the room.

And then the cry came again, and she remembered.

It was a baby's cry. Her baby.

She was no longer alone in the room. She had a son.

She was a mother.

He cried again and it tugged at her in a way she had never felt before. The thought that he was hungry or in pain or in distress of any sort was unbearable. Every instinct she had told her to help him, to stop whatever was upsetting him and make him happy.

She opened her eyes. He was lying next to her in a basket the man had brought.

'Hello,' she whispered. 'Hello, beautiful.'

2

Seb – she had named him immediately, had decided before-
hand that if it was a boy it would be Seb – was lying in a
wicker basket at the side of her bed. She stared at him in
disbelief that he was hers, that she had a baby, a son, then
turned and picked him up.

Pain tore through her abdomen and she felt a wetness
between her legs. She looked down. It was blood. She clutched
Seb to her chest and lowered herself back to the bed.

She groaned. He had been born an hour ago, an hour since
she had held him up and used the scissors and clamp the man
had left – she had not known why until she saw the cord
connecting him to her and understood – and become a mother.

An hour of pain and bleeding and fatigue beyond anything
she had ever dreamed possible.

An hour of disbelief and joy and love beyond anything
she had ever dreamed possible.

'Shhhh,' she said. 'Shhhh, Seb, shhhh.'

His cries grew louder and she felt her heart rate increase.
One tiny hand fluttered against the skin of her neck. *There's
something wrong with him*, she thought. *I'm doing something
wrong. Maybe he's hungry.*

She pulled her T-shirt up and exposed her breasts. They were large and swollen. She tried to guide him to her nipple. His mouth opened and closed against it, but he couldn't grip it. She tried again, chasing his mouth with her nipple. A bead of liquid formed and trickled down his cheek on to his lips.

He stilled, and she managed to press her nipple to his lips. They opened, and he began to suck.

She watched, in awe, as she fed, for the first time, a baby. It was painful, the suction more powerful than she had expected. After a few minutes, some instinct told her to switch to her other breast; Seb latched on immediately.

'You're a greedy little thing, aren't you?' she said. 'But you have as much as you want.'

Ten minutes later he was asleep. She lay there, watching him rise and fall on her chest. It was amazing how quickly and completely she had fallen in love with him. She knew that every parent felt this way, but to her he was the most beautiful person – the most beautiful thing – she had ever seen. She had no idea that it was possible to feel this way, to love someone to the point you would do anything for them.

The thought brought tears to her eyes, partly for herself and Seb and the situation they were in, but mainly for her parents. If they felt about her even one tenth of how she felt about Seb, then losing her must have been unbearable for them in a way she had not been able to understand until now.

And worse, they would not get to meet their grandchild. They would not even know he'd been born.

The man had asked her if she wanted an abortion when she realized she was pregnant. She asked how; he said he didn't know. He would not be able to get medical help, so maybe with some medication, or whisky? He offered to find a method.

But it might be risky, he said.

She had not wanted to. She understood what it meant to give birth in this place, what kind of a life her child would have, but she wanted to have the baby. Part of her thought the man might relent and let her go, but that wasn't the main reason. The main reason was nothing other than the feeling that she wanted her baby. It was inside her and she couldn't bring herself to kill it. She had nothing against abortion; if you'd asked her before she was abducted what she would do if she got pregnant at sixteen she would have said she would have got rid of the baby.

But that was before she knew how it felt. And it felt right. That was the word: it felt *right*. Everything else was as wrong as it could be, but this one thing was right.

And she did not want to end it.

So she decided to have the baby and the day had come and she'd given birth, which was, pardon her French in front of a child, a *fucking* miracle. She couldn't believe she – and Seb, for that matter – had survived. It was so *violent*. And so, so hard. Worse than hard. Worse than anything. Like having someone reach a hand into your body and turn you inside out.

She had done it all alone. The man had told her what to expect. Push on the contractions, rest in between. He gave her a pair of kitchen scissors to cut the cord, and a wooden peg to clamp it. Slap the baby if it's not breathing. Check the cord's not around its neck.

She wondered how he knew this stuff, if he was even right. She asked for a doctor.

What if something goes wrong? What if the baby needs help?

That's a risk you'll have to take. For you and the child.

And then it began. At first she wondered what all the fuss was about. The contractions were mild, just an increase in tension in her abdomen. She was starting to think this might not be all that big a deal when she felt like someone wearing iron-toed boots had kicked her in the stomach.

She lay on the bed, sweat forming on her forehead.

It happened again and again and again. For a time she found some relief by getting on all fours, groaning and moving her hips from side to side. That passed. Eventually the contractions were every few seconds and she could feel the baby between her legs, see the shape of her stomach change as it moved down.

She screamed through the next contractions and then it was out. She put her hands down and felt a head. The contractions continued, and shoulders then a torso then legs emerged. and she lifted and there was a baby on her chest, a baby who could move and was crying and was hers.

Hello, she said, crying herself. *Hello*.

And there were more contractions and more stuff came out – *The placenta?* she thought vaguely – and after a few minutes she reached for a towel and wiped the baby clean. She took the peg and the scissors and cut the cord and that was when she saw that it was a boy.

She had a son.

She wrapped him in the towel and held him against her chest. She studied him. He was asleep, his body moving up and down against her as he breathed. He had fine, black hair and ten fingers and ten toes and he was so fragile but so perfect.

After a while she felt her eyes closing. She didn't dare sleep with him in her bed; she was terrified she would crush him, so she clothed him and placed him in the basket the man had brought. By the time she got her head back on her pillow and closed her eyes, she was asleep.

3

She woke and was immediately alert. She looked at Seb. He was very still and she felt the beginnings of panic. Was he even alive? She watched for signs of movement, his chest going up and down.

There it was. The tiniest, tenderest lift of his narrow puppy-skin breast. He was alive.

Seb's peaceful expression changed to a pained one, and there was a gurgling sound. Maggie looked at him in alarm; seconds later his peaceful expression was back, but there was a faint smell coming from him.

His first poo, she thought. *First feeding, first sleep. Motherhood is a series of firsts.*

There was a pile of nappies by the basket. She leaned over and picked one up. She moved slowly; when she had the nappy, she sat up and stripped Seb naked, taking care not to pinch him or twist him or do anything which might cause him pain.

God, she loved him already. It was amazing.

The stuff that had come from him was green and sticky and it took her ages to wipe it from his scrawny legs and buttocks – scrawny legs and buttocks that were the cutest things she had *ever* seen – and then to fold him into his nappy. She threw the old one into the corner of the room and held him to her chest, rocking him in her arms. She smelled his head. She'd held a few babies before and he had the same new-born baby smell. How was it possible they all smelled the same? Seb was in a room in the man's basement, yet he smelled like every other baby in the world.

It was a miracle. Seb was a miracle. The whole damn thing was a miracle.

She heard the scraping sound, and froze.

She didn't want him here, not now. It would ruin the perfection.

But the door handle turned, and the door swung open.

4

The man stood and looked at her. He was holding a box of nappies. Pampers.

'Better to keep these down here. Don't want people in the house asking why I have them.'

So he had people in the house. She had assumed he never had guests. She wondered, Who would want to visit him? Who were his friends? Did he have an active social life? Host the local bridge club? But if people were there, maybe they would hear Seb crying and investigate.

It was a stupid idea. He would have thought of it. The basement would be soundproofed, she could be sure of that.

He pointed at Seb.

'How is it?'

'It's a he, and he's fine.'

'Good.' The man looked at her. 'And you?'

'Like you care.'

'Of course I care. You know I do. That's why you're here. Because I care. Because you need to be safe.'

Maggie looked away. They'd had this conversation before. She didn't need to have it again.

'Are you hungry?'

She nodded.

'I'll bring food. What do you want?'

'Anything. Something simple. And water. A lot. I'm thirsty.'

'Anything else. Are you . . . are you in pain?'

'Yes.'

'I'll bring some ibuprofen.'

Maggie looked at Seb. 'Don't you want to know his name?'

The man looked at her, his head tilted. He looked puzzled. 'No. Why would I want to know that?'

'I thought you might.'

'Well I don't. Call it whatever you want.'

And then he left.

5

She cradled her baby and kissed his soft lips. She watched his eyelids twitch as he dreamed. She couldn't believe she was a mother. There was joy, yes, unbridled joy, but also sadness. Sadness for him at where he was. For the moment, it didn't matter – this would be the perfect place for him. He would have everything he needed. Food, warmth, his mum. It was only as he grew older that he would really miss out. He wouldn't know what he was missing, not first hand, but Maggie would tell him. She would explain about playing football with your friends and swimming in rivers and lakes and gazing at the stars, so that when they got out he was as prepared as possible for the world he would find.

That would be her mission from now on: to get her son ready for the day they left. She would teach him to read and write and do maths. She would explain about kindness and compassion and love. She would tell him about his grandparents and uncle and all the other people who would be there for him when the time came.

That would be her focus. It would give meaning and purpose to her life. It would make everything worthwhile. And it would not be wasted, because they *would* get out.

She knew they would because one day Seb would be bigger and stronger than the man, and together they would be able to overpower him. It might take years, but it would happen.

The man had sowed the seed of his own destruction. So she would wait. And the longer she waited, the stronger she – and Seb – would become.

She felt, for the first time since she had been here, at peace.

Thursday, 21 June 2018

Two Days to Go

1

The man put two buckets on the floor next to the dinner tray. He stood up, wincing as he straightened his back.

'I'll be back for the stuff later,' he said.

Maggie waited until she heard the scraping sound that meant he was gone, then picked up the tray.

Two plates. Two slices of cold pizza and two bowls of mandarin slices. Eating was impossible. She wasn't sure if she was coming down with something but even if she wasn't – the sense of dread – it never left her now – about Max's birthday had destroyed her appetite.

She handed a plate to Max.

'Here you are,' she said. 'I'm not hungry at the moment.'

He picked up a slice of pizza and lifted it to his mouth. Maggie went back and picked up the buckets.

One of them was full of sand. In the other were two bottles, one of bleach and one of a blue liquid labelled 'Toilet Holding Tank Deodorant.'

It was Toilet Day.

One of the things she had had to get used to early on was the toilet. It was a bucket with a hinged seat on top. Next to it was a second bucket full of sand, mixed with the blue liquid. You did your business – piss or shit – in the toilet-bucket and then scooped sand in on top.

She lifted them up and carried them to the corner. She took off the hinged lid from the toilet and emptied it into the bucket without the sand in it. The man would come and take it away later. Then poured bleach into the toilet bucket, making sure it covered the sides, and put the bottle on the floor. She opened the bottle of blue liquid and started to add it to the sand. It worked well; whatever the blue stuff was, it masked the smell of the shit and piss in there.

And, oddly enough, the smell always brought a smile to her face. It reminded her of a camping holiday in France when they had used a chemical toilet for two weeks. Although the blue liquid was pretty foul stuff it had a sweet, strangely alluring smell. It was like petrol: even though you knew it would be horrible to drink, it smelled irresistible.

She had asked her dad why horrible things could smell good, and he had laughed. *Because we're not always attracted to what's good for us*, he said. *That's one of the things you have to learn to recognize when you get older. Things that look good but aren't.*

How do you know them? she said.

He shrugged. *Ask me. I'll tell you. I'll make sure you're safe.*

She'd believed him in the way that kids believed their dads, but he hadn't, not in the end. She was sure that would be one of the things that tortured him most about her disappearance. As a parent she had learned that, although you wanted all kind of things for your children, what you wanted most of all was for them to be safe.

And when they weren't you couldn't forgive yourself.

She'd thought a lot about her parents recently. Were they still alive, even? She assumed they were, but she didn't know. She didn't know anything about anyone out there. They could be ill, dead, divorced. James could be a famous actor or footballer – well, maybe not, but something that made him happy. She liked to think – hope – that they were as happy as they could be, given what had happened.

And she liked to think she would see them again, sometime. She dreamed about it often, and, when she woke, she wished she could go back into her dream. The only thing that made her open her eyes were her sons. They were here and real and in this world, not her dream world.

She poured the blue liquid in and watched it seep into the sand. It vanished, leaving only a blue stain behind. When she had vanished, she hadn't even left that. She had disappeared without a trace.

The way it pooled for a moment then seeped away into the sand was mesmeric. Max would be interested to see it. She turned to the mattress to beckon him over.

He wasn't there.

'Max?' she said.

She heard a noise behind her, then his voice.

'I'm here. Is this juice?'

He was sitting on the floor next to the bath, holding the bottle of bleach. He started to lift it to his lips and she realized two things.

She had left the lid off the bleach.

He was going to drink it.

A different memory came to her. When she was seven or eight she had climbed up on the washing machine, opened the cupboard above it and taken out a large white plastic bottle. It was fascinating; the cap turned and turned but didn't open. It clicked, but it stayed on.

And then her mum had come in and gasped and snatched it from her.

What are you doing?

There was a tone in her voice that Maggie didn't recognize, a mixture of anger and panic and fear that froze her.

203

Nothing.

That's bleach, *Maggie. You mustn't play with it.*

Why?

It can really hurt you. If you drink it – she shook her head – *it could kill you.*

Maggie remembered simultaneously wondering why they had something so dangerous in the house and understanding why it was so hard to take the cap off.

And now, just like she had, her own son was holding a bottle of bleach, except this time the cap *was* off.

'Max!' she shouted. 'Put that down!'

He frowned at her. She never shouted at him, and she never told him he couldn't have something. She wasn't spoiling him; they had so little she was hardly going to deny him what was available.

This time she was. She lunged forward and grabbed the bottle from his hands. He frowned and reached for it, but she held it away. The cap was by the toilet. She screwed it on, then picked him up and hugged him. He was shaking, and he started to cry.

'I'm sorry,' she said. 'I'm sorry for leaving that where you could get it. It's Mummy's fault. But everything's OK. I promise.'

He settled a little, keeping his face buried against her chest.

'Shh. It's OK. It was an accident. No harm done.'

It had been close. The bottle had been inches from his lips when she grabbed it. She wondered what would have happened if he'd drunk the bleach? Vomiting, almost certainly. Fever? A prolonged sickness? Death?

Had she nearly killed him?

But he hadn't drunk it. It was OK.

Sweat prickled on her back and arms. What if he *had* drunk it when she wasn't looking? No – it would have tasted horrible and he would have been spluttering as he tried to spit it out. He wouldn't have been trying to drink more.

She couldn't be sure of that, though.

'Max,' she said. 'Did you drink any of the stuff in the bottle?'

He didn't answer. He turned away from her. It was the first time she had ever been mean to him.

'You're not in trouble. Mummy needs to know. That's all.'

He stiffened. He turned his head so his face was totally hidden.

'Max, please. Tell me if you drank it.'

Did the fact he wasn't answering mean he had? Was he feeling guilty and didn't want to admit it? Shit, shit, *shit*. What had she done? Her son was in the safest place possible – she would have preferred him to be exposed to all the dangers of the outside world, of course she would, but the fact was the room was safe – and still she had been so fucking negligent that he had been hurt by the one danger there was.

She prised him away from her and looked at him. He turned away again.

'Max. Look at me. I need to know if you drank anything. That stuff is bad for you.'

He blinked, tears in his eyes.

'No, Mummy,' he said. 'I didn't.'

Of course, if he had done it, he would say that because he didn't want to get into trouble. On top of leaving the bleach cap off, she had created a stressful situation which meant she couldn't rely on what Max told her.

She took a deep breath.

'Are you sure? It's OK if you did. I'm not upset. I just need to know.'

'I *didn't*, Mummy.'

She stared at him. He looked serious. Honest. And he wasn't showing any signs of having drunk bleach. Even though it was early, she thought that some of the symptoms might start quickly – stomach pains, for example.

She smelled his breath. It was sweet, exactly like she

205

expected. She opened the bleach and smelled it. It was harsh and unpleasant, nothing like his breath.

Still, she had to assume he had drunk it. She picked up the bottle and read the label.

There was a warning symbol. A skull. She felt faint.

DANGER! POISON! CORROSIVE!

She read the label. There were instructions about what to do if it got in your eyes or on your skin. And what to do if your toddler drank it.

If swallowed, seek medical help immediately. Present this label.

That was it. No suggestions of what to do.

Only the instruction: *seek medical help*.

Which was impossible for her. She looked at Max. He seemed OK.

But all she could do – as always – was wait.

2

An hour later Max was asleep. He was lying on her, his chest moving up and down. He seemed normal, but she didn't know how long bleach took to have an effect.

She thought it would be pretty quick, though. Quicker than this.

She slid Max on to her bed and picked up the bleach. She read the label, then took off the cap and smelled it again. It really was vile stuff. Enough of it would kill you, or do you serious harm.

She paused. If Max had drunk it, she would drink it too. She wouldn't want to live with the guilt of having done that to him.

Maybe after Saturday she wouldn't want to live at all. The bleach might come in handy then. It would be a way for her to kill herself if the man took Max. She no longer doubted that was what she would do.

The problem was, the man wouldn't leave it with her and she had nothing to store it in. Even if she did have a storage container the man would see it and wonder what it was.

There was a faint rustle behind her. She turned round.

Max's ball of tinfoil had fallen off the bed, rolling out of his hand as he slept.

She could put some bleach in that. Fold the tinfoil into a bowl then pinch the top shut. She considered hiding it between her mattress and the wall, but that wouldn't work. It would be too soft. If she rolled on it in the night it would disintegrate. She needed somewhere solid.

She looked around the room. At the toilet and the bucket. At the water jug. At the plastic basin. At the pile of Duplo Lego bricks. At the walk-in barrel bath and the pipe that drained out of the bottom and ran out of the room.

The pipe that was lower than the floor of the bath.

There was a hollow space between the base of the bath and the carpet where the drain and the pipes went. If she could prise up the base of the bath, she could store the bleach in there. It would break the seal which would mean the bath would leak and the man would know, but that didn't matter. Bath day wasn't until next Tuesday, by which time she wouldn't care.

Either she'd have found a way out, or Max would be gone and she'd have drunk the bleach . . .

She walked over to the bath and looked down. The base was lined with plastic. At the sides was a line of white rubber. It was caulk – she'd helped her dad install their bath and recognized it from that. It was easy to apply and easy to remove.

She picked at it until she had a piece she could pull on. It came away quickly, and, when it was all up, she banged on the base. It came loose and she lifted it up. She looked at the pipes beneath.

Plastic. Not much use as a weapon.

But still, she smiled. Something, finally, had gone right.

She unwrapped the tinfoil, took the cap off the bleach and began to pour.

3

She took her pencil and the calendar. It was no longer necessary to mark the days, the calendar was all she could think of, but she did it anyway. It was a ritual, and rituals have power.

S	Su	M	Tu	W	Th	F
						~~1~~
~~2~~	~~3~~	~~4~~	~~5~~	6	~~7~~	~~8~~
~~9~~	~~10~~	~~11~~	~~12~~	~~13~~	~~14~~	~~15~~
~~16~~	~~17~~	~~18~~	~~19~~	~~20~~	~~21~~	22
23	24	25	26	27	28	29
30						

The door opened and she glanced up. Max was still sleeping. She was glad when she saw the man.

He was wearing his blue bathrobe. He stared at her, then picked up the tray – her food still uneaten – the bottles of blue liquid and bleach, and turned to the door.

For a moment she thought he was going to leave, but then he put the bottles and tray outside, closed the door, and walked into the middle of the room.

'Put him on the floor,' he said.

Maggie didn't move.

'On the floor,' the man said, a flicker of irritation in his expression. 'Now.'

'There might be a problem,' Maggie said. 'With Max.' When the man didn't reply she carried on. 'He may have drunk some bleach. It's bad for him.'

'I imagine it is,' the man said. 'How much?'

'I don't know. Maybe none. I left the cap off the bottle. He says he didn't, but I can't be sure.'

'Is he OK?'

Maggie nodded.

'Then there's no problem.'

'There might be.'

The man shrugged. 'There's nothing I can do.'

'You could take him to a doctor.'

The man gave a wry smile. 'Yes. I could. But that would make all this' – he gestured to the room – 'pointless. How would I explain his sudden arrival?'

'He could be ill,' Maggie said. 'You can't ignore that.'

'He could be.' The man shook his head. 'But I can ignore it.' He pointed at the bed. 'Lie down please.'

'Not today,' Maggie said. 'I – I don't feel well.'

'Did you drink bleach too?' His tone was mocking. 'No. I thought not. Now lie down. On your front.'

Maggie lifted Max from the bed and placed him on a pillow. She turned him so he was facing away from her bed, then lay down.

She looked at the bath. At the place the bleach was hidden. The bleach which was her way out of here. It might not take her home, but at least she would be free from this.

She felt the man's hand on her back, and she closed her eyes.

Eight Years Earlier:
Friday, 18 June 2010

1

James swigged the tea, then took a drag on his cigarette. Even though he was sweating in the hot summer sun the tea was refreshing, which was weird. It was also a good thing, given how much tea he, Pablo, and Ricky drank each day. A levels done, it was the first week he'd been working with them – landscaping, they called it, but it was mainly mowing lawns, trimming hedges and laying the odd patio – and they had probably already had twenty or more mugs of tea.

Pablo swirled the last of the brown liquid around his mug, then tipped it on the ground. He always emptied his cup like that – *Give something back*, he'd said, *don't be greedy* – before lighting another filterless cigarette.

'Gimme the mugs,' he said. 'I'll take them back to the kitchen. Give them to Angie.' Angie was the woman whose garden they were working in. When they'd arrived, Pablo had said *Hello, Mrs Turner,* but she had shaken her head. *Call me Angie.*

'Give something else to Angie,' Ricky said. 'That's what you're thinking. You've got no chance, mate.'

Pablo shrugged. 'Never know, Ricky. You never know. She might fancy a bit of rough.'

'Does that ever happen?' James said.

'Fuck yeah,' Pablo replied. 'All the time. Women that age are desperate. Forty, fifty. Not getting any from her old man. You'd be surprised. And you know what they say about the older ones?'

'What?' James asked, painfully aware of his naivety.

'Don't smell, don't tell, grateful as hell.' Pablo grinned. 'True, too.'

'Has it happened to you?'

Pablo nodded. 'Loads, mate. Fuckin' loads.' He held out his hands for the mugs. 'See you in a minute. Or maybe not. Don't wait for me. Get back to work.'

When he was gone, James looked at Ricky. 'You think he's got a chance?'

Ricky guffawed. 'None,' he said. 'And he's pulling your leg. He's never shagged a customer, other than in his dreams. He'll be in there now all polite. *Yes, Mrs Turner, thank you, Mrs Turner, delicious tea, Mrs Turner, we'll be out of your hair soon.* Give it twenty seconds and he'll be on his way back here.'

Ricky was right. It wasn't quite twenty seconds – maybe forty – but the back door opened and Pablo – whose real name was Paul – came out. He walked over and picked up his shovel.

'That was quick,' Ricky said. 'Even for you, Two Stroke.'

'She didn't fall for my charm,' Pablo said. 'I think she prefers the younger ones. Like Jimmy here.' He nodded towards the house. 'You have a go. Ask to use the loo. Leave the door unlocked and she'll be in there after you. She's a proper horny housewife.'

'You watch too much porn,' Ricky said.

'You can't watch too much porn,' Pablo replied. 'Gotta keep the pipes clean. So, you going to have a go or not, Jimmy lad?'

James felt his cheeks flush. 'I don't know,' he said. 'She's a bit, I dunno, a bit old for me.'

Ricky laughed. 'I remember when I could afford to be choosy. You got a girlfriend? That bird you were talking to last night in the pub?'

James shook his head. 'That was a friend. My ex, actually.'

'She was all right, mate,' Pablo said. 'You dump her or did she give you the elbow?'

She was Louise, and she had given him the elbow the summer before. Looking back, he could see she'd been right to. They'd been together a while and he'd become obsessed with her. He thought about her *all* the time. Every morning he called her before school; after school he made sure they met so he could walk her home. He started to hate it if she went out without him; he couldn't stop himself calling and texting to see how she was.

Mainly to see where she was, if he was honest. Who she was with.

Whether she was with another guy.

And when he saw her again he would interrogate her.

Where were you?

Out with my friends.

Which friends?

My friends. The ones I'm always with.

Were there any other guys there?

In the pub? Yes. Of course. But—

I can't believe it. You were flirting *with other guys?*

No!

And so it would go on. She would retreat from his questioning and he would interpret her retreat as evasiveness and ask more questions. It wasn't an excuse, but the truth was he was terrified of losing her, like he had lost Maggie, and in the end that had driven her away.

After she dumped him, things hadn't gone very well. He'd

215

been sure he could talk her round, if only he had the chance. She didn't want to give him the chance, so he had called her a few times. Sent some letters and emails. Text messages, too.

Quite a few.

A lot, in truth. Six or seven a day, along with a handful of unannounced visits to her house, the last of them after a night in the pub the week before he started his last year of school.

He managed to hit her window with some pebbles, but she didn't respond.

Louise, he called in a loud whisper. *I only want to say hello.*

After a while, the porch light came on and the front door opened. Finally. He could talk to her.

Her dad came out in his pyjamas, his face hard and fixed. *James*, he said. *You need to leave. Now.*

I just want to have a word with her.

He shook his head. *No. And you have to stop harassing her. I like you, and I know you had a hard time, which is the only reason me and her mum haven't called the police in the last few weeks – although Janet wanted to, I can tell you that – but it has to stop now. OK? Go and get on with the rest of your life.*

Which was what James had done. He'd woken up the next morning, head throbbing, and reached for his phone – see if she'd called, maybe try her with a message – and then stopped himself.

He pictured himself outside her window, drunk and pathetic.

Her dad was right. It had to stop.

And so he resisted the urge to contact her for the next week, and then started school and his last year of A levels and a life without Louise.

He thought about her many times a day at first, but after

216

a while she receded from his mind, her place taken by friends and nights out and beer and weed and whatever other distractions he could find.

But no other girlfriends. He couldn't go through it again, couldn't put himself in the position where he was so vulnerable. The loss of Maggie would never go away, but he was over Louise, finally, and he wasn't going back.

And he was finally over her. It had taken a year, but now he could see her when he was out and he was OK with it. Like last night in the pub. She had come over and smiled.

Hi, she said. *How are you? We haven't talked in ages. It's a shame.*

Good. You?

OK. You getting ready to go to university?

Yeah. Engineering at Warwick.

I'm going to do English at Liverpool. She touched his arm. *We should meet up before we go.*

Meet up? For a long time hearing those words had been the thing he wanted most in the world, and now he had heard them, and he felt nothing.

The relief made him dizzy.

I don't know, he said. *I'm not sure that's a good idea.*

There was a flicker of surprise in her eyes. The last time she had heard from him he'd been begging to talk to her, and now he wasn't interested in her offer of meeting up.

Sure, she said, *her smile forced. I was only thinking of a coffee. Nothing serious. Not like a* date *or anything.*

It's not that, he said. *It's just – I have a girlfriend.*

He didn't, but it seemed the easiest excuse.

Louise gave a little shrug. *Whatever.* She glanced around until she saw a friend, Rachel. *Enjoy summer. See you around.*

He watched her go. Life had moved on. He had moved on.

For a long time he had thought that would never happen, and he didn't want to put it in any jeopardy.

Pablo nudged him. 'So what happened? You going to get back with her? She's a looker, mate.'

James shook his head. 'Nah. That's all in the past. Thank God.'

2

The pub was packed. All the crowd was there. The ones who were off to university – James, Najla, Andy – those who had other plans – Toby, Heather, Mo – and others who James had known over the years.

James stood at the bar, trying to get the barman's attention. The barman nodded at him.

'Three pints of lager, two bitter, and two glasses of white wine, please,' he said.

The barman put a tray on the bar. 'You'll need that,' he said.

With the tray full, James made his way through the crowd, beer slopping out of the glasses as people jostled him.

When he got to the table he put the tray down and handed out the drinks. He'd had four pints and could feel the warm glow of the alcohol.

Najla took her wine. There was a girl sitting next to her who James didn't recognize. She was wearing all black, and had a ring in her nose.

'This is Vicki,' Najla said. 'She's new in town. She just moved to Stockton Heath. She works at my place. Thought I'd invite her out to meet you lot. This is James.'

'Nice to meet you,' James said. 'I would have got you a drink, if I'd known. I can go back to the bar and get you something?'

'That's OK,' Vicki said. She had an accent which James couldn't quite identify. Her eyes were very dark, which gave her an intense look. 'I'll get a drink in a bit. But thanks.'

James sat at the table. 'Where are you from?'

'Durham.'

'You go to university there?'

She shook her head. 'I'm from there. Left as soon as I could.'

'You didn't like it?'

She shrugged. 'You could say that. And I got a job here.'

'What do you do for work?'

'Data scientist.'

'Sounds impressive,' James said. 'Not that I know what it means.'

'Me neither,' Vicki said. 'But they pay well.'

'Next round on you, then,' James said.

Vicki smiled. 'Maybe.'

An hour later Vicki went to the bathroom. Najla sat beside him, grinning.

'Well,' she said. 'You and Vicki seem to be getting on. I thought you might.'

'She's nice.'

Najla raised an eyebrow. 'So? Summer fling?'

James shook his head. 'Nah,' he said. 'No point. I'm off to Warwick soon.'

'That leaves the whole of summer,' Najla said. 'And she's very nice.'

'Not my type,' James said. 'But thanks for thinking of me.'

'So,' Mo said. 'Are we staying here or moving on? It's ten now, so if we want to go somewhere else, we need to make a move.'

'Where do you have in mind?' Toby said. 'Town? Go to a club?'

'I can't handle a club,' Andy said. 'Too much bother.'

'Maybe another pub? The Lion?' Mo said. 'Or park here?'

'Here's good for me,' James said. 'But I'm easy.'

'Let's make up our minds,' Mo said. 'Stay or go?'

James was about to reply when he saw a tall, thin figure walking from the bathroom to the bar. It took him a moment to realize who it was. When he did, his stomach tightened.

It was Kevin.

Maggie's old boyfriend.

He glanced at James, then paused. He nodded a greeting; James raised his hand.

Please, he thought, *please move on. I don't want to talk to you.*

He had seen him on and off over the years, but they were not the same age and did not have the same friends.

And then, of course, there was the awkwardness. There had been rumours, for a while after Maggie's disappearance, that Kevin had a hand in it. He was her boyfriend, after all, and in the absence of any other suspects he was as good a bet as anyone.

Kevin turned and walked towards him.

'Hi, James,' he said. 'How's it going?' There was a hush around the table.

His voice brought it all back. High, thin, a little bit whiny: James had heard it over and over in the months following Maggie's disappearance, and he didn't want to hear it ever again.

'Good,' he said. 'You?'

'Not bad. Off to uni?'

James nodded. 'After summer.'

'I'm working at Dales's. Laying bricks.'

'Good for you.'

221

'I'm engaged. Getting married in a few weeks.'

'Oh,' James said. 'Congratulations.'

'She's here. Jenny. I'll introduce you.'

Don't, James thought. *I want you to leave me alone.*

'Sure,' he said.

Kevin walked over to the bar. There was a woman sitting alone, her back to them. He tapped her on the shoulder and said something, then she stood up.

When he saw her, James felt the world start to spin. He gripped the table and closed his eyes to steady himself.

'Jesus,' Mo said. 'What the fuck?'

Kevin's girlfriend – his fiancée – was the spitting image of Maggie. It was as though she was in the pub with them.

James pushed himself upright.

'I have to go,' he said. 'I'm sorry.'

3

He sat on a bench around the corner from the pub and lit a cigarette.

He could not get the image out of his head. For a moment – until he realized it was not actually her – he had thought Maggie was back. Kevin's fiancée – Jenny – was taller and had a thinner face, but the resemblance was unmistakable.

His hand shook as he lifted the cigarette to his mouth.

God, he wished it *was* Maggie. The moment he had thought it was her had been brief, but even so it was enough for a feeling of utter euphoria to engulf him. She was there! Maggie was there! Everything was restored, back to normal. Life was OK again.

And then, the despair. It wasn't Maggie. It was like losing her again, and all the grief and pain was right there, stabbing him in the heart.

He took a drag on the cigarette, then exhaled. He watched the smoke move and swirl. He was never going to get over it. Never. It would always be with him.

'You OK?'

He looked up. Vicki was standing by the bench, her arms folded. She was wearing a green rucksack.

'Yes,' he said. 'No.'

'What happened? In the pub?'

'It was that girl. Jenny. The guy she was with – Kevin – was my sister's boyfriend. A few years back.'

'Must have been quite a break-up.'

'You could say that.'

'Do you want to talk about it?'

James realized that he did. Even though he barely knew Vicki, he did want to talk about it. He might as well; after all, it was the only thing in his life he could think about.

'Do you remember Maggie Cooper?' he said.

Vicki frowned. 'The name's familiar.'

'She went missing.'

'Right. I remember now.' She caught his eye. 'I've got a horrible feeling about what you're going to say next.'

He nodded. 'She was – is – my sister.'

There was a long pause, then Vicki puffed out her cheeks. 'Holy shit.' She gestured at the cigarette. 'Got a spare?'

He handed her the packet.

She took one and lit it. 'Did seeing that guy bring it back?'

'Yes, but there's more. Jenny – his fiancée – looks exactly like Maggie. I mean, the spitting image.' James dropped his cigarette and crushed it under his toes. 'For a moment I thought it *was* her.'

'Fuck. I'm sorry.'

He shook his head. 'I thought my sister was back.'

Vicki sat next to him. She shrugged her rucksack off her shoulders and opened the flap. She pulled out a plastic bottle of vodka.

'Want a drink?' she said.

James did.

4

Sandra watched as Martin nibbled his toast, then pushed it to the side of his plate.

'He's eighteen,' she said. 'He can stay out at night.'

'I know. But I worry.'

'He sent a text. He went back to a friend's house. It's fine.'

Martin nodded. 'I like knowing where he is. That's all.'

It was understandable, given what had happened with Maggie, and on another day Sandra might have shared his concern, but her mind was elsewhere.

It was on the appointment she had at the hospital later that morning.

For a few months she'd felt bloated after eating. Not every time, but enough to notice. She'd assumed it was some kind of late-onset food allergy – a colleague had developed an allergy to apples a year or so back, so she knew that kind of thing happened – and tried cutting out various things: wheat, dairy, alcohol. None of it made a difference.

Then there was the weight loss. Not too drastic, but noticeable all the same. About ten pounds in total. She put it down to the bloating and change in diet.

But then, two weeks ago, she had gone to the toilet at the

gym and seen blood on the toilet paper. She'd looked at the stool.

Blood in there, too.

Of course, she made the mistake of googling 'blood in stool', and was convinced, mere minutes later, that she was going to die.

She calmed herself. There were many possible causes. Haemorrhoids. Benign polyps. It could easily resolve itself.

It didn't. The blood was there every day, so she went to see her GP.

Who told her she needed to get it checked out, and referred her for a colonoscopy.

Which was in about an hour and a half.

She hadn't told Martin. She didn't want to worry him, in case it was nothing, which it almost certainly was. It had been quite difficult to keep it from him, though, given that she had been sent a set of detailed instructions on 'prepping the colon', which basically involved taking a powerful laxative two days before and then not eating anything.

The abandoned toast on his plate looked *delicious*.

Martin caught her staring at it. 'You can have it,' he said. 'I'm not hungry.'

She shook her head. 'Me neither. I'll eat after the gym.' That was where she had told him she was going. 'I need to leave. See you later.'

'OK,' he said. 'I'll text you when James shows up.'

5

James opened his eyes. The room he was in was dark, but there was light coming from the edges of the curtains.

So it was daytime, then.

He lay still, listening to the throb in his head. He was on a mattress, on the floor. On the far side of the room was a bed. It was unoccupied, but the covers had been kicked off, so someone had slept in it.

Vicki.

They had sat by the canal drinking the vodka she had taken from her bag. He remembered telling her about Maggie, and about how he didn't want ever to be vulnerable to losing someone again, which was why he'd said he had a girlfriend, but he didn't, not really.

And she had said not to worry, she didn't want a boyfriend. She had a story too. The story of why she had left Durham to come here.

Her mum had died, and her dad was useless without her. Kind, and loving, but useless, and he had a friend, an evil pig called Jerry, who was not so kind and loving, and who took an interest in his friend's daughter, and told her he would kill her if she said anything.

And she believed him. If he could do what he did then why would he not be capable of murder?

So she fled, and made a life here. And she told him she could see he was hurt as badly as she was and that made them safe for each other.

Then they had come here, to her flat, and drunk the rest of the vodka and he had gone to sleep on the mattress, Vicki in the bed, both glad the other had no interest in anything other than that.

He stood up – he was still fully clothed – and swayed as his head swam. When he was no longer dizzy he left the room. There was a corridor leading to an open door. Through it he could see a fridge and sink.

Vicki was sitting at the kitchen table, smoking. She looked up at him and smiled.

'Feel OK?'

'A bit rough.'

'Me too. Coffee?'

He nodded. There was a cup in the sink; he rinsed it out and poured a coffee from a pot on the hob.

'God,' he said. 'I feel awful.'

Vicki tapped her cigarette ash on to a saucer. 'It's a hangover. It'll pass.'

'Doesn't do it justice.' He swallowed half his coffee. 'Thanks for letting me crash. I should get going.'

He reached for his phone. There were a lot of messages. The most recent was from his dad.

Hi. Let me know if you need a lift home. I've got work but can dip out.

His dad would be worried. He always was. He typed a reply.

228

I'm OK. Can take a bus.

He scrolled through the others. Toby, Mo. Andy. Asking where he'd got to, if he was with Vicki. If he'd got some action.

He felt sick. He didn't want to talk to them about last night. Didn't want to have to explain what had happened when he'd seen the girl who looked like Maggie.

He wanted to forget, but everything was a reminder.

'Are you leaving?' Vicki said. 'You have somewhere to be?'

'Not really,' he said. He gestured to the door of the flat. 'And I can't face it anyway. I want to disappear.'

Vicki stood up and opened a cupboard. 'I can't help you with that,' she said. 'But I do have this.' She took out a bottle. It looked like whisky. Cheap whisky; there was a picture of a boat on the label. She poured a slug into her coffee. 'Want some?'

James looked at her, then shrugged.

'Why not?' he said.

6

Sandra sat in the treatment room at the hospital and wished she'd told Martin so he was with her now. She was sure this was going to turn out to be nothing, but right at that moment she was *terrified*.

A nurse opened the door to the treatment room.

'Mrs Cooper?'

Sandra stood up.

'Come with me. I'm Jazz. I'll get you prepped for the procedure. It's quite straightforward. We'll pop a line in for the sedative and get you settled to wait for the doctor.'

Jazz took her into a room and indicated that she should lie on the bed. She took her hand and rubbed the skin until she had found a vein. Then she inserted a needle and taped it down.

'OK,' she said. 'All ready. I'll be back in a moment.'

She left the room. Sandra reached for her phone and checked her messages. Maybe Martin had figured out what was going on and was on his way.

Nothing.

Jazz came back into the room. 'We're ready. I'll take you down.' She pulled the bed through the door and pushed it down the corridor. Sandra felt like saying she could walk, but she lay back.

Maybe this is the future, she thought. *If something's wrong. Being pushed around in hospital beds.*

Which was a charm against it being wrong. If she accepted it was possible then it wouldn't happen. That was the opposite of what she had done when Maggie disappeared. Then she had thought, *This can't be happening to me, she'll come back.* It had taken days for her to accept that something serious really had happened. Maybe if she'd thought that immediately, Maggie would have been OK.

Jazz pushed the bed into a room full of screens and monitors. A doctor followed her in. She was in her fifties and had short bottle-blonde hair.

'I'm Dr Green.' She consulted a computer screen. 'You've had gas and bloating. Some weight loss. Blood in stool.' She looked at Sandra. 'Any pain?'

'Not really. Nothing too bad.'

'Not really? Or not too bad?'

'Not really.'

'OK. Let's take a look.'

Jazz put an arm on her shoulder. 'I'm going to give you some sedative now. You'll probably feel tired. Go to sleep if you like. Or you can watch the show.' She pointed at a screen. 'It'll all be up there.'

Sandra looked up.

'I think I'll try and watch,' she said.

7

She came around in the examining room.

She'd been planning to watch the procedure, but the voices had gradually faded and her vision had dimmed as the sedative took effect. She still felt a bit woozy; it was no wonder the hospital insisted you take a taxi or get a lift home. There was no way she should be driving.

The door opened and Jazz came in. She put a cup of tea and a packet of bourbon biscuits on the table next to Sandra.

'There you go. Take your time. Dr Green will be along to talk to you in a few minutes. She wants to discuss the results of the colonoscopy with you.'

'OK. Thank you.'

'Not a problem. Enjoy your tea.'

Sandra felt a small frisson of anxiety. Did the doctor want to talk to her because something was wrong? Or did she talk to all her patients? Maybe if you managed to stay awake you heard what she had to say during the procedure and it was only the patients who went to sleep who needed a special visit.

She sipped the tea. She felt its warmth spread through her body. She opened the packet of biscuits and took a large bite. God, it was good to get something inside her stomach.

There was a knock on the door. It scraped on the floor as it opened. Dr Green came in and sat on the chair opposite her.

'So,' she said. 'How are you feeling?'

'I'm good. Awake now. I didn't expect to fall asleep.'

'Yes. It's powerful stuff.' She put her hands in her lap, fingers intertwined. She caught Sandra's eye. 'There are some things we need to discuss, Mrs Cooper.'

She was unsmiling, her expression serious. Sandra felt her appetite drain away. She put the biscuit down.

'What?' she said. 'What do we need to discuss?'

8

Dr Green pressed her fingers together. 'I did find something during the procedure, Mrs Cooper. There's a large tumour in your upper colon. I took a biopsy and we'll get that to the lab right away.'

It took a moment for the words to sink in. Sandra had imagined the scene many times, gone through all the possibilities, but it was still a shock when the doctor said it.

'A tumour?' she said. 'Is it cancer?'

'We'll find out exactly what it is when we get the lab results, but that's a possibility.'

Sandra put her face in her hands. She rubbed her temples. Her legs felt weak. Was this it? Was this how it ended? Her dead, Maggie gone? It was so unfair to Martin. He was such a wonderful husband. She had loved him since they had first met, had always felt incredibly lucky to have a partner who was so decent. She would never have thought that was what she wanted in a husband – decency – but it turned out that was what mattered. Dependable, calm, loving, decent: not exactly Heathcliff, but exactly what she wanted.

And now he might be left a widower, father to a kidnapped girl and a damaged boy. What had he done to deserve that?

She looked up at the doctor.

'Do I—' she said. 'Will I – do I have any options?'

The doctor gave a reassuring smile. 'Plenty. I know this is unwelcome news, but there's quite a way to go before we get to that. Let's wait for the results and we can take it from there.'

'I want to know . . .' Sandra paused. 'You probably get this question from everyone, and you probably can't answer it, but I'd like you to tell me – honestly – if I'm going to survive. I have – I have a husband. And a son.'

'I know you want certainty,' the doctor replied. 'But it's too early. We'll get the test results and make a decision then.'

Sandra picked up her phone.

'Thank you,' she said. 'I need to call my husband.'

9

She got the news four days later.

It was cancer. Treatable, according to the oncologist, a slight man in his fifties with a goatee beard and a bowtie.

First, surgery to remove it. Then chemotherapy to make sure it didn't come back.

Then hope.

Hope was not a strategy that had worked for Sandra in the past. Hope had not brought Maggie back. Hope was a waste of time.

But she was going to have to rely on hope once again.

She put her hand on Martin's knee. He was driving them home from the appointment, both hands on the wheel, at ten to two, his eyes on the road.

Observing the speed limit and all posted traffic signals.

She squeezed his knee.

'I love you,' she said. 'You know that, right?'

He looked at her, his expression one of slight confusion.

'I do,' he said. 'I love you too. And we're going to be OK, Sandy. Whatever happens, we'll be OK.'

For a moment she almost believed him.

Eight Years Earlier:
Sunday, 27 June 2010

1

Sandra took a mango and strawberry smoothie from the chiller by the supermarket checkout. She twisted the top off and sipped it. She'd been to the gym, and she was hungry. She hadn't eaten for days. She didn't have much appetite.

Her treatment started the next day – Monday – and, despite the fact she wasn't hungry, she had decided to make a dinner. She finished the smoothie and smiled at the man behind the till.

'Don't worry,' she said. 'I promise I'll pay for it.'

She put the empty bottle on the belt and began to unload the rest of the groceries.

'Twenty-seven pounds and sixty-two pence,' the man said. 'Paying by card?'

She inserted her credit card into the machine and tapped in the pin. As it processed the payment she loaded the bags into her trolley.

'Can I help you with those?'

It was a familiar voice. She looked up.

'Mr Best,' she said. 'Nice to see you. How are you?'

Best smiled at her. His glasses were smudged and he looked

to have lost some weight. It had been a while since she'd last seen him and he'd aged.

'I'm well,' he said. 'You?'

'Excellent.'

'Your family?'

'They're good. James is getting ready to go to university.'

'How lovely! You must be glad to have him home for one last summer.'

'Yes,' Sandra said. 'It's always nice to have him around. Of course, he'll leave' – she shrugged – 'they grow up, in the end.'

She glanced at his trolley. There were only a handful of bags in it. She glimpsed a box of fish fingers, and some sugary cereal. She pictured him, eating alone in his house, and felt a wave of sympathy. He really should be eating better. And with people.

'You know,' she said. 'I'm sure James would love to see you. Your maths tuition helped him get the grades he needed. Why don't you come over for dinner?'

Best's smile widened. 'Gosh,' he said. 'What a kind offer. I'd be delighted.'

Sandra felt the warm glow of a good deed lighten her mood. 'How about later today? I'm making a roast.'

'If you're sure. I wouldn't want to impose.'

She waved his objection aside. 'Nonsense. It'll be a pleasure. Two o'clock?'

Best nodded. 'Two o'clock it is.'

2

Martin Cooper knocked on his son's bedroom door. 'You OK in there?'

There was no reply. He knocked again, but the door stayed closed. He was pretty sure James was home; he'd come back from a run about an hour ago and heard the sound of the shower. If James had left since then he would have told his parents. As a family, they were sensitive about people disappearing without explanation. They'd had enough of that to last a lifetime.

He considered trying the door but decided against it. It was probably locked – James had installed a small bolt on the inside the summer before – but if it wasn't, the last thing Martin needed was to walk in on his son masturbating, headphones on and phone in hand.

So he knocked again, louder this time.

He was about to walk away when he heard James's voice.

'Who is it?'

'It's me, Dad. Can I come in?'

'Sure.'

He opened the door. James was lying on his bed. He had

had his headphones on, although they were now lying on his chest.

'Sorry,' he said. 'I was listening to music. The Cure.'

Martin nodded. 'Great band.'

'You know them?'

'Of course I do. They were big in the eighties. I saw them live at the Liverpool Empire.'

'*You* saw them live?'

'Why so surprised, Jimbo? You don't think your old man's cool enough to go to music concerts?'

'Music concerts?' James said. 'Try gigs.'

'I've forgotten more about gigs than you'll ever know.'

'Right. I doubt that, Dad.'

'Let's see. The Cure, The Smiths, Joy Division, New Order.' Martin paused. 'UB40, twice. The Housemartins. Depeche Mode. There are others.'

'Really?'

'Really. And then there's Grandpa. He saw the Beatles at the Cavern.'

'That's not true.'

'It is. More than once.'

'That's unbelievable.'

'It seems so, now.' Martin sat on the bed. 'But they were just another band back then. So make sure you go and see the good bands of your generation. Then when you're my age you'll be able to surprise your kids with how cool you used to be.'

James laughed. 'You're still not cool, Dad. It'd take more than a Cure concert to make you cool.'

'You might be right.' He studied his son. 'Everything OK?'

James's eyes moistened and he looked away. It took a few seconds for him to reply.

'Not really.'

'Me neither,' Martin said. 'But Mum'll be OK.'

Martin's throat constricted. Tears came to his eyes. He put his arms around James. They hugged for a long time, then Martin leaned back. In some ways James might still be an adult but in others he was still his baby son. He would always be his baby son.

'By the way,' he said. 'Mr Best is coming for lunch at two, but that gives us a few hours. Want to go for a pint?'

'Best's coming? Why?'

'Mum bumped into him at the supermarket. She invited him over.'

James rolled his eyes. 'Today? The day before she goes for chemo? Why?'

'Because she thought it might be good for him? He's lonely.'

'But she goes to the hospital tomorrow!'

'I know. But I think she needs something to take her mind off things. And he's not *that* bad.'

'He's weird.'

'He's not. And he was a good tutor for you.'

'I guess. He used to ask all kinds of questions about you and mum. And Maggie.'

'What kind of questions?'

'Everything. Your jobs, if you had brothers and sisters, if your parents were still alive, where they lived. All kinds of stuff.'

'He was lonely, James. And it'll be nice to see him. Come on. Let's go and have a beer.'

3

They went to a pub in Thelwall, the Feathered Egg, where they had gone as a family for Sunday lunches. When they got back a few minutes after two p.m. there was a car – a blue Ford Focus – parked on the road outside the house. James recognized it from the times he had been to Best's house for maths tutoring.

'He's here,' he said. 'Right on time. I was kind of hoping he wouldn't make it.'

His dad nodded. 'Be kind, James.'

He would be. The beer – they'd had two pints – had taken his mind off lunch with Best. It was amazing how it did that, how it put a veil between you and the world. It was also good to be able to go out with his dad for a beer. He was interested to see how many people knew him, and how they all seemed pleased to see him; when his dad had gone to the loo, one guy had leaned over to James and muttered that his dad was a great bloke. James had swelled with pride.

Best was in the living room, sitting on the couch. He had a small glass of white wine. Sandra was opposite him; she had a large glass of water.

'You're back,' she said. 'Mr Best was asking how James

got on with his A levels.' She looked at James expectantly. 'So?' she said. 'How did you get on?'

'Great,' he said. 'Had a really good time. Results come soon.'

Best smiled. 'How were your studies? Went well?'

'Really well. It's very interesting.'

'Do you still enjoy maths?'

Had he ever enojoyed maths? He was going to study engineering; it was kind of required.

'Yes,' he said. 'I really love it. How about you? Are you well?'

'Oh, yes.' Best sipped his wine. 'I'm fine. Nothing much new since I last saw you.'

'Do you still live near the school?'

'I do. I doubt I'll ever move,' Best said. 'You get used to a house and it grows up around you. I have certain things I like to do and if I moved I don't think any other house would meet those needs.'

'Like gardening?' James said.

'Exactly.' Best nodded. 'And my darkroom. I still take film photos, even though digital is so much easier. And then there's all the stuff I've accumulated over the years. It all has a place. If I moved I don't know what I'd do with it all. Not that I need it all. There are things in that house that I acquired years ago and which have never seen the light of day since.' He shook his head. 'But we hold on to things, don't we? Even when we no longer need them, or they're taking up space we could use for something else, we don't want to let go.'

James glanced at his dad. He caught his eye.

See, he is weird.

His dad gave a little shake of his head.

'Another glass of wine?' he said.

'Are you having one?' Best replied.

243

'No. James and I went for a walk and ended up in the Feathered Egg, so I think I'll have a cup of tea for now.'

'I'll join you,' Best said. 'Tea would be wonderful.'

'James?' his dad said. 'You want tea?'

James nodded. 'I'll make it. Milk and sugar, Mr Best?'

'Milk. No sugar, thank you.'

James walked towards the kitchen. When he reached the door he glanced back into the room. Best was watching him, a wistful, almost longing expression on his face.

He didn't care what his dad said. Lonely or not, Best was *weird*.

Eight Years Earlier:
Thursday, 1 July 2010

1

Detective Inspector Wynne did not drink much. She was aware of the cliché of the troubled, alcoholic detective, and she was also aware that, like most clichés, it was a cliché because it was, in part, true. She'd known plenty of detectives who had no problem with alcohol, but also she'd known plenty that did, and she had no intention of following in their footsteps.

Still, she could see why you would. Sometimes it would make life easier.

Make it easier to forget the girl who was still missing. Anna Crowne, five years old, taken from outside her school. Gone. Her parents were distraught, obviously, but Wynne had no answers. They had no idea where the girl was. It reminded her of the last time this had happened.

It wasn't the only thing that day that reminded her of Maggie. A letter had come that morning, posted the day before in Wigan.

DEAR DETECTIVE INSPECTOR WYNNE:
    JUST ABOUT FOUR YEARS NOW. I MEANT TO POST
THIS NEARER THE ANNIVERSARY, BUT I DECIDED THERE

WAS A MORE IMPORTANT DAY FOR ME TO RECOGNIZE.
THE FIRST OF JULY – THE DAY YOU WILL RECEIVE THIS
– IS A BIG DAY FOR ME. FOR US.

I SEE YOU HAVE ANOTHER MISSING PERSON ON YOUR
BEAT. GETTING A LITTLE CARELESS, AREN'T YOU?

ANYWAY, HERE'S TO ANOTHER YEAR! I'LL RAISE A
GLASS TONIGHT.

YOURS SINCERELY,

???

It was the fourth letter. There had been one every year, all
posted from different locations, except for the third year.
Wynne didn't know why the kidnapper had missed a year.
She *did* know there was no forensic evidence on any of them.

And she knew she hated them. Hated the prim little colon
after her name. Hated the 'here's to another year'. Hated the
formal 'yours sincerely' and hated the stupid question marks.

Most of all she hated the feeling of powerlessness. She
was losing this game and there was nothing she could do
about it.

And what did he mean, the first of July was an important
day? For *us*? Who was us? Maggie?

She was being toyed with, and she *hated* it.

Then she saw him. The one person guaranteed to make
her day worse.

Best. Standing in front of the freezer cabinet, putting a
box of fish fingers into his basket. Two boxes. That was a
lot of fish fingers for a single man, but then again, they were
frozen. They didn't go off.

Funny to see him, this day of all days. He'd been a suspect
for a while when Maggie Cooper had gone, although there
was never any evidence against him. Not that the lack of
evidence had made Wynne any less certain he was involved.

She'd got carried away back then because she didn't like

him, and as she looked at him those feelings came flooding back. She walked down the aisle towards him.

'Mr Best,' she said.

He looked up, startled. 'Yes? Who? – Oh. *You*.' His eyes narrowed. There was real dislike in his expression.

She pointed at the fish fingers, remembered seeing him eating them at his house. 'Shopping?'

'Yes. As I am allowed to do.'

'Of course. I'll be on my way. Enjoy your meal.'

He smiled at her. For a second there was something sly, something secret in his smile, then it vanished.

'You too, Detective Inspector Wynne.'

She chose her pizza and walked towards the checkout. She had a feeling there was something she should have noticed, something unusual.

It came to her as she paid.

He remembered her name. Rank and name. Surely that was something he would have forgotten by now?

But no.

Clearly, Best had a good memory.

Why did that disturb her? What was it she was missing?

She couldn't find an answer. On her way home she stopped at the off-licence and picked up a bottle of red wine.

Then she picked up another. One wasn't going to be enough.

Eight Years Earlier:
Thursday, 1 July 2010

1

She heard the scraping sound. She took a deep breath. Seb's third birthday was coming up. She wasn't sure of the exact date – there were some gaps in the calendar – but it was close and she wanted to celebrate it. He didn't have any of the things he should have had. No presents, no party with his friends, no cake. The only saving grace was that he didn't know what he was missing. Seb was only three, so he had no idea what birthdays were. He would, though, as he got older, and so Maggie was determined to make the day as special as she could.

So she was going to ask the man for a few things. Candles. A cake. Maybe a toy. She would beg him if she had to.

It's your birthday soon, she told him, when they woke up. *You'll be three. You're getting to be such a big boy. I'm so proud of you.*

What's a birthday? he said.

The day you were born. You came out of Mummy's tummy.

He looked at her stomach. *I was in your tummy?*

I grew you in there.

Oh. Why did I come out?

You had to. And the day you did was your birthday. Three

years ago. She paused. *On birthdays you get presents. And I have a present for you.*

What is it?

A wish.

What's a wish?

It's when you ask for something and you get it. You might *get it. What would you like, most of all?*

He thought for a while.

To stay here with you, Mummy.

She had been worried about giving him a wish, since it would almost certainly not be granted. She could not provide toys or sunshine or a swim in a lake. It was a bitter irony that he had wished for the one thing that would actually come true.

Anyway, now she wanted to get him something more tangible. A real present.

The door opened, and the man came in. Seb was sitting on the end of the mattress.

'I want to ask something,' Maggie said.

He frowned. 'Go ahead.'

'It's Seb's birthday soon. He'll be three, and—'

'It's today.'

'Today?'

'Yes. That's why I'm here.'

Maggie stopped. What did he mean, that's why he was here? To celebrate? Give Seb a gift? Surely not. She was surprised he knew it was Seb's birthday, never mind bringing him a present.

'You have something for him?'

He shook his head and held up his hands to show they were empty.

'No. I've come for him.'

'What do you mean, you've come for him?'

'He's three now. It's time he left.'

Her mouth dried up. 'Left what?'

'Left here.'

'What do you mean?'

'The time has come.'

Maggie stared at him. 'You're letting us go?'

'No.' He licked his lips. 'I'm letting *him* go.'

'What about me? He can't leave without me.'

'He can. You're staying here.'

Maggie tensed. She reached for Seb and held him in her lap.

'No. You're not taking him.'

'I am. It's time. Don't you want him to be out of here? To be free?'

Maggie pulled Seb tighter. She did want him to be out of there, she wanted it more than anything.

The thought of him living a normal life, surrounded by people who loved him – even without her – was intoxicating.

But that was not on offer. The man was not going to provide that.

How could he? How could he explain the sudden appearance of a little boy in his life? People would ask questions, social services would get involved, the police would show up.

'No,' she said. 'You're not taking him from me. Never.'

'He has to leave. It's time.'

'What do you mean it's time? You keep saying that.'

The man shook his head. His mouth was a thin line, his brow furrowed. She'd seen the expression before, when she didn't do what he wanted.

'Give him to me.'

'Mummy,' Seb said. 'I want to stay with you.'

'You can,' Maggie replied. 'You can stay right here.'

'I don't want to go.' Seb started to cry. 'He's scary.'

'Now look what you've done,' the man said. His frown

deepened. 'You've made this difficult. I don't know *why* you have to make it so *fucking* difficult.'

He moved with surprising speed, uncoiling across the room. As he reached her, he raised his right fist and slammed it into the side of her head. She fell backwards on to the bed, then felt his hand around her throat. His other hand clamped over her mouth and nose. He squeezed, hard, until her breathing was shallow.

'You made this difficult, you stupid bitch,' he said. His voice was strained and angry, almost as though he was on the verge of tears, and, as he shook his head at her his grip tightened.

'Please,' she gasped. 'Please. Don't take him.'

'Too late.' He grabbed Seb in his right hand and picked him up, holding him under his arm. Seb was screaming, but his screams were fading as she struggled to breathe. 'Too late.'

'Please.' Her vision was blurring, Seb coming in and out of focus. 'Please. Don't take him.'

But the blackness at the edge of her vision thickened and closed in, and Seb was gone.

2

When she came round she had no idea who or what or where she was. She felt disembodied; the closest thing she could compare it to was waking from a very deep sleep and being confused, blinking away the slumber as your surroundings came into focus and you remembered where you were.

It was like that, multiplied by ten. She was no more than an observer of facts. There was a room. She was in it. She was alone.

None of them meant anything. At least, not at first.

And then what they meant came back to her. She was a prisoner. She had a calendar, and it told her she had been here for four years. She had parents and a brother.

She had a son.

A son called Seb.

The memories hit her in a rush. The man, choking her, grabbing Seb. Her crying out. The darkness bleeding into her vision and taking over.

Her son, gone.

She sat upright. Her throat hurt and she pressed her fingers to it. It was bruised and tender.

She didn't care.

'Seb!' she shouted. 'Seb! Are you there? Seb!'

The only answer was silence.

She wrapped her arms around herself, her eyes wide in horror. The man had taken him. He had taken her son.

And he would not be bringing him back. She would beg, of course she would, but it would make no difference. She knew that already.

Seb was gone, and she would never see him again. The boy she had given birth to, cradled and fed, kissed, read to, played with. The boy for whom she had dreamed of a future out of here, a future with friends and love and family. The boy she had loved, in a way she had never known was possible.

That boy was gone. It was as though someone had ripped away a part of her, the best and most important part, and left behind half a person, a shell, a worthless, pointless husk.

How could she live without him? How would it be possible?

She didn't know, and she didn't want to know. She didn't want to live, not without her son.

But the man would make her. He would force her to carry on.

She let out a low, keening moan and lay on her side, her knees hugged to her chest. This was worse than she had ever imagined possible, and it was never going to end.

Eight Years Earlier:
Wednesday, 18 August 2010

1

It's fine, Sandra had said. *You go. Colin can bring me home. I don't mind at all.*

It was her umpteenth chemo session. Martin had a meeting with a difficult client and he could not be sure he would be able to get away in time to bring her home. If she was honest, she would have liked him there, but they couldn't put their whole lives on hold because of her treatment.

And Colin Best had made it clear he would help whenever he could, which was why he was sitting by her hospital bed, reading a book. It wasn't the first time he'd helped out, either. He'd brought meals early on, fetched library books for her, come for a cup of tea when she was on her own.

The book was *The Collector* by John Fowles. It was a bit of an inappropriate choice, given what might have happened to Maggie, but she couldn't take offence at that. People could read what they wanted; it probably never crossed his mind that she might link it to her daughter. As with the treatment, life went on.

'Good book?' she said.

He nodded. 'I read it years ago. Made a real impression on me.' He turned the book over and looked at the cover. 'I found this in a second-hand book shop and thought I'd read it again.' He closed it and placed it on the table.

'I think I might go and get some tea. Would you like anything?'

'No thanks. No appetite.'

'Of course. I'll be back soon.'

By the time he returned she was ready to leave. She steadied herself against him while they walked down the corridor. At the exit, he paused.

'You wait here. I'll fetch the car.'

'That's fine. I can walk.' She looked up at the sky; it was blue and cloudless. It was always a relief to leave the hospital. It felt like a return to normal life.

'No, no,' he said. 'It'll only take a minute or two.'

She waited by the door until he pulled up. He opened the door for her.

'It's very kind of you to help,' she said. 'What do I owe you for the parking?'

'Nothing,' he said. 'I won't accept a penny. I already have the most precious thing you can give.' He put his hand on hers. His grip was surprisingly firm. 'Your friendship and trust. Now, let's get you home.'

2

'London,' Vicki said.

'London?' James watched a duck swim past on the canal. It was mid-afternoon and they had been drinking for a while already. He had started at Warwick but was spending a lot of time at home – with the blessing of the university – because of his mum. 'Why London?'

'Streets are paved with gold,' Vicki said.

'Right.' James closed his eyes. She was leaving. Moving to the capital. That was fine. She wasn't his girlfriend.

She was his friend, though.

'Not really,' she said. 'The streets are normal. But I've got a mate down there. And so why not?'

'Yeah,' James said. 'Why not?'

'Are you OK?'

He realized, now she had asked the question, that he wasn't, but since when had that mattered? Since when had the universe given a flying fuck whether James Cooper was OK or not? Maggie was gone, his mum might be next, and now this. It was the latest in a long line of shithouse treatment that he didn't deserve.

'Not really,' he said. 'I'll miss you.'

When he got home Best's car was parked on the road outside the house. Not again. Why would that fucker not leave them alone? He was a lonely old man, sure, but that didn't give him the right to show up at the house all the time. Besides, he was creepy. There was something in the way he looked at his mum that turned James's stomach.

She was blind to it, though. She saw him as a harmless pensioner who wanted to be helpful, and if she needed a lift somewhere and he was free, why not?

He opened the front door and went into the hall. He could hear people talking in the living room; when he closed the door they stopped.

'James?' his dad called. 'Is that you?'

'Yes.'

'Come and say hello. Mr Best is here.'

That was the last thing he was going to do. 'I'm tired.'

He went upstairs and lay on his bed. A few seconds later he heard someone coming upstairs.

His door opened and his dad came in. He stood for a second in the doorway, then came and sat next to him on the bed.

'That was a bit rude, James.'

'I don't care. I don't like him.'

'He's been very good to us. He doesn't have to ferry your mum around.'

'Whatever.'

'James.' His dad folded his arms. 'Have you been drinking? Do you think you're drinking a bit much at the moment?'

'No.'

'I think you might be.'

'I'm not.'

He knew his dad was right; he was drinking too much,

and for the wrong reasons. It was one of the things that made the pain go away. No – it was the *only* thing that made the pain go away.

Anyway, he could stop anytime he wanted. One day he wouldn't need it. But not today.

'OK,' his dad said, his voice quiet. 'If you feel like it later, come down and say hello.'

Friday, 22 June 2018

One Day to Go

1

Max coughed in his sleep. Maggie watched. She had barely slept, unable to waste any of her last moments with her son. After a moment, he coughed again, and his eyes opened. They were watery. He looked at Maggie and sneezed.

'Poor baby,' Maggie said. 'You're getting a cold.'

On this of all days. Tomorrow he turned three. Tomorrow, the man came. She had marked it on the calendar, struck through his last day.

S	Su	M	Tu	W	Th	F
						~~1~~
~~2~~	~~3~~	~~4~~	~~5~~	6	~~7~~	~~8~~
~~9~~	~~10~~	~~11~~	~~12~~	~~13~~	~~14~~	~~15~~
~~16~~	~~17~~	~~18~~	~~19~~	~~20~~	~~21~~	~~22~~
23	24	25	26	27	28	29
30						

She had held him against her all night, feeling the rise and fall of his chest, listening to him breathe in and out, in and out. She alternated between feeling paralysed by anguish and bouts of heart-racing panic. Sometimes she wanted to curl up into a ball with him and disappear; others she wanted to jump up and tear at the walls of the room and rip them down in her rage.

But she did the only thing she could. She lay there, arms around her son, feeling the seconds and minutes and hours slip past her, the end looming larger and larger.

At some point she'd fallen asleep for a few minutes and dreamed of a remote control with a pause button that could stop time. She'd be OK with that, OK if she and Max were frozen in one moment, as long as they were together. It wouldn't be perfect, but it would be better than the alternative.

Better than what awaited her tomorrow. She could hardly imagine it. It was too painful; the thought of being alone in this room, her three sons taken from her, caused her an anguish so intense it was a physical pain.

How much longer would she be here? How long until he let her out? Would he ever let her out?

She knew the answer to that. He would leave her here until he died, and then she'd die too.

So why wait? If that was the end of this, why wait? She wouldn't. If he came tomorrow and took Max, she would kill herself. She would bash her brains out or dehydrate herself or drink the bleach she had hidden under the bottom of the bath. Maybe she would drink that first and then hammer her head on the floor until she passed out.

Because she could not lose another child. It could not happen again.

Max sneezed again. He looked up at her, mucus all over his top lip.

'Mummy,' he said, and pointed at it. 'Look.'

Maggie reached for a tissue and wiped it away.

He sneezed again and his eyes widened in surprise. He smiled, and then laughed. 'This is funny.'

Maggie nodded. 'If you say so.'

Another sneeze; another laugh. 'I can't stop, Mummy!'

'That's what happens when you have a cold.'

'I like it.'

It was a novelty. He had never had a cold; there were no viruses in the room, other than those the man brought in.

'You might not, after a while.'

And then it hit her again. For a few seconds she had forgotten what was coming, but it all rushed back.

There would not be an 'after a while', not for Max. She felt dizzy; her stomach clenched and her hands shook. She steadied herself against the bed, then fell to her knees.

'Mummy?' Max's voice was alarmed. 'Mummy?'

'I'm fine,' she said, the words little more than a gasp. 'Just tired.'

He put his face close to hers, looking into her eyes. 'Mummy?'

'It's OK.' She hugged him to her, holding him tightly. 'Don't worry, Max. Mummy— Mummy had a little turn, that's all. I'll be OK in a second.'

But she wouldn't. She wouldn't ever be OK again.

2

'Mummy,' Max said. 'Can I have a story?'

'Of course,' Maggie said. She had no idea what it would be. She barely had the energy to breathe, never mind invent a story. And she was so distracted. All she could think of was what was coming; stories seemed so unimportant.

But they weren't unimportant to Max, so she had to try.

'I'm going to tell you about friends,' she said. 'Friends are the most important thing – after family – in the world.'

She thought of Chrissie and Fern. Of how they relied on each other, of how secure she'd felt when she was with them. They were a team, and like all good teams, they were much stronger together than the sum of their parts. She smiled at the memory of a boy, Christopher, a few years older who had kept asking Fern to go on dates with her. She said no; they were thirteen and starting to get interested in going on dates with boys, but she didn't like him. No one really did; he was sullen and aggressive and a bully, and when the kids his own age started to ignore him he turned to the younger ones.

At a school disco he had trapped Fern in a corner and tried to kiss her.

She refused, but he didn't let her go.

Maggie and Chrissie watched it happen.

What should we do? Maggie said.

We have to help her, Chrissie replied. *Come with me.*

They walked over and Chrissie tapped the boy on the shoulder. He turned around and scowled.

What do you want? We're talking, he said.

We want you to get lost, Chrissie said, then shouted. *We want you to leave her alone!*

A crowd was forming, and Christopher was starting to look uncertain.

You get lost, he said.

He's a cradle-snatcher! Maggie said. *Leave her alone!*

There was some laughter, and Christopher's face flushed. He backed away and walked towards the exit.

'Why are friends important, Mummy?' Max said.

Maggie hugged him. 'Because with friends,' she said, 'you can do anything. If you have friends, nothing can hurt you.'

'Do I have friends, Mummy?'

She pressed her hand to his heart. 'In there you do,' she said. 'In there you have all the friends in the world.'

'So nothing can hurt me?'

'That's right, Max. Nothing can hurt you.'

'Good,' Max said. 'That's good.'

She closed her eyes. If only it was true. Because there was something that could hurt Max.

And it – he – was coming tomorrow.

3

The day seemed to pass slowly, and yet it was a surprise when evening came and she heard the scraping noise.

The door opened and the man came in, two plastic plates and two plastic cups on his tray.

Max toddled over and looked at the food.

'Sausages,' he said. His voice was thick with the cold. 'And orange juice. Yum.' He picked up one of the cups and drank. The man stepped back towards the door.

'You can take mine,' Maggie said. 'I'm not hungry.'

The man shrugged. 'I'll leave it. You might change your mind.' He pointed at Max. 'Is he ill?'

'He has a cold.'

'Orange juice should help.'

'What do you care?'

The man caught her gaze. 'I suppose I don't.'

She watched him leave. She'd had many feelings towards him over the years – anger, of course, and hatred, but also pity and sympathy and wonder. Wonder at what made him do this, at the life he led.

Now, though, she saw only one thing. He was a monster. He had kidnapped and imprisoned a fifteen-year-old girl and taken and murdered – she was sure that was what had happened to Seb and Leo – two of her sons. Tomorrow he would take a third. To the world he seemed mild-mannered and calm but it was a veneer that hid the truth: he was violent and cold-hearted and selfish and utterly lacking in any sense of the harm he was doing to other people.

'Why are you doing this?' she said.

He paused, hand on the door.

'I'm only bringing food.'

'Not that. You know what I mean. This' – she gestured around the room – 'all of it. Why keep me here? Why take me in the first place? Why did you want a girl – and now a little boy – in your basement? How is this good for you?'

He frowned. 'I told you. You're safe here. Out there is' – he shook his head – 'it's a bad place. No harm can come to you in here.'

'Every day harm comes to me. Every second you deny me sunshine and laughter and family and love you are doing me harm. And Max.'

His eyes narrowed. 'You *never* listen. Why won't you listen? Sometimes I wish I'd not bothered with this, but then I remember. This is my duty. This is my burden.' His voice rose. 'I have to save at least one. I watch the girls. They start so *innocent*, so perfect, and then they change. They are corrupted. By boys and alcohol and cigarettes. And I couldn't let that happen to you. I tried with your mum, but I let her slip away. She was so beautiful, so perfect, and I was sure that she felt the same way about me, but no. The world took her from me. I realized then that I would never get what I wanted. What I *needed*. People like me didn't get such perfect prizes, so I decided I would have to take it. It was too late, though. Your mum was gone.' He smiled, a lopsided, clownish smile. 'But then I got the chance with you. And I was not going to miss it.'

'You haven't saved me,' Maggie said. 'You say I would

267

have been corrupted, but you've done worse. You've ruined me. Raped me. Dirtied me. You've destroyed my life.'

At the sound of his mum's raised voice, Max looked up from his sausages. Maggie smiled. 'It's OK,' she said. 'We're only talking.'

'OK, Mummy,' Max said.

The man was staring at her, his face flushed. She could see he was upset. Good. Maybe she could provoke him into an argument and he'd have a heart attack right now.

He shook his head. 'You're getting it wrong,' he said. 'I've not destroyed your life. I've *perfected* you. I've kept you pure.' He raised his hand. 'It doesn't matter what you say. You don't *know*. You were a girl when I rescued you. You have no idea what happens out there. If you did, you'd be grateful. I know that, so whatever you say, it won't bother me. Look at your mum. Look at what she became. And your brother.' He shook his head. 'He's wasting his life.'

Maggie stared at him. 'How do you know what my brother's doing? Or my mum?'

'I see them from time to time.' He smiled, although his eyes were hard. 'We're friends.'

It took her a while – she wasn't sure how long – to respond. 'Friends. You're *friends*?'

'Yes,' he said. 'We have been for a while. Ever since you disappeared. I tutored James in maths.' He pointed above his head. 'Up there. He did well. Went to Warwick University.'

This, she realized, was punishment. She'd hurt him and he wanted his retaliation.

'You're lying. You're only saying this to hurt me.'

'Why would I lie?'

'Because you didn't like what I said to you. So now you're making this up to hurt me.'

'OK. Then I'm lying. But if I am, you won't want to ask me how they are, will you?'

She tried not to, but it was too hard. Eventually, she spoke.

'What did you mean, he's wasting his life? What's James doing?'

'He's made some bad choices. Very bad choices. I think it upsets your parents to see what he's made of his life. But then he was hit hard when you left, and they know that. What else could they expect?'

'You fucking bastard,' she said. 'You did this to me, my parents, my brother, and then you stand there and tell me James made bad choices when it's all your fault.'

The man raised his hand again.

'Don't speak to me like that, you foolish little bitch,' he said. 'I'll be back for the tray later.'

4

Her family was out there. Close. If he knew them, they must be close.

Her mum. Her dad. James.

They were out there, her disappearance ruining their lives. She had to see them. She *had* to get out of here. There was a way, there had to be. She couldn't let him win. She felt a fierce, hard determination. She looked around the room. The bathtub. The bucket. The mattress. Max's Duplo. Their clothes. Her needle and thread. The bleach in the tinfoil.

Nothing she could use.

Could she get Max out? Throw him up the stairs when the man came, pull the man into the room? But where would Max go? What if there was a locked door at the top, the door that made the scraping sound?

He'd be trapped, and the man would still take him. It had to be something else. She visualized what would happen on his birthday.

The man would come in. He would look around the room. He would point at Max.

Give him to me.

She would say no and try to fight and lose.

And Max would be gone.

It was pointless. She couldn't protect him. She imagined how wonderful it would be if she woke up tomorrow and Max was gone, magically rescued. The man would come in and look around and frown.

Where is he?

I don't know. I don't know where he is, but he's gone. He's free.

But that was impossible. There would be no magical rescue. The best she could do was hide him for a few minutes. She could put him in the bathtub, like the day before when, for a second, she had not known where he was. That was her only option, but the man would find him immediately.

She could hide him under the *bottom* of the bath. It would take the man a little longer to find him there.

But he would still find him, and it would be over. It wouldn't work.

Maybe not, but it might buy her some time.

Which was a start.

And a start was all you needed. She remembered something her dad used to say when she complained about not knowing how to do something: *Get started, Fruitcake. If you're not moving then you can't get anywhere, but once you're up and running you've got something to work with. Once you're in motion, all you have to do is steer.*

He was right. Suddenly things felt different. The man would come in and Max wouldn't be there. She would know where he was; the man wouldn't. For a change, she would be in control.

And the germ of what she might do with that control began to emerge.

Four Years Earlier: July 2014

James

1

Hey.

The instant message popped up on his screen. It was from Penny. She had started the graduate programme at Spinks, an engineering firm in Manchester, at the same time as him. He liked her; she was funny and smart and tough, which he imagined was something to do with her upbringing as a police officer's daughter in a village in Yorkshire. She had a long-term boyfriend, but from the start they had connected. Sometimes there was a spark when you met someone. It was hard to know why it happened with that particular person – why not one of the other graduates, Janet or Angie or Vanessa, who, at first glance, were equally as attractive as Penny. Why not Mary, who was much more attractive?

James didn't know, and he doubted he would ever find out, but he was glad it was Penny. He was glad because she was already taken and he didn't want a girlfriend. He didn't want any connection to anybody.

He had lost enough in his life, and he didn't intend to lose any more.

He typed a reply.

Whats up?

Lunch?

Sure. Canteen?

I was thinking of getting out of the office. Maybe the burrito truck in the park?

He looked out of the window. The leafy crowns of the trees swayed gently in the summer breeze. It would be good to get some fresh air.

It would help with his hangover. He had woken up with a stinging headache. He was used to hangovers, but this was a big one. Most nights he and Carl, the guy he shared his flat with, drank a few beers and a bottle or two of wine while they watched YouTube videos of football goals and rugby hits and famous gigs. Last night Carl had taken a bottle of vodka from the freezer and handed him a glass of that. Then there'd been some weed and he'd woken up feeling like shit. Some fresh air and a walk away from his desk sounded good.

You're on. Five minutes?

2

Penny was standing by the revolving door, looking at her phone. She was wearing tight, dark jeans and a grey, long-sleeved sweater with a V-neck. A pendant glittered at the base of her throat. James imagined what it would feel like to kiss her neck.

She saw him and smiled and they walked out of the revolving door. Outside, James tilted his face to the sky, enjoying the warmth of the sun.

'Happy Friday,' she said. He noticed her eyes were puffy and red. 'You have plans for the weekend?'

He shrugged. 'Pub with Carl tonight, probably. Then I'm not sure. The usual. Hanging around. You and Bryn doing anything fun?'

Her eyes caught his. 'Not this weekend. We split up.'

'What? What happened?'

'It's been coming for a while.'

'Really? I thought you guys had been together for ages?'

She nodded. 'We have. That's part of the problem. Bryn's a lovely guy, but he's – he's a bit clingy. He wants to settle down. Have kids. His parents were married at nineteen so twenty-three for him is high time to tie the knot, but I'm not ready. Not even close.'

'You don't have to split up. You could agree to wait.'

'That's the problem. The more we talked about marriage and kids, the more I realized I couldn't picture it. I couldn't see us as parents together. When I tried, it felt wrong. I've been thinking of breaking up with him for the last six months. Last night he brought it up again and I kind of came out with it.'

'What did you say?'

'I said I didn't want to marry him anytime soon. He said, well then, when? and I said I don't think ever. He said in that case let's break up for good. I think he was calling my bluff, but I agreed. And that was that. It was a rough night.'

'I'll bet.'

'He slept on the couch, but our flat is tiny and you can hear everything. I was up all night listening to him crying. I was glad when he left for work. He went early, at like five a.m. I felt awful.'

'Sorry to hear it.'

'Don't be. It's for the best.'

They reached the burrito van. James looked at the menu; Penny didn't bother.

'Could I have a beef burrito?' she said. 'Extra chilli.'

'You got it, love,' the man said. 'And you, mate?'

'I'll have the same,' James said. They waited for their food and walked to a bench.

'Where are you going to live?' he said. 'Will you move out?'

'No. He will. At first I thought he was being a gentleman, but now I think he just wants to know where I'm going to be. He's called eight times today. And sent four texts asking if I'll be home tonight and if he can come to talk. I will be home, but I feel like going out so he can't find me.'

'Not taking it well, then?'

'You could say that.'

'Well,' James said. 'At least you did it.'

'Yeah. It feels good. I feel good. I'm sorry for him, but better now than later.'

'For you. He'd probably have preferred to postpone the inevitable.'

She lifted the burrito and took a bite. It left a smear of chilli sauce on her bottom lip. James brushed his own lip with his forefinger to indicate where.

'You've got some chilli on your mouth.'

She dabbed it with a tissue. 'Thanks. Bryn would have wiped it away for me. You know, I feel really good about breaking up with him. Guilty and weird, but good. I'm *so* glad it's done. It's strange – I thought about breaking up with him for ages, but I kept coming up with reasons why not. He wasn't that bad, we had a lot of history that it was a shame to throw away, but now – now I can't believe I waited this long. I have no regrets at all. It's like I came out of a long, dark tunnel and I have no intention of going back. You know what I mean?'

He knew the feeling of being in a long, dark tunnel. It had been like that since Maggie disappeared. He didn't think he would ever come out.

'I've never been in that situation. Not with a relationship.'

'I hope you never are,' Penny said. 'Anyway, I learned my lesson. I'm not going to waste my time any more. If I want to do something, I'm going to do it.' She caught his eye and looked at him. 'So, how about a date this weekend? Saturday? Or tonight? Give me somewhere to be?'

He looked away. He felt a mounting panic. He liked Penny; more than liked, he was very attracted to her, but that was the problem. He'd get attached, and then lose her in some way. She'd dump him or fall for someone else. It didn't matter how it happened, only that it would. Or *might*. Even the risk

277

was too much. He couldn't risk losing someone else he cared about.

And what about when he told her about Maggie? That would make it almost certain she would leave him. He never told people. He didn't want their sympathy. But he would have to tell Penny, and then she would look at him differently. At first she might pretend it didn't matter, but over time she would see him as damaged goods. She might not think that, she might just think she was growing apart from him, but it would be because of what had happened. Who wanted to be with someone with that kind of baggage?

'No,' he said. 'No. I don't think so.'

'Oh,' Penny said. 'That's pretty definitive. Is there a reason? It's only a drink. Trust me, I'm not looking for another relationship right now.'

He shook his head. 'It's not that. I can't.'

She nodded slowly. 'James. It's only a drink, but fine. Another time, maybe.'

'Maybe,' James said. For a moment he considered telling her the whole story, but the words died on his lips. 'Maybe.'

3

Carl took a drag on his spliff. 'Have you got a photo of her?'

'I think so. We had a team-building day.' James scrolled through his photos. There was one of him, a guy called Paul, and Penny. 'That's her.'

Carl looked at the screen. In the photo, Penny had her hair scraped back in a ponytail. She was wearing a green T-shirt and tight black leggings.

'You turned her down?' Carl said. 'Are you fucking crazy? Or secretly gay? It's cool if you are. I'll still be your mate.'

James regretted telling him at all, but they'd had at least six or seven pints of strong lager before coming home and starting on the weed, and he'd found himself explaining what had happened.

'No, I'm not,' he said. 'I'm just not that interested.'

'Give her my number if she's looking for someone to help her get over the break-up,' Carl said. 'I'll do it.'

There was a knock on the door. Carl nodded at it. 'You go,' he said. 'I'm still in shock.'

James opened the door of the flat. A tall, thin man in a leather vest looked at him with dark, sunken eyes. He had a shaved head, the veins in his forehead visible.

'All right, mate,' he said. 'Carl in?'

'Yeah. I'll get him.'

'No need. I'll come right in. Don't worry, chicken. He knows me.'

James nodded and walked into the living room. The man followed him.

Carl clicked his tongue when he saw him. 'Well, fuck me,' he said. 'Davy. When did you get out?'

'Two days ago.'

'Welcome back, mate.' Carl looked at James. 'This is Davy. Been a guest of Her Majesty. Davy, this is James.'

'He living here?' Davy said.

'He is. Where you staying?'

'At my mum's. Looking for something permanent. Thought you might want to give me my old room back, but looks like it's taken. Anyway, let's celebrate.' He pulled a plastic bag from his pocket. 'Borrowed a few quid from the old woman,' he said. 'And got this.'

He emptied the bag on to the coffee table. There was a small vial of liquid and a needle.

'Oh,' Carl said. 'You're a bad man, Davy Simpson. I've not been near that stuff for a few years. And I don't want to go back.'

'Yes, you do,' Davy said. 'You *always* want to. You might tell yourself you don't, but that's bollocks.'

James looked at Carl. He was staring at the bag with yearning in his eyes.

He swallowed and rolled up his sleeve. 'Come on then,' Carl said, his voice low. 'Let's celebrate.'

4

It was – what? Like getting drunk but ten times better? A hundred times? A thousand?

Definitely, but it was more than simply *better*. It was different. It made you feel perfect, flawless, like nothing could touch you. And it was so quick. There'd been the prick of the needle and then he had felt it rushing through every cell in his body and pointing them all in the same direction.

All the thoughts and questions and worries that had been running around his head dissolved. Should he have said yes to Penny? Was his job how he wanted to spend his life? Was the hole inside him, the Maggie-shaped hole, ever going to be filled in?

All gone. None of it mattered. All the anxiety and sadness and conflict – gone. Vanished, in an instant. Replaced by bliss, and the knowledge that he was safe and nothing could hurt him. He'd been happy, for the first time in years.

He'd woken and his first thought had been of the heroin and he'd smiled. For a while, he lay in bed, watching the sun stream in through the gap in the curtains. It was a lovely summer day. He could go for a walk. Head up to the countryside. Maybe hike up Kinder Scout and look down on

Manchester below. He imagined lying on the rocks, feeling their warmth against his back, the sound of a brook lulling him to sleep, a gentle breeze keeping him cool. Or maybe sit and read the paper in his garden with a cup of tea.

Maybe call Penny and say, *Sorry about yesterday, do you still want a drink?*

No. Why bother? That was too complicated. Too difficult. Too risky. Something might go wrong.

He knew what he wanted. He wanted that feeling again.

He'd be back in work Monday, but why not spend one weekend happy? It wasn't like he'd get addicted. You couldn't get addicted doing it twice.

He swung his legs out of bed. The house was quiet, but Carl wouldn't mind being woken up.

Four Years Earlier: July 2014

DI Wynne

1

Wynne's phone rang. A number she didn't know, with an unfamiliar area code. Probably some telemarketing bullshit.

But maybe not.

'This is Wynne.'

'Detective Inspector Wynne? This is DS Liz Dales, from Alsbury.'

Wynne straightened in her chair. She reached for a pencil.

'Yes. How can I help?'

'We received a request related to a letter posted two days ago somewhere in the village. We were asked to review any CCTV footage that might show who posted it.'

'That's right. The request came from me.'

'Well, we think we have it. We think we have the letter being posted.'

'Who was it?'

'A man in his late fifties, maybe early sixties. He lives here in the village.'

'Thanks,' Wynne said. 'We'll be there as soon as we can. Do nothing until we arrive.'

2

The letters had continued to come every year around the anniversary. There was no letter on the seventh year – like the third year – but other than that they came. Mocking, boastful, sick. They were posted in various locations around the north of England, dropped into a postbox by the man – she assumed it was a man – who had abducted Maggie Cooper.

Wynne had spent hours reading them, looking for some clue, but there was nothing. At least nothing in the letters themselves. She *had* wondered why he had missed the third and seventh anniversaries. There must have been a reason. It could have been as simple as illness, or laziness, but Wynne didn't think so. She thought something had prevented him from sending them, something like prison, or a stint working abroad.

So she had checked the prison admissions in those years, looking for someone from the Warrington area who had been locked up in the third year, free in the fourth, and back inside in the seventh. There were one or two, but it had come to nothing. She checked the same with the Army; again, nothing.

And now she had the latest letter.

DEAR DETECTIVE INSPECTOR WYNNE:

EIGHT YEARS, DETECTIVE INSPECTOR. COMING UP ON A DECADE AND YOU'RE NO CLOSER TO FINDING ME OR MAGGIE. I SEE YOU IN THE NEWS FROM TIME TO TIME, COMMENTING ON YOUR INVESTIGATIONS. ARE THEY AS MUCH OF A FAILURE AS THIS ONE? YOU WOULDN'T SAY SO, WOULD YOU?

I'LL RAISE A GLASS AGAIN THIS YEAR! EIGHT LONG YEARS. AND THERE'LL BE ANOTHER EIGHT. OR MORE. YOU HAVE NO CHANCE, DETECTIVE INSPECTOR WYNNE, NONE AT ALL.

AND YOU KNOW IT, WHICH IS THE BEST THING OF ALL.

YOURS SINCERELY,

???

But this time, the sender had made a mistake.

And Wynne was not going to waste the opportunity.

3

The letter was postmarked Alsbury, a small village in North Yorkshire.

A *tiny* village. No more than a road, a pub, a few houses and a petrol station. How many postboxes could there be in a village that size?

Wynne had asked and there were two. One near the pub, and one opposite the petrol station. The petrol station had CCTV and the camera covered the postbox, and, according to the DS who had called, the CCTV had recorded a man in his fifties or sixties posting a letter.

It was *him*. Wynne knew it.

The drive took over two hours. On the way, DI Wynne explained as much of the case as she could to her partner, DS Chan. When they arrived at the police station it was closed, but as they pulled up the side door opened and a woman in her late forties stepped outside.

'DI Wynne?' she said.

Wynne nodded and shook her hand. 'Thank you for waiting.'

'DS Liz Dales.'

'Nice to meet you. This is DS Paul Chan.'

'Come in.'

They went into a small office at the back of the building. Dales sat at the desk in front of a computer.

'I must say, it was a very intriguing request,' she said. 'Was there any footage of someone posting a single C4 envelope on Wednesday afternoon? I didn't hold out much hope. I thought there would be a lot of people doing it.'

'But there weren't?' DS Chan asked.

'No. Quite a few people posting letters, but only one posting a large white envelope.' Dales pressed a key and a window popped up. On it was a still image of the garage forecourt, the postbox to the left. She pressed another key and a man walked on screen. He was wearing loose-fitting chinos, a short-sleeved shirt, and a flat cap. He approached the postbox, took an envelope from his back pocket, and put it into the slot.

'That's the only person who posted a letter Wednesday afternoon?' Wynne said.

'Yes,' Dales replied. 'As I say, others posted things, but they were multiple letters, or smaller format ones.'

DS Chan looked at Wynne. 'Probably passing through. Stopped here to post it then moved on.'

'Oh, he's not passing through,' Dales said. 'That's Fred Taylor, lives in the village. Would you like his address?'

4

Wynne rang the bell of a large detached house. It was the perfect place – big, private, secluded – to hide someone away. She didn't want to jump the gun, but she felt they were getting closer. If this man had sent the letter, even if he wasn't the one who took Maggie Cooper, he must have some connection to whoever had.

She and DS Chan waited as the echoes died down. She was about to ring it again when she heard the drawing of a bolt.

The door opened. A man – almost certainly the one from the CCTV – looked at them.

'Hello,' he said. 'Can I help you?'

'Mr Taylor?' Wynne said.

'Yes.'

'I'm Detective Inspector Wynne,' Wynne replied. 'This is DS Chan. We were wondering whether we could ask you some questions?'

'Of course,' Taylor said. 'Could I ask what it's about?'

'A letter you posted,' DS Chan replied.

Taylor frowned. 'A letter? What letter?'

'Perhaps we could discuss it inside,' Wynne said. 'It'll all become clear.'

They sat in a large living room. Even though it was summer, the room was chilly.

'So,' Taylor said. 'A letter?'

Wynne took a folder from her bag. She pulled out a photocopy of the envelope that had arrived at the station.

'Do you recognize this?' she asked.

Taylor studied it. When he looked up, his expression was puzzled. 'I do.'

'We have CCTV footage of you posting a letter that looks a lot like this one,' DS Chan said. 'Did you post it?'

'Yes, I did.'

He didn't seem concerned. Didn't seem like a kidnapper who had been caught out.

Wynne shifted in her chair. 'Do you have anything to say about it?'

'I do,' Taylor said. 'It's quite an odd story, as it happens. I didn't think too much about it at the time, but now I see there's more to it than I thought.'

'Didn't think about what?' Chan said.

'The letter. You see, I found it.'

'Did you open it?' Chan said.

'Of course not. I don't open other people's letters.'

'Mr Taylor,' Wynne said. 'I'm not saying I don't believe you, but I think you should know that we have tested the letter for DNA and there is some on it. If that matches your DNA then we will be questioning how you came into contact with the contents of an envelope you did not write or open.'

'Fine. It won't. I found the letter, and I posted it. I assumed someone had dropped it.'

'Where did you find it?'

'In Leeds, near the town hall. I had a meeting there last

289

week.' Fred Taylor folded his arms. He clearly prided himself on knowing how to deal with petty officials. 'Is there anything else? Would you like some of my DNA for your tests?'

'We would,' Wynne said. 'Just in case. An officer will arrange to collect it.' She felt deflated. Taylor was nothing to do with this. Still, it was worth asking. 'Mr Taylor, does the name Maggie Cooper mean anything to you?'

Taylor thought for a second. 'It rings a bell.'

'She was a girl who went missing,' Wynne said. 'Eight years ago.'

'Yes,' Taylor said, drawing out the word. 'The teenager?'

'That's right.' Wynne let him ask the obvious question.

'What has this got to do with her?'

'That letter was from the person who took her. They send one every year. To me. Mocking me.'

She was pleased to see him go pale.

'Thank you, Mr Taylor. We'll see ourselves out.'

5

They drove in silence. Wynne didn't want to talk. It had been a waste of time.

After a while, DS Chan spoke. 'We're not much further along. All we know is it was someone who was in Leeds on Wednesday.'

'Or the day before, or the day before that,' Wynne said. 'The letter could have lain there for a while.' She tapped the steering wheel. 'It does solve one mystery though.'

'What's that?'

'Why there isn't a letter for every year. If his method is to drop them and hope someone picks them up to post them then sometimes it won't happen. Sometimes the letter will be trampled or kicked down a drain or put in a bin.'

'It's smart,' Chan said. 'He drops the letter somewhere and waits. It's almost impossible to trace.'

Wynne stared at the road ahead. She'd been hoping this was the lead that would break the case open. She wanted Maggie back.

And she wanted the letters to stop, but she couldn't help wondering how many more there would be.

One? Two?

Twenty?

Four Years Earlier: July 2014

Martin

1

COOPER ELECTRICAL

It was written in large capitals on the side of a van. Martin paused and watched the van go down Deansgate. The driver was Stephen Anderson, one of the first trainees he had taken on. That was seven years ago, and Stephen now oversaw all the projects they did in Manchester. Martin took care of the others – in Liverpool, Lancaster, Preston, Warrington – but was gradually handing them over to Karen Richardson, another trainee he had recruited when he had decided to branch out from doing jobs for other people and become an electrical firm.

It had been slow at first but in the last few years it had gone better than he had ever dreamed possible. He had a simple approach: he was careful who he hired, he was totally honest, and he never cut corners.

It seemed people liked it, and he now had a firm with over twenty full-time electricians and a turnover in the millions. It had attracted the attention of a national building firm, which was why he was in a shirt and trousers, about to go into the offices of an accounting firm in Manchester.

A woman in her late thirties was waiting by the front desk. She held out her hand.

'Melinda Jameson. Pleased to meet you.' She gestured towards a door. 'We can talk in there.'

They sat at a polished metal table. There was a file in front of Melinda Jameson, which she picked up and opened.

'So,' she said. 'You were contacted by Weaver Construction about acquiring your firm. I understand you would like to discuss having us represent you in this transaction?'

'Yes,' Martin said. 'I have a lawyer and he gave me your name.'

'Who was that, if you don't mind me asking?'

'Peter Sidwell.'

She nodded 'I know him well. Will he be handling the legal side?'

'He will.'

'Then I'd say you're in safe hands.' She opened the folder. 'Shall we review the offer Weaver made?'

The offer was to buy Cooper Electrical for three million pounds.

Martin enjoyed what he did and didn't particularly want to sell, but it was a lot of money. He didn't know how it could be worth so much, but when they had contacted him they had talked about revenue multiples and brand scalability and a bunch of other stuff he didn't fully understand or care about.

The problem was that work – the constant hustling for new jobs and hiring new people and visiting new sites – was what kept him sane. It gave him the sense he was moving forward. At night he would still wake up, suddenly and completely, and think, *She's gone. My little girl is gone.*

And then he would lie awake and imagine her working alongside him and wonder what kind of a person she would have become, who she would have married, the grandchildren she might have given him and Sandra.

And the sense of loss and grief would be as strong as ever.

Sandra was the same, but she found her distraction in exercise. Yoga, spinning, training for marathons and triathlons. She read magazines about diets and training programmes, went to clinics to work on her swimming, researched new bike technologies.

She was in remission from cancer and focused on living life to the full.

And maybe it was time for him to do the same. Maybe it was time to let go of work and move on, spend time with his wife, try to sort James out.

Melinda Jameson closed the folder.

'Do you have an initial position? I assume from the fact you're here that you have some interest?'

'It's a lot of money,' Martin said. 'I think I should accept.'

2

So,' Sandra said. 'How was it?'

She had come in from the gym and was drinking a glass of water. She was wearing running shorts and a T-shirt from a triathlon in Chester. Her arms and legs were lean, the muscles defined and visible.

'They want to buy the firm,' Martin said. 'For three million pounds.'

Sandra put the glass down.

'Three million?'

'The lawyer suggested negotiating. We might get four.'

'Holy shit. Then why do you sound so morose?'

'Because I can't decide if I'm doing the right thing.'

'I can think of three – or four – million reasons you are.'

'I know, but I had no intention of selling until the offer came in. I don't want to sell. I enjoy it.'

'You could enjoy something else. Set up a new business.'

'I suppose. And it is a lot of cash. A fortune.' He gestured around the room. 'But the thing is, I'm happy with what we have.'

'Me too. But it'll be nice to have the money. We can travel.

See some of the world. And you can get a sports car. Really go for it with your midlife crisis.'

Martin pursed his lips as though considering it. 'And maybe a younger wife. Now you're talking.'

'You better be joking, Cooper,' Sandra said.

'About the sports car, yes. The wife – maybe not.' He put his arms around her. 'Of course I'm joking. You know I love you. More and more the older we get. I can't imagine life without you.'

'Then sell up,' Sandra said. 'Work for them for a while, maybe go part-time, and we can spend some time together. Let's live life.'

He kissed her head. 'OK. We'll sell. Travel. I just wish we could do it with Maggie and James. Go to Asia, New Zealand, the Rockies. It'd be perfect. I still miss her, Sandy.'

Sandra sipped her water. 'Me too. I often imagine Maggie watching me. If I'm running and I feel like giving up, I imagine her there, telling me to carry on. And if she was here now, she'd be telling us to take the money and enjoy ourselves.'

'I think you're right,' Martin said. 'That's what she would say. But I'd give every one of those three million pounds and more for one chance to hug her again.'

Four Years Earlier: July 2014

Maggie

1

Leo was a slow waker. She watched him every day – he slept later than her, unlike Seb, who had been her alarm clock – so she was used to watching his body start to jerk and move, his feet kick and his lips twitch, his eyes open and focus as a new day began.

Today he was three. She had been thinking about it for weeks, the memory of Seb's third birthday still an agonizing, raw wound.

The only thing worse was the fear it might happen again.

But it might not.

'Happy birthday, Leo,' she said.

He looked at her for a while, then climbed off the bed. He was wearing his Batman underpants and a faded blue T-shirt. His legs, longer and leaner than Seb's, were bare.

'I'm thirsty,' he said. 'Water?'

He was very different to his brother. Seb had smiled often, and, for a toddler, was very even-tempered. He rarely got upset, rarely flew off the handle.

Leo, though, had tantrums. Maggie remembered the first one. After breakfast, she had asked if he wanted to hear a story.

No, Mummy.

He folded his arms and stared at her.

I do not want a story.

OK. What do you want to do? Draw? The man had brought some paper and crayons, and Maggie had drawn pictures for Leo to colour in. She picked up one – a dragon – and offered it to him.

He slapped it down.

'No,' he shouted. 'No, no. NO.' She tried to pick him up and comfort him, but he twisted in her arms and kicked and scratched her, hitting her with his fists. When she put him down, he ran from wall to wall, banging into them so hard she was worried he would hurt himself. She called to him, sang to him, shouted at him to stop, but none of it made any difference. While it lasted, he was totally unreachable.

Eventually – like a storm – it faded. She picked him up and held him for a long time. He said nothing. He lay motionless, eyes closed, in her lap.

It had happened a few times since. She wondered whether it was something she was doing, but she couldn't think what. She never shouted at him – there was enough misery in here without her adding to it – and constantly told him how much she loved him. It was simply his temperament.

Same mum, same situation, two totally different children.

And she loved them both the same. For different things and in different ways, but she loved them with the same terrifying intensity.

Leo frowned. 'I'm thirsty,' he said again.

Maggie reached for the jug and poured some water into one of the plastic cups. She handed it to Leo and he drank it.

'So,' she said. 'My little boy is three years old. I can't believe it. You're growing up so fast.'

She didn't have a present. With Seb, she had begged the

man for something to give him. He had given nothing; instead he had taken him away. She had often wondered if her begging had brought it about in some way – for a time she had been sure it had, and the guilt had tortured her – maybe, if she'd kept quiet, he would not have even known it was Seb's birthday.

So this time, she said nothing. In the last few weeks she had acted as though everything was normal. The man came with breakfast and dinner. Sometimes he came in his blue bathrobe and sometimes he left her alone.

She never mentioned Leo's birthday.

He never mentioned Leo's birthday.

And she thought, maybe, hopefully, that he had forgotten. And if having no present for her son was the price of that? Well, it was a price she would happily pay. And when she got out of here she would make it up to Leo with all the presents money could buy.

2

She heard the scraping noise. She beckoned to Leo and he came and sat on her lap. The door opened and the man came in.

He put a tray on the floor. Two bowls of cornflakes. A new jug of water.

He gestured at the old one. 'Leave that by the door later,' he said.

Maggie watched him, waiting for him to say, *Happy birthday, Leo* or *Give him to me*, but he said nothing. Her heart skipped; the weight in her stomach lifted.

He backed out of the room. The door clicked shut behind him.

'Leo,' she said. 'Let's have breakfast.'

3

'Hands out,' she said. 'Watch the socks.'

Leo stood in front of her, his hands cupped in front of his chest. She sat cross-legged, a balled-up pair of white socks in her hand.

'Ready?'

Leo nodded.

'One, two, three . . . catch!'

She threw the socks in a gentle arc. They hit his hands and his fingers closed around them.

'Well done! What a great catcher you are! You throw to me.'

Leo launched the socks into the air. They flew to Maggie's right; she dived to catch them.

As she landed on the carpet, she heard the scraping sound.

It wasn't time for the man to come. It was only an hour since breakfast. It was still morning.

She stared up at the door, the socks in her outstretched hand. The handle turned, and it opened.

The man walked in. He looked at her and frowned, then shook his head dismissively. His hands hung by his side. They were empty. He was not bringing food or cleaning equipment or anything that explained why he was here.

He pointed at Leo.

'Come here, Leo,' he said.

Maggie sprang upright and grabbed Leo's hands. She pulled him tight to her.

'No,' she said. 'He's not going with you.'

The man's face was expressionless. 'Give him to me.'

'No.' She backed up and climbed on to the bed. 'He's staying with me.'

'Don't make this worse than it needs to be. Give him to me.'

'Why? Why do you want to take him?'

'Because he's three. It's time.'

So he did know it was Leo's birthday and this *was* happening again. Well, so be it. The first time she'd been taken by surprise. Not again. This time, she wasn't going to let it happen.

She had a plan. She'd thought this through. She'd keep him talking then, as soon as he made any move towards her, she'd attack him. Hit him in the balls, scratch his eyes: whatever it took. And then she'd get out of here.

'What's so special about him being three?'

He didn't answer. Without warning he darted towards her, hands outstretched, and grabbed her shoulders. He was very quick; she was surprised by his speed.

And his strength. He threw her on to the floor with a flick of his wrist. Leo was on the mattress and she reached out for him, but the man pinned her to the floor with his knees. With his hands free, he leaned over and picked up Leo.

'No!' Leo screamed, his face red. 'No! No! No!' He started to scratch the man's face, leaving red lines on his cheeks.

The man watched him. 'What's he doing? What's wrong with him?'

'Leo,' she said, her shoulders agony under the weight of the man's knees. 'Leo, it's OK.'

It made no difference. Leo screamed, banging his fists against the man's chest.

The man slapped him, hard. For a moment, Leo was silent, then he started to howl. The tantrum was over; now he was just a frightened little boy.

'Shut up,' the man growled. 'Shut up, you stupid child.'

Maggie was about to tell him to leave Leo alone when the man threw Leo on to the mattress. He clamped a hand over her mouth, and pinched her nose, hard. She tried to bite him and tasted the salt on the man's hand, before the pressure increased and her jaw was forced shut.

Panic flared.

Her breathing stopped.

And then, darkness.

Four Years Earlier: July 2014

Sandra

1

Sandra slipped her hand into Martin's. His fingers squeezed hers, then he let go and put his arm around her waist. They walked in silence for a while. The air was warm, although the sun struggled to make it through the thick branches of the trees overhead.

The path through the trees – one of many in Delamere Forest – was dusty and firm. In the spring and autumn – and summer too – the forest paths could be muddy, but it had not rained much and all the paths were dry, even the one they had taken, which went deep into the trees. Some of the paths were for horses and bikes and were busy; she and Martin preferred the narrower, less well-trodden ones.

Martin let go of her waist. 'Do you want to eat?' he said. 'I packed sandwiches. Or drink? I made a flask of tea.'

Sandra wasn't hungry; she'd not had much of an appetite for a while, but she nodded. 'Sure.' She pointed to a fallen tree-trunk a yard or so off the path. 'We can sit there.'

They sat on the rough bark. Martin opened his rucksack and pulled out a large Stanley flask and two tin mugs. He filled them and handed one to her.

'Sandwich? They're ham and mustard.'

'I'm OK for now,' Sandra said. 'Tea's fine.'

Martin unwrapped a sandwich and took a bite. 'What time's James coming?'

'Six. I'll make a fish pie.'

'OK.' Martin put his hand on her knee. She was wearing shorts, and his palm was warm against her bare skin. 'We'll be back around four, so we'll have to wait until after he leaves.'

'Wait for what?'

He slid his hand up her thigh and under the hem of her shorts.

'Maybe we can do it now.' He pushed his hand higher. 'There's no one around.'

'Martin!' She put her hand on his arm to stop it going any further. 'I'm going to spill my tea!'

'Put it down,' he said. 'And there's plenty more in the flask.'

For a moment – a brief moment, there was no way she was really going to have sex with him in the forest, and she doubted he would either – she considered it, and then she caught a glimpse of some movement further up the path.

She slid away from him. 'Stop it! There's someone coming.'

He turned to look. There was the sound of twigs breaking, and then a man came around the corner.

Sandra stared at him.

'My God,' she said. She felt herself flush. 'That's Mr Best! Imagine if he'd caught us.'

He took a few more steps before he saw them, then he jerked to a stop. He was carrying a large rucksack, and was pale and out of breath.

'Oh,' he said. 'Sandra. Martin.' He blinked a few times, looking around. He seemed on edge, almost startled. 'What are you doing here?'

'Same as you,' Martin said. 'Out for a walk.'

308

'Yes,' he said. 'Out for a walk. That's right.'

'How are you?' Sandra said. She stood up. 'It's been a while since we saw you last.'

'I'm well.' He hefted the rucksack. 'Although I've been a little under the weather recently. You probably don't want to get too close!'

'I'm sure it's OK,' Sandra said. 'You look fine.'

'I don't know. I'm feeling a little warm. A little dizzy.'

'Probably that big bag you're carrying,' Martin said. 'Do you want me to take it? We can accompany you back to your car?'

'No, no,' Best said. He shook his head. 'It'd ruin your walk. I wouldn't dream of it.'

'It's no problem.' Martin got to his feet. 'Here. I'll take it.'

Best took a step backwards. 'Please. No. I'll be fine.'

'If you're sure,' Martin said. 'But we're more than happy to help.'

'That's very kind. But you needn't worry.' Best took a mobile phone from his pocket. It was an old flip phone. Sandra hadn't seen one for a while. 'I've got this. If I need to, I can call someone.'

He started to walk away from them.

'Anyway, it was lovely to see you. Enjoy your day out.'

Sandra watched him walk away.

'I feel for him,' she said. 'Living alone. You can see it.'

'What do you mean?'

'I don't think he's taking care of himself.'

'In what way?'

'Did you see his hands?'

Martin shook his head. 'What about them?'

'They were filthy. Dirt under the fingernails. And his trousers looked like they needed washing. They had mud on the knees and the hems.'

Martin shrugged. 'Maybe he'd been foraging in the forest.

309

Looking for mushrooms, or digging up roots. That might be what he had in his bag.'

'I don't know,' Sandra said. 'But he's getting older, and he needs someone to look out for him. And he was so good to me when I was ill. I'll go round and see him. Take a look at his house. We need to take care of him.'

'Sure,' Martin said. 'It's very neighbourly of you.' He leaned forward and kissed her on the lips. 'And don't think I've forgotten what we were talking about.'

She returned the kiss, then put her hand on his lower back and pulled him against her.

'I won't forget,' she said. 'I'll be looking forward to it.'

2

Sandra glanced at her watch. On the countertop the fish pie she'd made was cooling. It was James's favourite – had been since he was young – so when she had texted to say We're selling the business, come over to celebrate, she'd followed it up with I'll make fish pie, C U at 6?

Yum, he replied. See you there.

Now, though, it was six thirty and he wasn't here. She picked up her phone.

Are you coming?

She half expected a text saying Sorry, *went to the pub and lost track of time. Maybe save me some pie for tomorrow*, which would have been fine. She understood he didn't want to waste his Saturday night with his parents. But he *had* said he was coming, and she *had* made a meal and it would have been nice for him to let her know if his plans had changed, and it—

She stopped herself. She could hear the hectoring tone in her thoughts. If he wasn't coming, he wasn't coming. It didn't matter. Let him have fun. One thing she'd learned from

Maggie's disappearance was that life was too short to get upset about stuff like your twenty-two-year-old son not showing up for the dinner you made. What mattered was that he was happy.

Or as happy as he could be. When Maggie went, it wasn't only her they lost. For a while, James had disappeared. He'd become someone different. Quieter, more thoughtful. Wounded. She wasn't sure he'd ever fully recovered. She'd discussed it with her therapist, who had told her that he probably was changed forever, but that wasn't necessarily a bad thing. Everything changed us, one way or another, everything left its mark. Everyone had to deal with grief and loss and pain. So, yes, maybe he wasn't fully recovered, but that was who he was now, and the best he – and her and Martin – could do was to help him be the best version of that person he could be.

Which was probably right, in theory. In practice, though, not everyone did go through the same things. Not every teenage boy lost his sister in the way James had. Yes, we all had wounds, but his was deeper and more abiding.

And it was still there. So Sandra wasn't going to waste time arguing with him about a missed dinner.

Hey. Guess you're not coming? No problem. Maybe tomorrow, if you feel like it? xoxo, Mum.

She added the *xoxo, Mum* so that he would know she was not upset with him. She and Martin could eat together. She took out two plates, a bottle of white wine, and headed for the kitchen table.

'No James?' Martin asked, as he sat down.

'He said he was coming. I texted him, but he didn't reply.'

There was a long pause. Since Maggie, anytime James was unavailable or didn't reply or was missing in any way, however

312

innocent, there was a moment when the panic and terror of her disappearance was right in front of them again.

'I'm sure he's OK,' Martin said.

'Probably in the pub.'

Sandra spooned some of the fish pie on to Martin's plate. He glanced at his phone. 'What time was James supposed to be here?'

'Six.'

'I'm going to give him a call. Check what he's doing.'

'Don't make him feel bad. It's not a problem if he doesn't want to come.'

'I won't. But I'd like to know where he is. Just in case.'

Four Years Earlier: July 2014

James

1

'I'm not sure about this,' James said. 'We might get caught.'

He didn't really want to do it at all – it seemed unfair – but that wasn't something he thought Davo and Carl would care about. Getting caught, though, might be.

Davo sniffed. He had a permanent cold, his nose constantly running.

'It'll be easy money,' he said. 'Don't worry. Carl'll look out for anyone coming while me and you get it done.'

The plan was to mug a window cleaner Davo had noticed. He had seen him working and come to the conclusion that it would be simple to relieve him of his takings. He'd be in the back garden of some big house, hidden away at the end of the day when no one was in, walking around with a load of cash in his pocket.

He was also in his late sixties, and about five foot six, so he wouldn't put up much of fight.

Davo grabbed his elbow. His grip was stronger than James expected, given how thin he was.

'Come on,' he said. 'Let's go.'

They were standing on a quiet road opposite a large

detached house. The window cleaner was working around the back. Davo tugged him towards the driveway.

'Go on,' Carl said. 'I'll keep an eye out. You hear me whistle and you leg it, OK?'

James followed Davo around the side of the house. There was a gate but it was unlocked. Davo shook his head.

'People make it easy for you, they really do,' he whispered. 'They deserve whatever they get.'

He walked slowly along the length of the wall, then peeked around the corner. He looked at James and gave a thumbs up, then beckoned him to follow.

They stepped out on to a wide patio. The window cleaner was working on the patio doors, his back to them.

They watched as he slowed. He looked at their reflections in the window and turned to them.

'All right, lads,' he said. He had neat grey hair and glasses and small, precise features.

'All right,' Davo said. 'You can make this easy or hard, mate. I know you've got money, so hand it over.'

'I haven't,' the window cleaner said. He was calm. 'I've got about forty quid on me. It's not worth it.'

'You've got more than that,' Davo said. 'You must have. You've been at it all day.'

The window cleaner laughed. 'I don't get cash, mate. This is the twenty-first century. I use apps. You think I want to walk around with a load of cash when there's scum like you about? So why don't we call this a day? You leave me to my job and go on with your life, and no hard feelings?'

Davo shook his head. 'We'll take the forty quid,' he said. 'And whatever else you're hiding.' He took a step towards the window cleaner. 'Hand it over.'

James did not have much experience with this kind of thing, but he knew he wasn't supposed to stand behind his friend – accomplice – doing nothing. He stepped forward.

The window cleaner shook his head.

'Don't do this, boys,' he said. 'It's really not a good idea.'

Davo twitched. 'Now,' he said.

The window cleaner held up his hands. 'Don't say I didn't warn you.'

Five minutes later they were on their way back to the flat. James's throat was agony, but all in all he'd got off lightly. Davo was hobbling, his face green.

They were also penniless.

The window cleaner had turned out to be some kind of ex-soldier and, before he and Davo could move, he had kicked Davo hard in the balls – it had made a kind of crunching sound that James could still hear – and then elbowed James in the throat.

He stood, watching them writhe in agony.

Fucking idiots, he said. *Get out of here before I decide to hurt you properly.*

They did. They scuttled around the house and on to the street where Carl was waiting.

He asked if they had the cash. James had to give him the bad news; Davo was still groaning.

They stopped by a bench and sat down.

'That went well,' Davo said. 'My fucking balls are killing me.'

'What are we gonna do?' Carl said. 'We need some money.'

As he spoke, James's phone rang. It was his dad. He rejected the call. He could speak to him later.

There was a buzz as a text message arrived.

Are you coming for dinner?

He hadn't been. He wasn't hungry.

At least, not for dinner.

'I might have an idea,' he said. 'I can go to my folks' place.'

He'd eat then get out of there as soon as he could. And his dad would give him some cash, or he could steal some.

He typed a reply.

Yes. On my way.

Four Years Earlier: July 2014

Maggie

1

Maggie woke up. She opened her eyes but the room was pitch-dark. Her mouth was dry; she tried to swallow but there was no saliva. Her nose ached. She lifted her hand and felt it gingerly. It was swollen and sore to the touch.

Where the man had grabbed her and suffocated her into unconsciousness.

Before he had taken Leo.

'Leo!' she shouted, her voice comically nasal. 'Leo!'

There was no reply. She felt around her on the bed, her hands reaching in vain for his warm, sleeping body, then rolled on to the floor. In the darkness she crawled from wall to wall, covering every inch of the floor with her hands. She felt inside the bath and around the bucket and on every corner of the mattress.

Leo was gone.

There was no escaping it.

The man had taken him. It was Seb all over again.

Where was Leo? In the man's house right now, eating chocolate and marvelling at the wonder of television? Or sleeping in a soft, warm bed of his own? No. The man could not be seen with a three-year-old boy. So what had he done?

Left Leo by the side of a road for someone to find and take to the police? She had a momentary fantasy of her parents hearing about the little boy who was found and adopting him, unaware that he was their grandson.

Or worse. What if Leo was dead? Thrown into a deep lake or buried in some remote forest? She curled up in a ball on the mattress, her hands covering her face.

'No!' she screamed. She banged her fists against the wall. 'No! No! No!' She wanted to destroy this place, get out of here and kill the man, but she couldn't. She was trapped. Stuck, with no way of getting out.

All she could do was destroy herself.

She curled her hands into claws and dug her nails into her cheeks. The pain was shocking; she felt the blood run down her face.

She dug in harder, pulling downwards, until the pain was too much to bear, and then she stopped, and lay on her side as her tears mingled with her blood.

'Leo,' she said, her voice a whisper. 'Leo. I love you. Be happy, my son.'

Saturday, 23 June 2018

No Days to Go

1

It was today.

Maggie picked up the calendar and drew a line through the last date.

S	Su	M	Tu	W	Th	F
						1
2	3	4	5	6	7	8
9	10	11	12	13	14	15
16	17	18	19	20	21	22
23	24	25	26	27	28	29
30						

Max was three.

He was sleeping next to her, his face turned to the wall. She lay behind him, watching his chest rise and fall. He'd wake soon, and smile, and laugh and ask for a story or to play with his Duplo or do some exercises. And she'd do it, but all the time she would feel heavy, numbed by the knowledge of what was to come.

The scraping sound. The handle turning. The man looking for him.

Where is he?

Her, shaking her head, refusing to say.

The man finding him anyway.

Her fighting. Him overpowering her, choking her into unconsciousness, leaving her lying there while he disappeared with her son.

Her waking up, realizing Max was gone, getting the bleach from under the base of the bath.

Unwrapping the foil. Drinking it.

She imagined a sour, bitter taste that burned as it went down her throat and into her stomach. She saw herself doubled over on the mattress in pain, foam flecking her lips, her body gradually slackening as the life left it.

She pictured the man coming in and seeing her lying there, running over and feeling her pulse, understanding what she had done.

Would he be sad? Did he love her, in some twisted way? Would he kneel by her body and wail in grief?

She doubted it. She thought he would frown, his lips pressing together, thin with anger. And then he would have to get rid of her body. Maybe he would cut it up into pieces which he could remove easily. Or perhaps he would drag her out in the dark of the night and discard her body in some remote place.

She shook her head. That wasn't going to happen.

Because she had a *plan*.

Next to her Max twitched. His eyes opened. Slowly they focused on her.

'Mummy,' he said.

'Max. Happy birthday. You're three!'

Max looked at her for a while before a smile spread over his face.

322

'I'm three!' he said. 'What comes after three?'

'Four,' Maggie said.

'Will I be four tomorrow?'

'No,' Maggie said. 'You'll be four in a year.'

'Oh,' he said. 'A *year*.'

And he would be. In a year, he would turn four, somewhere far from here.

Because finally she had a plan. It was going to hurt her, to take all the courage and determination she could find, but she would do it, one way or another she would do it.

She didn't know what time the man would come. She guessed he would take Max when – if – he brought breakfast. He would know that this time she would have no doubts what he wanted, so he would not want to come down to the room twice.

Which meant she had to be ready. As soon as she heard the scrape she had to be able to hide Max in the bath. She had removed the wooden base and measured the space between the floor and the base; he would fit, just. Then she could put the base back and cover him. And then, when the man was here, she would take whatever advantage of his confusion she could.

First, though, she needed Max to learn his part in the plan.

'Max,' she said. 'I have a new game for your birthday. It's called hide and seek.'

'What is it?'

'You hide and I look for you. When you're hidden you have to be very quiet. Want to try?'

2

She called Max over.

'This is a really great place to hide. I'll show you.'

She picked him up and put him in the bath.

'Lie down.' Max did as she said and she picked up the base. 'I'm going to put this in place,' she said. 'It'll be dark, but don't worry. And then you stay *quiet*. Whatever I say, you have to be silent, OK?'

Max nodded. Maggie lay the base on top of him. A cursory glance would have shown it to be out of place, but it was something. The man would have to walk over to the bath to look and maybe that would be an opportunity for her. For what, she didn't know. But for something.

'Are you OK?' she said.

There was no reply. Good. He knew to be quiet. It was ironic, but one of the results of living in the room was that Max was not scared of the dark. As a small girl she'd been terrified of sleeping without a light on in her room. If she ever woke up in darkness she would scream until her mum or dad came to her room and turned on a light.

Max had no such luxury. If the man switched off the light, the room was pitch-black until he switched it on again.

'Max?' She put on a deep voice, imitating the man. 'This is the man speaking. Are you there?'

Max did not reply.

She stomped around the room. 'Where are you, Max? I need to talk to you.'

Still no reply.

'Max.' She spoke louder, putting a threatening tone into her voice. 'You'd better come out *now* or there'll be big trouble. Do you hear me?'

There was a long silence. After a few minutes had passed, she walked to the bath and lifted out the base.

Max grinned up at her. 'Was I good?'

She lifted him out and hugged him. A phrase her dad used to say when she was very young came to her.

'Good as gold,' she said. 'You were good as gold.'

3

Maggie clicked a square red Duplo into place.

'There,' she said. 'A Duplo birthday cake. Let's sing you a song.'

She sang 'Happy Birthday'. Max watched her, grinning, and she forced herself to smile back, but it was nearly impossible. She was too on edge, waiting for the scrape that would announce the man's arrival.

Tears came to her eyes and she reached for her son. He laughed and jumped away, but she beckoned, both hands outstretched.

'I need a cuddle, Max.'

She was sitting cross-legged and she got to her knees to reach for him. There was a sudden, sharp pain in her calf.

'Ow!' she said. 'What is that?'

She felt under her leg and pulled out a yellow Duplo. It was upside down and the edge had dug into her flesh.

'Mummy? Are you OK?'

'I'm fine. These things are *really* hard, Max.' She ran her finger along the plastic. 'It's a good job it's not sharper.'

And then she looked at him.

'Max,' she said. 'Max, my beautiful, beautiful boy. I think I may have an idea.'

Saturday, 23 June 2018

James

1

James woke up slowly. He lay on his back, looking up at the ceiling. It was stained with water damage. His eyes traced the patterns and he imagined the water dripping through into the room.

He licked his lips. Fuck, he was thirsty.

He sat up on his mattress – he'd had a bed but at some point it had gone, probably sold – and got to his feet. There was a bolt of pain in his ankle.

'Shit,' he muttered. 'What the fuck was that?'

He looked down at his feet. His right ankle was swollen, a dark bruise running up the inside of his foot. He tried some weight on it and the pain came again. When had that happened? It must have been last night. He must have fallen and twisted it. He wouldn't have felt it. Heroin had that effect. It blotted everything out.

Everything.

It made you feel as though you were hovering outside of

the world watching what was going on. Nothing was happening to you. You were merely an observer. A happy, blissed-out observer.

But not now. Now his ankle throbbed with pain.

He was still wearing the jeans – grey, loose around his thighs, the crotch stained with God knew what – and hooded top he had worn the night before. He was barefoot, though; maybe he'd stripped off his socks after he'd buggered up his ankle.

He limped into the living room. There was a rich fetid smell and he held his breath. He knew what it was. He'd smelled it often. Davo stayed over most nights, and often he'd shit himself. James thought it smelled worse than it should have, as though Davo was rotting from the inside. It wouldn't have been a surprise if he was. All he consumed were endless cups of tea and cigarettes, the occasional box of fried chicken, and as much narcotics – opiate pills, heroin, methadone – as he could lay his hands on.

It was a diet he shared with James and Carl.

James hobbled – the pain was getting worse – into the kitchen and poured a glass of water. The flat was cold. They had not paid their gas bill for a few months so there was no heating. He flicked on the kettle. They still had electricity, but it was only a matter of time before that was gone. Davo knew someone who worked at the electric company and had persuaded her to help out, but eventually she would not be able to put off the inevitable.

He grabbed a teabag and a mug and poured in the water. There was no milk, and when he sipped it the hot liquid scalded the top of his mouth. It didn't matter. It'd hurt for a while but the drugs would take care of it later.

If he could get some. Carl still had a job, washing vans for a friend he used to play football with. He didn't work much, but his friend didn't care. If he showed up for a few hours there were always vans to be washed and he could scrape together enough cash to buy what he needed. Davo didn't work but he left the flat most days and came back with drugs he had got from somewhere – stolen or begged, James never knew which, and never asked.

James though, he only had one source of cash.

He felt in his back pocket and pulled out his phone. He would have sold it long ago but he knew he needed it. He tapped out a message.

Want to meet up later?

His dad replied almost instantly.

Of course. How are you?

OK. Farmers' Arms in Padgate at 11?

How about a coffee instead? Costa in town? 11 is good.

Whatever. He'd been hoping for a few beers to take the edge off, but coffee it was.

Sure. See you there.

2

His dad was sitting at a table when he arrived, two coffees in front of him. There was a sandwich next to one of them. He was reading something on his phone, and when he saw James he stood up.

He looked him up and down. Took in the dirty jeans. The torn coat.

He held out his arms. 'Come here,' he said.

James hugged him. He was aware that he was smaller than his dad, thinner and weaker. He let go, but his dad pulled him close.

'I miss you, James,' he said. He leaned back and smiled at him. 'I could hug you all day. Although the smell might become a little too much.'

'Shower's not working.'

'I could come and fix it.'

James caught his dad's eye. He was smiling, but there was a mixture of worry and sadness in his expression. He couldn't bear the thought of his dad seeing the place where he lived, smelling Davo's shit, looking at the needles and pill packets that littered the countertops and tables.

'It's OK,' he said. 'Davo said he'll get to it.'

'Davo,' his dad said. 'Of course.'

'He's all right,' James said. 'He's a good bloke.'

'Maybe.' His dad gestured at the sandwich. 'BLT. Eat something.'

James took a bite. It was good, the bacon salty and rich. He swallowed and then put it down. He felt nauseous.

'I had a big breakfast.' He could see his dad's pain at the lie and he felt an overwhelming urge to get up and run and find some drugs to make it all go away. 'Dad,' he said. 'Really. I did.'

'It's OK. How are you?'

'Good. But the shower – it's not broken. We don't have heat. They turned the electric off.'

'Why?'

'It wasn't our fault. We missed a payment. By accident. And now we're behind and – you know how it is.'

'You need a bit of money?'

James nodded. 'For the 'leccy. I'll pay you back.'

I'll pay you back. He said it every time they had these conversations, a pathetic formula to cover up the fact he was begging his own father for money to buy drugs and his father was giving it to him so he could check his son was still breathing.

And his dad would always reply the same way, absolve him of his guilt with a simple 'You don't have to'.

But this time he looked at him, his eyes narrowing.

'You can pay me back by stopping taking those damn drugs,' he said. 'And coming home.'

James swallowed, his mouth dry. 'I don't take them much,' he said. 'And I'll stop soon. This is temporary – I'm having a hard time at the moment. It's not as bad as you think.'

'It's every bit as bad,' his dad said. He put his hands on James's. 'Why do you do it, son? Why do you take them?'

'Because . . . because . . .' James felt the warmth of his

333

father's hands on his. 'It helps. I lost my way a bit, and it helps.'

'I can help. Mum can help. There's a way out of this, James. All you have to do is say the word and we'll be able to get you through this. We can get the right treatment, take care of you at home. You can recover. You can take as much time as you need. You're still young. You have your whole life ahead of you.'

'I know. I know. And I will, but . . .' But all he could think was *I need the prick of that needle and the rush and then the oblivion, everything else is too hard, too damn hard, and I can do that later, recover later, get help later, but now, now I need the needle and the pain to go away and the darkness that follows.*

'You can start to work again. Take your time learning a trade. Become a teacher. Anything. The world is a wonderful place, James. Life is a wonderful gift. Don't waste yours.' His dad cupped his chin. His hand was warm. It smelled clean. 'And I can help you. Come with me and leave that life behind.'

James was gripped by an all-consuming panic at the thought of going with him, of walking away from what he knew, from his friends.

From the next high.

'Sorry,' he stammered. 'Sorry. I can't. Not now.'

3

He fingered the notes in the pocket of his jeans. Ten twenties; two hundred pounds. It was what his dad normally gave him. They met about once a fortnight, and it was enough to get him through.

And he needed it today. Needed it more than normal after the conversation with his dad.

Life is a wonderful gift.

He didn't know how his dad could say that. How he could even *think* it, not after what had happened to Maggie. James thought about her every day. He had since she had gone. He had wondered where she was and what had happened to her and in his head he saw her suffering violent and endless torture, heard her screams and cries for help and was powerless to do anything.

In his dreams, he rescued her. In the daytime he endured her suffering.

And his dad said *life is a wonderful gift*? It wasn't. It was anything but.

He'd made up his mind that his was over. In truth it had been over for a while. There was nothing worth living for.

Every day was such a *fight*. All he had was the drugs, and that was no life.

He was going to get a massive dose. Take it all. Dissolve into a state of bliss.

Mum and Dad would be sad, but it was better for them in the long run. He was worthless, a pathetic, useless excuse for a son who caused them nothing but trouble and pain. It was time to set them free.

It was time to set himself free. The sense of relief now he had made the decision was overwhelming.

He felt the notes in his pocket. Two hundred pounds. More than enough to buy what he needed.

Thanks, Dad, he thought.

Martin

He didn't cry until he was back in his car. He would have preferred to wait until he got home but the car was as far as he could make it. He had walked through the town centre, eyes ahead, back straight, lips pressed together, holding his face as expressionless as he could, rehearsing what he would say if he bumped into someone he knew who wanted to stop for a chat.

· *Great to see you but I'm late for a train. Sorry. Have to run!*

No one had stopped him and he was grateful to the universe for that small mercy. He wasn't sure he would have been able to get out even those few sentences without his words dissolving into tears.

He sat behind in the front seat, hands gripping the steering wheel, and cried, loud and hard, his shoulders heaving with each fresh sob.

His boy – his son, the baby he had held – was vanishing before his eyes. Maggie had gone quickly; James was slowly fading away. He'd been shocked to see him. His face was drawn, his eyes sunken and red. There was a grey pallor to his skin, and the smell – they'd been camping once in France

337

and in one corner of the campsite there was a stream that he discovered was effectively an open sewer. That was what James reminded him of.

He didn't know why. Why James was doing it, why Maggie had been taken, why he was being punished. What had he done to deserve this? Why him?

He wiped the tears from his eyes. While he was with James he'd wanted to stay calm, let him know he was loved and that his parents were there for him, whatever happened. What he wanted to do was grab his son and drag him home and lock him in his room until he was better, but he'd spoken to a bunch of different experts and one thing was clear: James could only get better if he wanted to. It had to come from him. Martin could try to get him to see how desperate the situation was – stage an intervention of sorts – but it would only work if James wanted it to.

That was the crux of it all. James had to want to stop. He had to see the drugs as a problem and not a solution and then they could start to get rid of them.

But he was a long way from that. Martin had seen the hunger flash across his eyes when he suggested that James come with him. He had seen that – for now – his son's first love was the high he needed, and his recovery would have to wait.

If it came. That was the worst of it. The uncertainty. The not knowing whether his son would survive. Whether his son *wanted* to survive.

And he could not go through it again. He could not lose a second child. When Maggie had gone it was as though his world had ended. He had carefully pieced together a life: a career, a wife, a house, his kids, and then it had been taken from him. He had seen how flimsy it all was. And, slowly, he had put it back together again.

It had been all he could manage to avoid doing what James

was doing now. He had flirted with it; he had sat in the darkness alone with a bottle in his hand and stared into the abyss, but for whatever reason – and he took no credit, it was no more than dumb luck – he had pulled back from it. Maybe it was James: maybe he knew his son needed him. Whatever it was he had escaped it.

Now James would have to do the same.

And, if it came to it, Martin would make him. He knew that by meeting his son and giving him money he was simply enabling his addiction, but that was fine by him. The alternative was to refuse and leave him penniless. James would then have a choice – give up, or fund his habit by other means. Means that would get him in more trouble, in an even deeper hole. No – it was better, far better, to see him every week or two, make sure he did not need to steal, try to get him to eat something, check he was still functioning.

But the time was coming when Martin would have to find a way to get him out of his squalid flat and into a rehab facility. He wanted that to come from James. He wanted his son to be cured, whole again. He didn't want him forced into sobriety and fighting it every day of his life.

But it might come to that. And soon. James had looked worse than he had ever seen him. He put his key in the ignition and started the car. He pulled out of the parking space. James's smell lingered on his clothes.

He shook his head and picked up his phone. He searched for the number of the electric company.

He'd call them and pay the bill. He knew James wouldn't use the money for that, and he wanted his son to have hot water.

DI Wynne

The letter was on her desk when she arrived. She knew what it was immediately. Plain A4 envelope, printed address, her name on top.

DETECTIVE INSPECTOR WYNNE

She left it there while she went to get some gloves and an evidence bag. She doubted there was any forensic evidence to be had, but it paid to take care. There'd be some DNA on the envelope belonging to whoever had picked it up and posted it, but that was no use. It was possible they would get a match – two years previously they had matched the DNA to a woman who had been convicted of killing a swan in Lincoln – but all that told them was who had put the letter into the postal system, not who had written it.

For a moment she considered throwing it away. It was the last thing she needed; three days earlier a local magistrate had come across the body of a woman in her late twenties who had been burned to death and then left in a field.

It was the second such murder and it seemed there might be some ritualistic element. The press were all over it; there was near hysteria in the town. She did not need any distractions.

But she had no choice. She snapped on the gloves and picked it up. She slit the top and pulled out the letter.

DEAR DETECTIVE INSPECTOR WYNNE:

SO, IT'S BEEN TWELVE YEARS. YOU MUST BE GETTING USED TO YOUR FAILURE BY NOW? I NOTICE YOU HAVE ANOTHER FAILURE ON YOUR HANDS. SOMEONE BURNING YOUNG WOMEN? IT'S AWFUL. GOOD LUCK CATCHING THEM. I SUSPECT YOU'LL NEED IT, IF YOUR PERFORMANCE IN FINDING MAGGIE COOPER IS ANYTHING TO GO BY, BUT I WISH YOU WELL ALL THE SAME. YOU MIGHT FIND IT HARD TO BELIEVE, BUT I THINK IT'S APPALLING THAT SOMEONE IS KILLING THESE POOR GIRLS. IT'S WANTON DESTRUCTION OF BEAUTY OF A TYPE I ABHOR.

I ALSO - IN A STRANGE WAY - WANT YOU TO HAVE SOME SUCCESS. I'VE GROWN QUITE FOND OF YOU OVER THE YEARS AND I CAN SEE THAT IT MUST BE HARD TO HAVE TO LIVE WITH A CASE LIKE MAGGIE HANGING OVER YOU. I SUPPOSE IT'S STILL OPEN, WHICH PROBABLY MAKES IT EVEN WORSE. YOU POLICE LIKE CERTAINTY. YOU LIKE TO STAMP 'CASE CLOSED' ON YOUR FILES. WELL, YOU CAN DO THAT ON THIS ONE. YOU MIGHT AS WELL. YOU'LL NEVER FIND HER. I'VE THOUGHT THROUGH ALL THE WAYS YOU COULD, AND THEY'RE ALL IMPOSSIBLE.

SO, GOOD LUCK, DETECTIVE INSPECTOR. AS USUAL, I'LL BE RAISING A GLASS TONIGHT!

YOURS SINCERELY,

???

It was different in tone to the previous years. Chatty, friendly almost. Was that because it had been more than a decade? Or was he simply getting complacent, and, as a result, careless? And that *Maggie* – it was so familiar, like he knew her. Like she was there, still alive.

Wynne read it again, slowly.

One sentence stood out.

IT'S WANTON DESTRUCTION OF BEAUTY OF A TYPE I ABHOR.

Which suggested that whoever it was had not killed Maggie. That would be wanton destruction of beauty.

And if he abhorred its wanton destruction, might he not want to preserve it? Keep it safe?

Which meant Maggie was alive, and in captivity somewhere. That had always been a possibility, but so too had murder. They had nothing to point them in either direction.

Until this letter. It wasn't much, but it was enough for Wynne to be convinced that this was a kidnapping and captivity case, which meant that she wasn't dealing with a crime that had taken place ten years ago. She was dealing with a crime that was still going on.

And that meant they needed to keep looking for Maggie.

Sandra

Sandra sat in the waiting room. She felt nauseous, sick with anxiety.

A few days back, she had started to have stomach pains. They were different to the first time around but, understandably, she was very sensitive to any kind of stomach issue, so she went straight to her doctor, and she booked her in for another colonoscopy.

She was under no illusions about what might happen. She had been through this before. The first time she had cancer the treatment – chemotherapy, followed by surgery to remove the tumour from her upper colon, followed by more chemotherapy – had seemed to work. But then, at her six-month check-up, the doctors had bad news.

It was back. Not as bad as the first time, but back none the less.

Which meant a whole new round of treatment.

That too, had worked.

Ironically, the stomach pain was gone. After she got back from the doctor's office she'd had diarrhoea and now everything seemed normal. But she had learned the hard way that that meant nothing.

Her phone buzzed. It was a text from Martin.

Saw James. He's OK. Struggling a little. On way to the hospital.

James. He wouldn't see her. She thought he was too embarrassed of what he had become in front of his mum. Martin was different; he was softer, more accommodating. She had been to James's flat once and told him straight out what a disgrace it was, what a disgrace it was for a boy like him to live in filth.

She had not been back, and James had refused to see her. She missed him, but part of her was also relieved. It was too hard to watch.

She put her phone down, and waited.

Maggie

1

She heard the scraping noise. Max was playing on the floor. She picked him up. Pain flared in her left hand. Her eyes watered and she took a deep breath. Every second was agony, her hand like a ball of fire.

It was no surprise given what she had done to it. It was her chance, though, and she would have to put up with it. One way or another it would be over soon.

'Remember,' she said. 'Stay quiet, whatever happens, OK?'

She put him in the bathtub and laid the base over him, then walked over to the mattress. She got under the covers.

She picked up the tinfoil ball – although it was much more than that now – and kept her hands hidden.

The man could not see them. Not until the right moment came.

The door opened and the man came in. His eyes narrowed. 'Where is he?'

'Who?' Maggie said.

'You know who. The boy.'

'I don't know where he is. I don't feel well.' She tried to make her voice sound weak and strained, as though she was suffering.

It didn't take much effort. The pain in her hand was so intense it was hard not to whimper.

The man shut the door. He put the key in the pocket of his chinos.

'Stop this,' he said. 'Give me the boy.'

Maggie groaned and turned on her side. He walked towards her.

'Don't make this more difficult than it needs to be,' he said. 'You know what happens when you disobey me.'

She did. She knew all about what happened.

The rapes. The captivity. The darkness. The motorbike helmet. The *rat*.

The sons, taken and killed.

And in her hands, her throbbing, aching hands, she held the means to end it.

'I'm not disobeying you,' she said. 'I don't feel well. I really don't.'

'God,' he said, disgust lacing his voice. 'Don't you *ever* learn?'

Maggie shifted so she was facing him.

'That's it,' she said. 'That's the problem, right there.'

'What do you mean?' he said, confusion creeping into his expression.

'I don't,' she said. 'I don't ever fucking *learn*.'

The look of confusion turned to one of alarm as she threw the covers back and sprang to her feet, her left hand – the painful one, the one she had mutilated – outstretched, thrusting towards the man's face.

His eyes followed it, widening as he saw what she had done to it and understood the situation he was in.

346

Understood that things had changed.

The movement sent pain shooting up her arm, but she was able to ignore it. In fact, she *welcomed* it. It was the price she had to pay for freedom, and she paid it willingly.

Her hand reached the man's face and she clawed at it, listening to him squeal in pain.

She screamed in triumph. There was blood everywhere.

Lots of blood.

His blood.

For she was transformed.

She had *talons*.

2

The man screamed and jumped back. He clutched his face, his right hand covering the wounds. Blood oozed out from under his palm. He backed towards the door, his other hand scrabbling for the key.

'What?' he said. 'What are you – how?'

Maggie stepped towards him. She looked at her left hand. Her fingers were mottled and bruised and the pain was like a bright light, but she didn't care. It was working.

And she was only getting started. In her right hand she had another surprise.

The idea had come when she had stood on the Duplo. The brick was large, about two inches by two inches, and the plastic was hard.

These are hard, she had said to Max. And she had thought *I'm glad it's not broken. The edge would be like a knife.*

It had all come to her in a rush. She had put Max on the mattress.

Stay there. Mummy has to do something.

She picked up the Duplo brick and took it to the bath.

She lay it on the carpet, then lifted the wooden base of the bath and slammed it down on the Duplo.

It squirted away, unbroken. She placed it against the floor and hit it again, then again and again and again. The hard plastic Duplo split in two.

She picked it up and ran her fingers along the edge. It was as sharp as she had thought it would be. She took it and drew it across the skin of her forearm, pressing it down hard. It left a thin red line. As she watched, blood welled up in it.

Max was indignant. *Mummy! What are you doing? That's my toy!*

It's OK, darling. I'll get you some more.

Maggie stared at the broken Duplo. This was it. This was the weapon she needed. She could make lots of them, pick the sharpest and use them to attack the man. But how? She was hardly going to do much damage by coming at him with a piece of Duplo Lego held in her hands. She needed something to attach the plastic to, some kind of club.

She looked around the room. She already knew there was nothing. Just the clothes and the bleach and the sewing kit.

The sewing kit.

She took a deep breath.

It might work. It really might.

But it would *hurt*.

She looked at her left hand. The hard, sharp pieces of Duplo had blood on the ends where they had gouged the man the first time. They were holding well; it was one of the things she had worried about when she attached them to her fingers, winding the cotton thread around them in a lattice that held them in place.

She had tried it a few times before she got it right. She had attached one to her forefinger, but it had fallen off as soon as she started to scrape it down the wall – her trial run for the man's face – and it had not been until the fourth or fifth that she got one to stick.

And she learned that the cotton had to be so tight it felt like someone was slicing her finger apart. The thin thread bit into the flesh of her finger so hard that it drew blood, which brought a new level of agony. It *burned*.

And then there was the stitching.

To make sure the Duplo truly held she pushed the needle through the end of her finger, drawing the thread through her flesh, then wrapping it under her finger, before putting the needle back into the same hole and repeating the process until her hand was slick with blood and she was sure the Duplo would hold.

When it was done, she looked at Max, the pain leaving her short of breath. She had three more fingers and a thumb to go, but she wasn't sure she could bear this until the man came. She wasn't sure she could bear it for another second.

But she had to. This was for Max. For his life. His entire life. This was the way she would make sure he saw his fourth birthday.

An hour – two hours? A day? A week? – of pain, for a lifetime with Max?

No question.

She picked up the biggest, sharpest piece of Duplo and started on the next finger.

'What?' The man looked at her from behind his hand. His expression was a mixture of fear and shock. No doubt he had expected her to argue with him when he came for Max, maybe try to fight him, but he had not expected *this*.

He held out his other hand, palm up.

'No,' he said. 'Stop.'

Maggie feinted with her left hand and then jumped

350

forward, slamming her right hand into his face. In it she was holding the tinfoil ball of bleach, and the liquid smeared all over his face, mixing with blood and turning pink.

He screamed again, swiping his face in an attempt to wipe the bleach from it. It was pointless. The bleach was in the wounds and all he was doing was rubbing it in further.

He staggered back; when he was off balance, Maggie jumped forward and pushed him on to the floor. She looked down at his face, saw the blotches and patches of stubble and wispy hair growing from his nose, saw how he had aged, saw just how much time had passed, and she understood what he had done to her, what he had taken from her and from her brother and from her parents.

She grabbed the side of his face, the shard of Duplo on her thumb digging into his lower lip, her other four fingers forming a semi-circle stretching from his eye to his chin, and she squeezed.

The sharp points of the hard plastic made little troughs in his skin, then, one by one, they broke the skin and slid into the muscles and flesh of his face. She screamed, and pulled her fingers together, as though making a fist. They left deep gouges. She freed her forefinger, then plunged it into the man's right eye.

He bellowed, and twisted away from her, then hit her in the ribs with his right hand. He lifted his knees and kicked her away, then scrabbled backwards.

Winded, she stared at him. He stared back. The right side of his face was a mess, his eye already closed.

She got to her feet and took a step towards him. He backed into the corner.

'Please,' he said. 'You can go. Please. Go. But no more.'

She shook her head. She stood over him, and raised her left hand, the Duplo talons bloody.

He stared at it, his one good eye wide in fear.

And then, with her right hand, she snatched the key and pulled it as hard as she could.

She backed towards the door and unlocked it. The man twitched.

'Stay there,' she said. 'Or I'll take your other eye.'

She felt a sense of elation.

She had done it. This was it.

All she had to do was unlock the door, then go to the bath, get Max, and they would be free.

And then there was a noise.

A banging coming from the bath.

'Mummy,' a muffled voice said. 'Where are you?'

Martin

Martin pulled into a car parking space at the hospital. It was hard to be back here. This was the third time, and he had hoped it was over for good.

But maybe that was another hope that would not be granted to him.

He walked into the consulting room, two cups of tea in his hand.

Sandra was sitting on the bed. She smiled. 'I'm not sure I feel like anything,' she said. She put a hand on his forearm. Her hand was dry and warm, the veins prominent. She looked at him. Her hair was beginning to grow back, but it was still short. 'I'm a bit nervous.'

'Me too,' Martin said. 'Me too. But it'll be OK,' he said. 'It really will.'

She didn't reply. When he looked at her there were tears on her cheeks.

Maggie

There was the sound of wood scraping on wood, then a blond, curly-haired head appeared over the lip of the bath.

'Mummy?' Max said. 'Are you OK?'

The man thought – and reacted – more quickly than Maggie did. They were an equal distance from the corner of the room with the bath in, and, before she could move, he half-sprang, half-ran to it. He reached out and grabbed Max, then held him up.

His hands and face and clothes were covered in blood. His one remaining eye was wild, his mouth parted as he panted for breath.

'The key,' he growled. 'Put it on the floor.'

Maggie shook her head. 'No.'

He gripped Max's neck. 'Then he's dead.'

'Ow,' Max said. 'Stop it! You're hurting.'

Maggie took a step towards them. Her left hand – the one with the talons – lifted.

The man shook his head. 'Don't take another step. I'll break his neck.'

Maggie blinked. Tears came to her eyes. She couldn't believe she'd got so close, only to fail at the last step. It was going to be even worse now. The man would take Max – that was for sure – and then what? He'd leave her in darkness for days? Weeks? Torture her? He'd have to go to the doctor for his eye – no doubt he'd make up some story about getting mugged – and then he'd take it all out on her.

And she would not be able to avoid his punishment. The bleach was gone. Even that way out was lost to her now.

So close, but all she'd done was make things worse.

'Put the key in the door,' the man said. 'Then go and lie on the mattress, face down, your hands behind your head.'

'Please,' Maggie said. 'Leave Max with me.'

The man laughed. 'Key in the door.'

So this was it. The same story, yet again. She'd managed more of a fight this time, but Max was gone either way. She could try to attack the man again, but she had no doubt he would snap Max's neck.

Then, though, there would be nothing stopping her from killing the man.

No. She couldn't do anything that would harm Max. She had to keep him alive.

'Key in the door,' the man said. 'Then walk slowly to the bed and lie down.'

Maggie turned to the door, the key between her thumb and forefinger. She inserted it into the lock. She'd dreamed of this moment so many times, dreamed of standing by this door, key in her hand and now here she was.

As trapped as she had ever been.

She would lie on the bed and the man would take Max and this would be over.

And she would be alone. She paused.

She looked at the man. She looked at Max.

She had to try. If she didn't Max was dead anyway. She had no choice. She had to leave him.

She had to leave him with the man.

She stared at him, drank in the beauty of her son, maybe for the last time.

'I'm sorry,' she said. 'But don't worry. I'll be back for you.'

It was the hardest thing she had ever done. She unlocked the door and walked through it.

James

Sitting in his flat only confirmed that he was doing the right thing. For the first time he could see how squalid it was. Filthy mugs of week-old tea, over-flowing ashtrays, the rotten, fetid smell of decay permeating everything – this mess, this obscenity, was his life.

He had everything he needed. Two hundred quid's worth of smack. It was enough to kill a horse. There'd be some left over for Davo and Carl. He wondered whether they would miss him. Probably for as long as it took to get high from whatever was left. Once that happened they would no more care about James than they would anything else.

That was exactly the problem. All James cared about was the next fix, and he understood now that was no kind of life. He also understood there was no way out of it. He wasn't strong enough to dig himself out of the hole. His pain went too deep, went back to the day his sister hadn't come home.

He'd lost more than Maggie that day. He'd woken up a fourteen-year-old boy who messed around with his friends and wondered if he'd ever kiss a girl and thought the world was basically a fun, safe place and he'd gone to bed a fourteen-year-old boy who looked at the world with fear.

He'd gone to bed scared of what was out there, and the fear had never gone away.

Until he took heroin.

So that was his choice. A life lived in fear, the ghost of his sister – who he had loved, had idolized – forever tormenting him, or *this*. This squalid, filthy flat.

He picked up a needle and straightened his arm. He looked at the vein, anticipated the prick and rush and bliss.

He smiled. Finally, this was the end.

Maggie

She opened the door and looked up the stairs. There was a square of yellow light at the top. She stepped on the first step and glanced over her shoulder.

Max was on the floor and the man was running towards the door.

'Stop!' he screamed. 'Come back here!'

She ran up the stairs. They emerged from a rectangular hole on to the concrete floor of a garage. Next to the hole was a heavy piece of wood, the source of the scraping sound she had heard so often. To her right was a white door. There was a window on her left; rain ran down it.

Rain.

Actual rain.

The garage door was closed, so she ran to the white door. It must lead to the house and then to the outside world.

She grabbed the handle. It was unlocked; she stepped through into a kitchen. On the counter was a phone. It was a flip phone, modern, sleek and grey. She'd not seen many of those before. Still, she knew how to use one. She grabbed it. As soon as she was away from the man she'd call the police.

The man. She realized it was quiet behind her. She looked back. The door to the garage was open and she could see the stairs that led to the room. The wooden cover was still off.

Where was the man? Was he still in the room? Was he hurting Max? Or was he hiding in the garage?

She took a step towards the door. Slowly, she pushed it wide open.

The garage was empty.

Which meant the man was with Max. He was waiting down there. She opened the flip phone and dialled 999. Once she had done that and the police were on the way she could go back down and protect him. She would be able to do that for long enough to free them.

The phone rang once, twice.

'Which service? Police, Ambulance, or Fire?'

'Police.'

She waited for someone to answer.

There was a loud bang. Maggie turned to her left; the man was standing in the back door, his face contorted in anger. He was holding a shovel in his hand.

And she realized her mistake.

There was another door in the garage that led out to the garden. He'd gone through that and got the shovel. There was no sign of Max.

'You stupid little bitch,' he said, spitting out each word. 'Why did you have to do this?' He stalked to his right, blocking Maggie's path out of the kitchen. He lifted the shovel, the blade level with his ruined face.

There was a voice from the phone. It was brisk and official. 'Hello. What can I help you with?'

The man charged towards her. Maggie held the phone to her ear.

'Maggie Cooper,' she said. 'Maggie—'

And then the shovel hit her hand and the phone flew to the floor. The man picked it up and closed it. He raised the shovel again.

'You stupid, stupid little girl,' he said.

DI Wynne

DI Wynne sat at her desk. Her first Saturday back at her old job and she was in the office. DS Chan was at the next desk.

'So,' he said. 'It didn't work out down south?'

'Not exactly,' she said. 'So here I am.'

'What happened?'

Wynne pursed her lips. 'This and that.'

'Sounds pretty serious.'

'Look,' Wynne said. 'It wasn't for me. That's all.'

There was a knock on the door. A uniformed officer came in.

'Hey,' she said. 'You worked the case of that missing girl, right?'

'Which one?'

'Maggie Cooper.'

Wynne sat up in her chair. 'Yes. What about it?'

'We received a notification from dispatch. They had a pretty weird call come in. Someone rang 999. It was a girl, and all she said was "Maggie Cooper", before the line went dead. The dispatcher recognized the name and flagged it to us.'

'Do they know whose phone it was from?'

'Yes. A mobile. Belongs to someone called Best. Man in his sixties. Known to us.'

Wynne stared at the PC.

'Still at 7 Dover Street?'

'How do you know?'

'Because,' Wynne said. 'I know that bastard from years ago.'

Martin

Martin sat in the waiting room. He had a magazine – it was about golf, and had a picture of someone he didn't know holding a trophy he didn't recognize on the front – on his lap, but he wasn't reading it. He couldn't. He'd only picked it up to keep his hands busy.

He flicked through a few pages, then put it back on the table. He got to his feet and walked to the window. It looked over the car park. He searched for his red Audi. An S4. Fast. Expensive, but not too flash. Great engineering. A good use of the money he had.

Nothing other than a bauble. It meant nothing to him at all.

He wanted Sandra to be OK. That was all he asked.

Maggie was gone, he was resigned to that now. He had been for a while. James – well, James was alive, at least. Not doing well, but not getting worse. It was time to sort that out. Whatever happened with Sandra he was going to bring James home. He wasn't going to lose all of them.

He'd tried, over the years, not to feel sorry for himself, he really had. After all, he had plenty going for him. Good health, plenty of money, a wife he adored. Yes, James was a worry, and of course there was Maggie, but he still had his blessings.

Now, though, he wondered whether a bit of self-pity wasn't in order.

He took a deep breath. It wasn't time for that yet. She might be fine; Maggie might come home James might get well.

Yeah, right.

But for now he needed to focus on Sandra.

He walked back to his seat. The receptionist smiled at him.

'She won't be long, love,' she said.

Martin sat down. He felt sick.

Wynne

DI Wynne held her hand on the horn. The light was red and she didn't see any other cars approaching but if you were going to ignore a red light it was worth letting people know.

There were squad cars on the way, but she was not waiting for them. There was no time to waste.

A woman's voice on Best's phone, saying the name Maggie Cooper. There were possibly other explanations, but Wynne could only think of one.

Best had been holding Maggie Cooper captive and she had somehow escaped. The fact the call had been cut short meant Best knew she was out and had stopped her cry for help, and that meant Wynne had to get there as soon as possible.

The speedometer was a few clicks shy of ninety miles per hour when she went through the light. Next to her DS Chan was gripping the sides of his seat.

'How much further?' he said.

'Two minutes,' Wynne replied.

Almost exactly two minutes later she braked to a stop outside Best's house. A house she knew well. There was no car outside, although the garage door was closed, so it could be in there.

She ran to the front door and rang the doorbell. There was no answer.

'Best!' she shouted. 'Open the door!' She turned to DS Chan. 'Ready?'

He looked at her. 'Are you sure we should do this?'

'Now,' she said, and raised her foot, sole facing the door.

Chan lifted his and they kicked the door. It juddered, and they kicked it again. The lock gave and it banged open.

Wynne ran inside. The house was quiet; she checked the living room and dining room. Nothing.

'You check the kitchen,' she said. 'I'll look upstairs.'

She was in the bathroom when she heard DS Chan calling her name. When she reached the kitchen he wasn't there.

'DS Chan?'

'In the garage,' he called.

She walked through a white door. DS Chan was standing in the middle of the garage, looking down at a set of steps.

'This is it,' he said. 'This is the place. But there's no one here.'

Martin

Martin's phone rang. He frowned.

It was DI Wynne.

He hadn't heard from her in a long time. He let it ring to voicemail. He didn't want to deal with her at the moment. He'd call her later.

The phone rang again. Wynne, again.

It must be important.

After all these years, it must be Maggie.

He put it to his ear.

'Mr Cooper? This is DI Wynne. I worked—'

'I know,' Martin said. 'I'm a bit tied up. How can I help?'

'I have some news,' DI Wynne said. She sounded nervous. 'There's been a development in your daughter's case.'

Martin sat up. 'What? What kind of development?'

'Your daughter – Maggie – was imprisoned,' Wynne said. 'She was held captive.'

'Captive? How do you know?'

A nurse opened the door to the waiting room. 'Mr Cooper?' she said. 'Your wife is out. You can come through.'

Martin looked at the nurse then at his phone then back at the nurse. He covered the phone with his hand.

'One second,' he said, then lifted the phone to his ear. 'I'm at the hospital,' he said. 'I have to go and see Sandra.'

'Is everything OK?' Wynne said.

'I'm about to find out.'

'Before you go,' Wynne said, 'let me tell you what happened.'

'Go ahead.'

'Someone – a young woman – dialled 999 and said your daughter's name. That was all they had time to say before the line was cut off. However, we have the number she rang from. It's a mobile phone belonging to Colin Best.'

'Best? What does he have to do with this?'

'We think it was him who took her. We found a secret room under his garage, but it was empty when we got there. We think he knew she'd called 999 and fled with her.'

Martin's legs shook; he sat down heavily.

'Is she alive?'

There was a pause. 'We have every reason to think so. We have all available resources looking for her.'

'My God,' Martin said. 'I don't believe it.'

'Mr Cooper? Are you all right?' The nurse walked over to him, frowning in concern.

'Yes,' he said. 'I got some – some unexpected news.'

Wynne spoke again. 'You should go. I'll ring as soon as I have any kind of update.'

'Thank you,' Martin said. He cut the connection and stood up. His legs were still weak and he steadied himself against the arm of the chair. 'OK,' he said. 'Let's go.'

Wynne

The first few hours were critical. Best would likely have a place he could go to ground. Once he was there it would be hard to find him. It was while he was on the move that they had the best chance of catching him.

They had found a passport photo of him in a drawer in the house and that, along with the make, model and registration of his car, was now circulating among every police force in the country. Border Control also had the photo, as well as an alert on his passport. In case he had a fake, they had been told to look out for a man in his sixties travelling with a girl in her late twenties.

Wynne didn't think he would try and leave the country, though. It was too risky, especially since the description didn't stop at a man in his sixties and a woman half that age.

It also included a toddler.

There wasn't much in the room under the garage, but what there was included a child's clothes and some toys. She hadn't mentioned to Martin Cooper that he might have a grandchild, but it looked as though he did.

There was also a lot of blood, which must have left someone with some injuries. Such an unusual group travelling together, one of whom would look like they'd been in a boxing match, would draw a lot of attention to them.

So he may have got rid of them. Wynne doubted it. Not after so much time. Still, she'd make sure that the alert included the instruction to look out only for Best.

All in all, Wynne didn't think Best would be leaving the country. Where he was going, she didn't know. But it was important they find him before he got there.

Martin

Sandra's room was at the end of the corridor. Martin felt dazed as he walked along it, the nurse by his side.

Maggie had been held captive by Best? It was impossible. He'd been at their house. James had been at his house. He was their friend.

He felt sick. If it was true then it meant Best had done more than simply take their daughter. He had taken some perverse pleasure in watching them suffer.

And he still had her.

But she was – or at least might be – alive.

First, though, he had to see Sandra. He put his hand on the door, and pushed it open.

Wynne

There was a knock on the door of DI Wynne's office. DS Chan walked in. He was holding his car keys.

'They found it,' he said. 'They found Best's car.'

'Where?'

'On the Sparkedge industrial estate. It was parked behind a warehouse. There's a canal that runs past it and someone was jogging on the towpath. They called it in.'

'And?'

'No sign of them. The industrial estate is abandoned. Been that way for years.'

'Do we have anyone there?'

'Two officers. Another two are on the way. We've also called in the armed response gang. You never know.'

Wynne nodded. 'Let's go and check it out.'

Best's Ford Focus was hidden from the road. Wynne walked around it, taking in the details. Two forensic technicians were working inside it, methodically collecting whatever evidence there was to collect.

She looked around the industrial estate. There was a car park, grass growing through the tarmac where it had buckled and split, and four large buildings, their corrugated rooves rusting. Beyond them was a brown, fetid-smelling canal.

She gestured at the buildings. 'Have you been in?'

'All locked up,' said one of the PCs. He took off his helmet and scratched the back of his head. 'We've contacted the owners. They're sending someone who can open them.'

'There may be an entrance,' Wynne said. 'A side door, or window.'

'We had a good look,' the officer said. 'But it's possible.'

'Let's have another look,' Wynne said. 'Best must have brought them here for a reason.'

They divided the buildings up. Wynne and Chan took the one nearest. There was a double door at the front. The glass was grimy, but they could make out a reception area through it. The name of the company was still on the wall above the desk.

The door was secured by a chain.

'They didn't come through here,' Chan said. There was a large window to the left. At some point the glass had been broken and it had been covered with a board. 'And I don't think they got in there, either.'

They walked down the side. There were a series of high windows at least thirty feet above the ground. At the far end was a loading bay. It too was secured with a padlocked chain. Wynne picked up the padlock. She pulled it; it was locked.

'Not here either,' she said. She looked down the other wall of the building. There was a door about halfway along.

'Let's check that out,' Wynne said.

They walked along the building. The door was metal, and had the words 'Fire Escape' printed on it in faded red letters. There was no chain, and no padlock.

Chan glanced at Wynne. He walked up to the door and gripped the handle. It twisted and the door swung open.

'Get an officer,' Wynne said. 'I want backup.'

374

Martin

Sandra was lying on the bed. There was a cup of tea and a packet of biscuits on the table next to her. As the door opened, she looked at Martin.

The whole of his life seemed to crystallize in that moment. There were two possible futures, the left fork of illness and treatment and maybe the premature loss of his wife and the right fork of good health – for now, at least – and travel and growing old together.

And then there was Maggie. He didn't dare believe it yet, but if she was alive and Wynne could find her, what would she come home to? Would she be reunited with her mum, only to lose her again? It seemed impossible that the universe could be so cruel, but Martin had learned from bitter experience never to underestimate the capacity of the universe for cruelty.

He took a step into the room.

'So?' he said.

Sandra smiled.

'It's OK,' she said. 'I'm clear. I guess it really was just an upset stomach.'

Wynne

There were no lights, but in the beam of the torches they could see that the building was empty. It was a warehouse of some description, and, apart from a thick layer of dust, an unpleasant, animal smell and a stack of pallets in the far corner, there was nothing.

'There are offices at the front,' Wynne said. 'Where the reception is. Check those.'

Two officers – a man and a woman – headed for the front, their torches bobbing in the darkness. It was not long before they called out that there was nothing – and nobody – there.

Wynne and Chan walked out into the sunshine.

'Not in that building,' Chan said.

'There are three more,' Wynne said.

'I know.' Chan looked around. 'But there's no one here. No one's been here for years. You can tell.'

'You can't be sure.'

'No, but why would they go into one of these buildings? They'd be trapped,' Chan said. 'There's no way out. This place'll be crawling with uniforms soon.' He shook his head. 'Best wouldn't be here. He knows he'd get caught.'

Wynne nodded. 'Unless he doesn't care about that.'

'What do you mean?'

'Maybe being caught makes no difference to him. Maybe he brought them here to end it.'

'To kill them?'

'Murder–suicide,' Wynne said. 'It makes sense. Because if that isn't why he came here, then I don't know what the hell his reason could be.'

An hour later there were eight squad cars in the car park and every building had been searched.

There was no sign of Best, or Maggie, or a child, whether alive or dead, and there was no sign any of them had been in any of the buildings.

Wynne stood in the car park and tried to think. Chan walked over with a coffee and handed it to her.

'Why did he come here?' she said. 'Why come to this place in particular? What's special about it?'

'Maybe it's something close to here,' Chan said. 'A house? Or something else?'

Wynne turned to look at him. 'Right,' she said. 'Which means this is not his destination. It's a stopping point. He must have known that one day he might need to run. And he would have had a plan. He'd know that we would be looking for his car, so he'd need a new one. That's what this is. It's where he kept another vehicle, and that's where he is now. In some nondescript car on his way to wherever he's going to hide.'

She inhaled deeply.

'We need to go through everything in his life. Every document in his house, every photo, every record of anywhere he's been and anything he's done. Get his bank records. See if there are transactions clustered in a particular place. Cash withdrawals. We need to find somewhere he's visited more than normal. He's going to need a place, property of some

377

sort. If he has property there'll be a record of it. Something he inherited, maybe.'

Chan nodded. 'Or somewhere he has access to that nobody knows about. Something abandoned.'

'No.' Wynne sipped the coffee. 'I think he'd want control. An abandoned cottage or something like that would be too risky. He'll want his own place. And we'll find it. There'll be a trace, somewhere, and when we find it this'll be over.'

Sandra

'I'm fine,' Sandra said. 'I can walk to the car.'

Martin was holding her arm. The nurse had said she might be a little woozy, and he had taken it to heart. What she mostly felt was elation.

She was clear. It was a stomach upset and not a return of the cancer. There would be blood tests and check-ups for a while, but for now, she was in perfect health.

'OK,' he said. 'But there's something I have to tell you.'

There was a seriousness in his tone which she was not expecting. She was expecting joy and happiness and laughter. She stopped walking and turned to him.

'What is it?'

'Let's wait until we get to the car.'

'Martin. What is it? Tell me.'

His eyes flickered right and left, before he caught her gaze. For a moment she wondered if he was going to confess to something. An affair, maybe.

'DI Wynne called. You remember her?'

'How could I forget. What did she want?'

'She said they think Maggie has been held captive. They

found the room.' He took a deep breath. 'It was in Mr Best's house. Under his garage.'

It was a good job he was holding her. Whether it was the sedative or the news or a combination of both, she stumbled and he had to catch her.

'Best?' she said. '*He* took her? But – but he ate with us. He was my *teacher*.'

'I know. It's almost unbelievable.'

'Are they sure it's him?'

Martin nodded. 'They seem to be.'

Had his friendship all been a sham, then? It was hard to believe, but then she remembered the book he had been reading that time at the hospital. *The Collector*. It had struck her as odd at the time, but now she understood what had actually been going on. He had been toying with her, stringing her along for his own amusement.

Sandra felt something drain away from her – belief in the goodness of other people, maybe – as well as a rising anger – at Best, but also at herself. How had she missed it? How had she let him get away with it?

'Should we have known?' she whispered. 'Could we have seen it?'

'I don't know,' Martin said. 'But we can save that for later. Wynne said Maggie escaped and called 999. They traced the call to Best, but by the time they got to his house, he was gone. Maggie too.'

'So what are they doing?'

'Looking for them.'

'Oh, God. Is she alive?'

'They think so.'

'But with Best?'

'Yes.'

'Our little girl,' Sandra said. 'She's alive, Martin.'

'I hope so.'

'I know,' Sandra said. 'I always knew. We have to go home. She might get away from him again. We need to be there.' She stared at Martin. Why did he look so worried. 'Martin. You know what this means. She's alive! Our daughter's alive!'

'Yes,' he said. 'But she's with Best. And until she's back with us, I won't be celebrating.'

Wynne

Every airport, ferry terminal and other kind of border crossing was alerted to the possibility that Best might be trying to leave the country with Maggie Cooper and a toddler, either male or female, one or more of them with significant injuries.

They were also alerted to the fact it might only be Best and Maggie.

Or Best alone. In that case, they were looking for a man in his sixties, travelling alone.

And there were plenty of them. She pictured him on the Eurostar to Paris, settling into his seat with a cup of coffee and a newspaper, one more businessman in a suit making his way to a meeting.

Leaving Maggie Cooper in an unmarked grave, her child beside her.

No. He had dumped the car and left in another vehicle. He had a destination in mind and it wasn't abroad. But they had no idea where it was. They had found no records of any property he might have had. Of course, it could be in another name, a fake identity, and finding that could take a long time. Time they did not have.

The truth was, Best could be *anywhere*.

She banged her desk in frustration. DS Chan looked at her.

'I know,' he said. 'I can't believe we missed him. We were so close.'

'It's more than that,' Wynne said. 'It's the whole thing. I was involved in this at the beginning, and I went to Best's house. He was known to be interested in school girls, taking photos from his window, that kind of thing. We searched his house – without a warrant, I bullied him into it – and we missed her. I went in the garage. His car was there, parked over the fucking trapdoor.'

'You couldn't have known,' Chan said. 'He must have excavated that room himself.' He shook his head. 'He must have been planning this for years, getting ready for the right opportunity.'

'I should have known,' Wynne said. 'If I'd only taken more time.'

'No,' Chan said. 'There was no link to Best. It's not your fault.'

'It feels like it is. And now we – I – have missed him again. I'm starting to think it's not meant to be.' She picked up her phone. 'Time to call the Coopers. Give them the bad news.'

Martin

The phone rang as they were pulling into the house. Martin put it on speakerphone.

'DI Wynne,' he said. 'Is there any news?'

'I'm afraid not.' She paused. 'We did find Best's car. It was on the Sparkedge industrial estate. He'd abandoned it.'

Sandra leaned forward. 'Was there any sign of Maggie?'

'No. We had a lot of officers on the scene and they did a thorough search of the premises and the surroundings. There was nothing. We think Best left his car there and switched to some alternative means of transport.'

'He had a second car?' Martin said.

'That seems the most likely explanation.'

'So he was planning this?' Sandra asked.

'Perhaps not for today,' Wynne said. 'But it wouldn't be a surprise to find out that he had a contingency plan should he need to flee. And this could be it.'

'So where is he?' Martin said. 'Where are you looking?'

'We have a description of Best out nationally, along with what we think Maggie would look like now. All border control officials have been alerted to stop any couple who fit their description.'

'He might have changed his appearance,' Sandra said. 'And Maggie's.'

'They're looking for any older man and younger woman.' Wynne cleared her throat. 'There is something else.'

Martin glanced at Sandra. From her expression he could see that she too had picked up on the tone of Wynne's voice.

'What is it?' he said.

'There was evidence in the room where Maggie had been held that she might have had a child. A toddler. Aged from two to four.'

The world seemed to stop. For a second there was only silence.

'A child?' Martin said. 'Maggie has a child?'

'Possibly. If so, then it should make them easier to identify.'

Sandra was shaking her head. 'No,' she said. 'No. She can't have. He can't have done that to her. Not my little girl.'

'I'm sorry to break the news this way,' Wynne said. 'But it's important you know the facts. You should also know that we are looking into every aspect of Best's life to see if there are any indications as to where he might have gone. We will have all available resources on this. You can be assured of that.'

'Thank you,' Martin said. 'And please call if you have news. Anytime.'

He ended the call and turned to his wife.

'Holy shit,' he said. 'I can't believe this is happening.'

'She has a child,' Sandra said. 'Our *grandchild*.' She closed her eyes. 'They have to find her, Martin. They have to.'

'It's his child too,' Martin said. 'We need to think about that.'

'I don't,' Sandra said. 'I will love any child of Maggie's. But we need her back. That's all that matters now.'

'I'm going to tell James. I want him here with us.'

'OK,' Sandra said. 'Good idea.'

James

James wrapped the rubber band around his bicep and cinched it tight. His pulse sped up. Saliva filled his mouth. God, he wanted this.

His phone rang. He looked at the screen. Dad. He rejected the call. It rang again. He ignored it. Nothing mattered any more.

There was a buzz as a text message arrived.

Call now. Urgent.

Shit. Was it mum? She'd been ill. Maybe she was sick again. Well, if she was, all the more reason to go through with this. He picked up the needle and looked at the point, examined its sharpness, got ready for the prick and the rush.

His phone buzzed again.

Call me. It's about Maggie.

Maggie? What the fuck was this? He put the needle down and called his dad.

386

'Dad? It's me. What's up?'

'Where are you?'

'At the flat.'

'I'm on my way. I'll pick you up there.'

'No.' He didn't want to see him. 'What did you mean, it's about Maggie?'

There was a pause.

'They found her.' His dad sniffed. 'But then they lost her again.'

'They what?'

'It's a long story. I'll tell you when I see you.'

'Tell me now.'

'James—'

'Dad! Tell me now! I want to know what happened!'

'OK.' He heard the sound of an engine starting. 'I'll be there in a few minutes, but I'll fill you in on the way.'

'Best,' James said. He was sitting in the front seat of the car. 'That *fucking* bastard. If I ever get my hands on him I'll rip his *fucking* throat out. I was *at* his house, and she was there, under his *fucking* garage.'

'That's what DI Wynne said,' his dad replied.

'And he ran away?'

'Yes. He had a plan. He must have wondered if this day would come. They found his car at the Sparkedge industrial estate. He must have had a spare one hidden there.'

'So now he still has her but no one knows where he is.'

His dad drummed his fingers on the steering wheel. 'I know. I feel like someone has their hand in my stomach and is twisting it around and around.'

'Can we go to Sparkedge? I want to see.'

'I don't think there's much—'

'Just go, Dad. I want to have a look. She's my sister.'

His dad nodded. He turned left at the next roundabout.

Ten minutes later they were approaching the gates of the industrial estate.

A PC was standing by a car, arms folded. He walked over to James and Martin.

'I'm afraid you'll have to move on,' he said. 'This is a crime scene.'

'I'm Martin Cooper. Maggie's my daughter.'

'Oh. I see. I'm sorry, sir, but the premises are still off-limits.'

James listened. His hands shook. He looked at them, surprised at the physical manifestation of his need. For the last hour he hadn't thought of the needle or pills; all he had thought of was Maggie.

For the first time in years he felt alive. For the first time in years, he felt there was something worth doing.

He sat on his hands and made himself a promise. If Maggie was returned he would clean up. The drugs would be history.

His dad pointed towards the industrial estate. 'They think he kept a spare car here. One not linked to him, that he could use to flee if he needed it.'

He looked out of the front window at the four sprawling, derelict buildings. On one side was a scruffy field; on the other was run-down housing estate. Behind was the slick, oily canal.

James stared at it.

Best had talked to him once about canals, when he was tutoring him. What was it he'd said? Something about what he'd do if he won the lottery?

He grabbed his dad's elbow.

'Dad,' he said. 'I know where she is.'

Wynne

DI Wynne stood by the gates of the industrial estate. She had met James Cooper years ago and it was hard to believe this was the same person. He was thin, his hair patchy, his eyes sunken in a pallid, slack face.

'So,' she said. 'You have an idea where your sister may be?'

James shuffled from foot to foot.

'Maybe,' he said. 'Sort of.'

'Talk us through it,' Wynne replied.

'It's the canal,' he said. 'He brought her here because there's a canal. He didn't switch to a car, he switched to a boat.'

Wynne folded her arms 'You think he kept a boat here?'

'Yes.' James looked at her. 'When he was my tutor we were doing probability. He used the lottery as an example. He asked if I thought there was more chance of a set of random numbers coming up than a sequence of numbers – say one to six. I thought it was random but he showed me why it was mathematically the same. Then I asked him what he would do if he won the lottery. He told me he would get a canal boat and live on it. I remember him saying how you could go anywhere you wanted on the canals and no one would know. They go over the whole country . . .'

'Did he have a boat?' Wynne said. 'Did he ever mention that?'

'No,' James said. 'But I've not seen him for years. He could easily have bought one.'

'And if he had,' Wynne said, 'using it to conceal them would make sense. He'd know we'd be looking for a car.'

James Cooper turned to his dad. 'Them?' he said. 'He has more than one prisoner?'

DI Wynne glanced at the PC. 'Let's go and look for evidence of a boat,' she said. She turned to Martin Cooper. 'I think you might need to talk to your son for a few minutes.'

Wynne stood by the bank of the canal. At the far end of the industrial estate, and hidden from view unless you happened to be standing at this exact spot on the towpath, the canal widened. It was some kind of turning circle. It didn't look like it got much use – this whole stretch of the canal was not exactly popular with the pleasure boaters – and at the far end a large section of it was overgrown with thick, brambly bushes.

She walked over. If someone wanted to conceal a small houseboat they could do it there. It wouldn't exactly be hidden, but it would be obscured, and there was no one here to see it anyway.

Her heart rate rising, she approached the bushes. As she did the ground grew softer, the moisture kept in by the foliage.

She stopped and stared at the ground.

'Shit,' she said. 'He was right.'

In the soft ground there were sets of fresh footprints.

Saturday, 23 June 2018

Evening

Maggie

They were on a boat. The man had dragged her from the boot of his car and led her across some kind of wasteland to a white boat, moored on a canal. In those few moments she had stared at the sky. Breathed in the air. It was the first time she had been outside in more than a decade.

There was a cabin in the front and he had thrown her in. Max was still in the car and she had tried to ask about him but the words were muffled by the gag. The man slammed the door and left.

Maggie's arms were bound at the wrists and her ankles were tied. There was a gag stuffed in her mouth – *I'll do something more permanent later*, the man said – and she had a throbbing headache where the shovel had hit her.

The door opened and the man pushed Max into the cabin. He, too, was gagged. She had managed to pick him up by putting her bound wrists over his head and under his bottom. His face was dirty and streaked with tears; she pictured him, eyes wide with panic, as the man tied the gag around his head and shoved him into the cabin.

It was the first time he had ever been outside. Not a great way to start.

Then the engine had fired up and the boat had started to move. It was slow, and, in a small mercy, the gentle rocking had sent Max to sleep.

Leaving her alone to try and think what the man was planning.

Clearly, he was hoping to hide. The police would have come to the house and worked out what had been going on, and they would be looking for the man everywhere. The boat was perfect; nobody would think anything of another canal cruiser moored up for the night. He could keep them here as long as he wanted. She might be on a boat instead of in a cellar, but other than that her situation had not changed at all.

She lay down, Max asleep on her chest.

There was a bump and the rocking of the boat ceased. The hatch opened, and the man stepped into the cabin. He was wearing a hat and sunglasses.

'Well,' he said. 'You went and messed it all up.'

Maggie gestured to the gag. *Take it out and we can talk.*

The man gave a sardonic laugh. 'And have you start screaming? I can't trust you, Maggie. I thought I could, but I was wrong.' He pressed his palms together and held his forefingers against his mouth. 'You know, I thought, at first, that we could have a normal life together. Man and wife. Once you understood what I'd done for you, I was convinced you would see past my age and see that I was a good person. That I had your best interests at heart. Think about it for a second, you ungrateful bitch. Have you any idea how much work it was to excavate that basement? And you threw it back in my face. You were too ungrateful to see it. And too stupid. Too self-absorbed.' He folded his arms. 'But then, this. How could you do it?'

He took off his sunglasses. His eye was gone, a gaping red hole where it had been.

He winced in pain. Maggie was amazed he could stand it, but then he was not the same as other people. He was insane in ways she barely comprehended.

'How could you?' he said. 'How could you do this to me? All I wanted was to take care of you, and this is how you repay me?'

Maggie stared at his eye. It didn't repulse her; she wished she had done the same to the other one.

'Well,' he said. 'There's no way back after this. An argument I could have forgiven. Even an attack. But not this. This is too much. I'm afraid it's over between us, Maggie.'

She tilted her head. Over? What was over?

'If I can't have you, nobody can.'

He reached up to a shelf by his head and picked something up.

It was a knife, the blade long and sharp.

'You brought this on yourself, Maggie, you really did. I can't go home now – the police will have been there – and I can't keep you two with me. If I'm to survive, I need to be on my own. I could let you go, but you know about my boat and you can't be trusted. So I'm afraid I have no option.'

He looked at the knife, his eyes running up and down the blade.

'I've thought it through and I have no choice.'

Maggie kept her eye on the knife. She knew now what was coming, but that was fine. Death was better than the life she'd had.

She nodded, and shrugged.

Wynne

Wynne turned to DS Chan. 'How far can they be? Those boats are pretty slow, right?'

'Four miles an hour,' Chan replied. 'Maybe five.'

'And Best has two or three hours' start? So they're within ten or fifteen miles. We need to look inside every boat within twenty miles of here. Get a map of the canal and get officers on bikes pedalling every foot of them.'

Chan nodded. 'He may have ditched the boat, too,' he said. 'He could be back on the road.'

'We'll keep that search ongoing,' Wynne replied. 'Either way, we'll find the boat and we'll track the bastard down from there.'

PC Oliver Reid

PC Oliver Reid had come off his shift at six a.m. and slept until one in the afternoon. Then he'd spent a few hours watching his son's rugby match, and arranged to meet a friend for a pint after he walked his dog, Benjy.

The springer spaniel ran ahead of him, sniffing in the hedges and picking up this trail or that before moving on. Reid lived in a small village south of Warrington, and his dog walks took him deep into the Cheshire countryside. It always surprised him how remote it seemed. Liverpool was thirty miles to the west and Manchester thirty miles to the east, but out here felt like the middle of nowhere.

Up ahead, a humpback bridge crossed the Bridgewater canal. He normally picked up the canal towpath at the bridge and followed it back towards the village. As he approached, his phone rang. He glanced at the screen.

It was the station.

'Olly,' it was Pete Faro, the duty sergeant. 'You still sober?'

'I'm tempted to say no,' Reid replied. 'In about an hour I planned not to be. I'm assuming you need something?'

'Yup. People in. Feet on the street, so to speak. Big search about to happen.'

'For who?'

'You remember that teenage girl who went missing, years ago? Maggie Cooper?'

'Yeah. Something new turn up?'

'It did. She'd been held captive. They found the place, but it was empty. Whoever took her fled with her. That's who we're looking for. Guy in his sixties.'

'OK. I'll be in. What's the drill? Roads, railways, ports?'

'No,' Faro said. 'Canals.'

It was about two miles back to his house. He walked quickly; PC Reid wanted to get into the station as soon as he could. He knew that time was critical in this kind of search; if they were going to find the girl their chances were at their highest early on.

The canal curved to the right. As he rounded the bend he saw a boat. There was a man standing on the towpath next to it, securing the mooring.

He was in his sixties. But then there were a lot of people that age on canal boats.

Probably settling down for the evening. The sun was getting low in the sky. As he climbed aboard the boat he glanced back at Oliver, then he disappeared below deck.

Maggie

The man's dark eyes held Maggie's gaze. He lifted the knife so the point was right in front of her nose.

This was it. This was the end.

Outside the canal boat she heard a dog barking. It was the first since she was fifteen. It was a beautiful sound. She was happy to have heard it before she died.

The frosted window in the cabin darkened as the dog passed.

If she died. She felt a sudden spring of hope.

Where there were dogs, there were owners. Owners who could get her out of this.

Maggie jumped up and launched herself across the boat. Her head thudded into the plastic window. She turned to the side to keep Max from slipping from her grasp, then banged her head into the window again.

'Help!' she screamed through the gag, although the words came out as a muffled shout. 'Wearrhg!'

The man jumped forward and clapped his hand over her mouth. He twisted her head savagely to the side and held the knife to her throat. She felt like her neck might break.

'Quiet!' he hissed. 'You stay fucking quiet. I'm going to

397

enjoy killing you. It's your own fault. You're too much trouble.'

Maggie looked up at the window from the corner of her eye, waiting for it to darken as someone walked back.

There was nothing.

PC Oliver Reid

Reid heard a thud and stopped a few feet past the boat. Probably just the man he'd seen putting something away.

The man. There was something odd about him. Reid pictured him, tying the boat to a mooring then – with a glance at Reid – climbing aboard.

There'd been no friendly wave, or call of 'good evening', which was typical of canal boaters.

And the man was wearing sunglasses, which was odd, because the sun was setting and he was moored in the shade of a large oak tree.

There was another thud from the boat.

Reid whistled softly. Benjy ran up to him.

'Come on, boy,' he said. 'Let's take a look.'

He turned, and walked back towards the boat. At his heel, Benjy barked.

Maggie

The window darkened again. There was barely the hint of a shadow, but it was there. She pulled Max tighter against her. The knife was sharp against her throat.

There was a knock on the hatch.

The man held his hand tighter over her mouth.

'Hello?' he said. 'Who is it?'

'Just checking everything's OK,' a man's voice said. 'I heard a bang. Wondered whether you'd slipped.'

'No, I'm fine. Dropped a kettle, that's all. But thanks for asking.'

There was a pause. 'Could I come in?'

'No,' the man said. 'I don't think so. My wife's getting dressed.'

'I can wait. I only want to help if there's a problem.'

The man tensed. 'It's really OK,' he said. 'And to be honest, I don't want you on my boat. I don't know who you are. You could be anyone.'

'Oh, I'm no one. A concerned citizen.'

'If you don't leave, I'm going to call the police.' The man waited a second, then changed his tone, as though he was speaking to someone in the cabin with him. 'Darling, could you pass my phone? I've had enough of this.'

He was going to do it, Maggie saw. He was going to get rid of this man and then move the boat somewhere else and then kill her and Max.

This was, without any question, her last chance.

She gripped Max's big toe, pressed her nails into the skin, and dug in, hard.

His eyes flew open and he looked at her in shock. He opened his mouth and screamed. It was muffled by the gag, but it was still loud.

It was still a child screaming.

There was a bang on the hatch, then another. Someone started to shake it. The lock was weak and there was a splintering sound as it ripped open. A man's face appeared against the light and looked at her, then the man, then Max.

'Hold it right there,' he said. 'Police.'

The man had moved his hand from her mouth to her chin and lifted it, exposing her neck. He pressed the tip of the knife against it.

'Stay there,' he said. 'Or I kill her.'

The man in the doorway – who'd said he was police, but was not wearing a uniform – shook his head.

'Don't be stupid,' he said. 'This is over. Put the knife down.'

The man drew the knife over her skin. She felt warm blood run down her neck and over her chest.

'Jesus,' the man in the doorway said. 'You fucking fool.'

He stepped into the cabin and stood opposite the man.

'My name is PC Oliver Reid. I—'

The man let go of her and lunged forward, slashing at the policeman with the knife. The PC dodged out of the way, then grabbed the man's hand and bent it backwards at the wrist. There was a loud snap like a branch breaking and the man screamed.

Maggie backed away, holding Max, and watched as the policeman forced the man face down on the yellowing carpet.

'Listen, mate,' the policeman said. 'I'm trained in this and you're an old fella, so let's be sensible, OK?' He looked at Maggie. 'Are you Maggie Cooper?'

She nodded. The policeman beckoned her towards him. He untied the gag, and, with the knife the man had held at her throat, cut through the rope binding her wrists and ankles.

'And who's this?' he said.

'My son. Max.' It was the first time she had spoken to anyone other that Max, Seb, Leo or the man in over a decade. She could barely believe it was happening.

The policeman glanced at the man. 'I see,' he said. He nodded at a coil of green rope hanging on a hook by the sink. 'Could you pass that to me?'

Maggie put Max down and got to her feet. As she did, the man twisted. There was another loud crack – something else breaking – and he screamed, but he managed to get on his back. He kicked the policeman hard in the stomach and, for a second, he was free.

It was enough. The man scrambled to his feet and grabbed Max, then clambered through the hatch and on to the deck of the boat.

Maggie

'Max!' Maggie shouted. 'Max!'

The policeman jumped to his feet and followed the man outside. Maggie climbed out after him. She saw the man running down the towpath. She frowned. The policeman wasn't chasing him. He was looking at the canal.

'Shit,' he said. 'Fuck it.'

And then he jumped into the muddy brown water.

Maggie looked over the side of the boat and saw why. Max was in the canal, coughing and spluttering. The man had thrown him overboard. She watched as the policeman picked him up.

She turned. The man was about fifty yards away, running as fast as he could.

Which wasn't very fast. He was limping badly. She looked at the policeman. Max was clinging to his neck, coughing.

'Here,' the policeman said, holding Max out. 'Take him. I need to get after that bastard.'

'No,' Maggie said. 'I'll get him. I want him to know that after all these years, I still beat him.'

* * *

403

She made up the ground quickly. The man looked over his shoulder and tried to speed up, but it was pointless. She was much faster.

And then, without warning, he slowed to a walk.

A man and woman were walking towards him. They were in their late sixties, the man wearing a green tweed hat, white hair poking out from under it, the woman a quilted gilet. Each one of them was holding the hand of a small, blond-haired boy.

The man pointed at Maggie.

'Help,' he said. 'She's a thug. She's tormenting me. Can you stop her?'

The man in the hat frowned. He stepped in front of the two small boys. 'Stay back, Harry and George,' he said. He looked at Maggie. 'What's going on here? What are you up to?'

Maggie thought for a moment about explaining, but she was suddenly too tired. This had to stop. And what the man had done to Max had given her an idea.

She lunged at the man and shoved him as hard as she could. He stumbled, and fell into the canal.

The woman gasped. 'What on earth—'

A voice interrupted. 'Everybody stay calm.' Maggie turned. The policeman was walking up to them, Max in his arms. He handed him to Maggie. He was dripping wet. 'Everything's fine. I'm a police officer.'

The woman folded her arms. 'What on earth is happening here?'

Maggie squeezed Max tight.

'I'm Maggie Cooper,' she said. 'And this is Max.' The black-and-white spaniel sniffed her knee. 'Is this your dog?' she said.

'Yes. He's called Benjy.'

Maggie put out a hand and the dog licked it. It felt wonderful.

'Max,' she said. 'This is a *dog*.'

404

Maggie

She could see that Max was happier when they were alone in a room again. It was a room in the police station, and it had windows and a door that she could walk out of any time she liked, but it was at least a setting familiar to Max, and once they were in there he started to calm down.

He had found the activity – and it had been a whirl of police officers swarming over the boat and asking her questions then leading them to a police car – overwhelming. When the car started to move he began shaking, his eyes wide with fear. Maggie held him tight and whispered in his ear that everything would be OK.

And it would.

They were free.

They were out of the room.

The man – Best, she had heard them calling him – was gone from her life.

There was a knock on the door and a woman came in. She had short hair and bags under her eyes and was wearing a dark suit.

'Hello,' she said. 'Can I sit down?'

Maggie nodded. She and Max were sitting on a couch and

the woman took an armchair facing it. Next to Maggie was a table with two glasses of orange juice on it; she took one and for the first time since the man had taken her, she drank from a glass.

'Would you like anything else?' the woman asked. 'Something to eat?'

Maggie shook her head. 'No, thank you.'

'OK. Well, let me know if you do.' The woman clasped her hands in her lap. 'I'm Detective Inspector Wynne. I've been working on your case for a long time and at some point I'm going to want to talk to you about what happened, but not now, and not until you're ready. For now, we're going to focus on getting you whatever you need.'

'I want to see my mum and dad,' Maggie said.

'They're on their way. We contacted them as soon as we found you and they're coming. I think your brother is with them as well.'

Her mum and dad and brother. She'd thought of them so many times when she was in the room, wondered what they were doing, how they looked, if they were happy.

If they were even alive.

And now she was going to see them, and she couldn't wait. Her stomach was a ball of nerves; it felt like the anticipation of every exam and every Christmas and every date all rolled into one.

'Are they – are they OK?' she said.

The door opened and a woman looked in. She nodded at the detective.

'Well,' DI Wynne said, and smiled. 'You can find out for yourself. They're here.'

Martin

They had been in this same place at the beginning.

In these corridors, in these rooms, meeting police and lawyers and journalists, their world collapsing around them.

It was here it had become clear they had lost Maggie. And now they were back.

She was back.

He had accepted long ago it would never happen. At first he had believed she would be found, then he had hoped she might be found, then he feared she wouldn't be found, and finally he had accepted she was gone forever.

A PC, a man in his twenties, led them to a door.

'This is the room,' he said. 'And I don't know if this is the right word, but congratulations.'

Martin held Sandra's hand in his left hand and James's in his right.

'Thank you,' he said.

The PC opened the door.

She was sitting on a brown couch. Her feet were bare and she was wearing grey tracksuit bottoms and a black coat. She was thin, and very pale.

She was holding a little boy. He looked up at the noise, his eyes fearful.

She looked up.

Those blue eyes. They hadn't changed. The light was still there.

She smiled, then her lips started to quiver and tears came to her eyes and she started to get to her feet and he ran across the room and they were hugging, all of them, Sandra, James, him and Maggie, the little boy, back together, a family again after so, so long.

'Fruitcake,' he said. 'My little Fruitcake. I love you. I missed you.'

Maggie heaved with sobs. He held her to him again. He inhaled deeply. Despite what she'd been through, despite where she'd been, she smelled exactly as he remembered. He inhaled again.

He felt something kick him in the stomach. The boy started to cry.

'Mummy,' he said. 'I want you, Mummy.'

Martin stepped back and looked at him. He kissed Maggie again.

'Who's this?' he said.

'This is Max,' Maggie said. 'My son.'

Sandra wiped tears from her eyes.

'Hello, Max,' she said. She put a hand on the back of his head. 'He's beautiful. He looks just like James did at that age.'

Max shrank away from her touch.

'He's not used to all these people,' Maggie said. 'He doesn't know you're his grandparents.' She looked at James. 'Or his uncle.'

'He can take all the time he wants to get used to us,' Martin said. 'Let's go home.' He turned to DI Wynne. 'If that's OK?'

She smiled. 'That's fine. I'll get Maggie some shoes. I think we have some trainers she can wear.'

She left the room. Martin looked at his wife and son and daughter and grandson and his heart swelled with love for them all.

He put his arms around his daughter. She pressed her face against his neck.

'Welcome back, Fruitcake,' he said. 'Everything's going to be OK, I promise. Better than OK. It's going to be perfect.

Epilogue

Six months later

Maggie had chosen to wear bright colours for the funeral. There had been enough darkness in the last twelve years to last her a lifetime, and she felt it was right to be dressed in red or green or yellow or whatever she wanted.

The two small coffins were at the front of the funeral parlour. She did not want a church funeral; she had never been much interested in religion and whatever vague faith she might have had, had been extinguished in the room. No god she wanted to worship would do that to her.

Or Max.

Or Seb, or Leo.

They had found their remains in Delamere Forest. The man – Colin Best, he was called – had refused to divulge the whereabouts of Seb and Leo's bodies at first; but then another prisoner had broken into his cell – it had been left unlocked in an unfortunate oversight – and the next day Best said he was ready to tell the police where the bodies were.

The police exhumed them, and they were not the only bodies they found. There was a pet cemetery of people's dogs and cats, along with the body of a woman in her twenties.

The police thought it might be a prostitute who had gone missing in the late nineties.

She sat at the front, and looked at the two coffins. They were closed – there was not much left of Seb and Leo – and she was glad. She preferred to remember them as they were. She had described them to James and her parents, although they would never know what their other two grandsons looked like. There were no photos. That was one of the many things that Colin Best had taken from them and from her.

Her dad sat on her left, his hand on her arm. He was exactly as she remembered him. Warm, thoughtful, loving, and still telling his terrible dad jokes. There was a wariness to him that was new – he didn't let her go anywhere alone, which she was going to have to talk to him about – but other than that he was the dad she remembered.

Mum had been ill, it turned out, and you could see it in the lines on her face. According to the doctors she was fine now, but it had left its mark.

And James. Her little brother, James. He was over his addiction, although she still saw the hunger in his eyes from time to time.

Max was – incredibly – fine. At first he had asked about the room and the man all the time, but that had gradually slowed until he didn't mention it at all. He still saw a child psychiatrist; she told Maggie that, although he had some developmental delays, they would resolve themselves on their own and he would grow up a normal, well-adjusted child. Maggie marvelled on a daily basis at how easily he had adapted. He went to a pre-school, had a group of friends, watched television, and sat, for hours on end, watching his grandad build a huge, electric train set for him.

And her? She saw a psychiatrist too. She had nightmares; she didn't like sleeping with the door open; she struggled to trust people, especially men. The weirdest part had been when she had, for a few days, started to *miss* the room. Everything felt like a threat; she didn't dare take her eyes off Max. At least the room was safe.

Except it wasn't. It was slowly destroying her, and the man would have killed Max. He was going to do it that day. She had the scars on her fingers to prove it.

And the feeling of missing it didn't last. Now she was glad, every day, to wake up and look out of a window and see a tree or the rain on the glass or a bird in the sky. She'd taken Max to see some of the things she'd described to him: the sea, the forest, the mountains. He'd especially loved the animals at Chester Zoo.

It was time for Seb and Leo to be cremated. She had wept when Best confessed where their graves were, images of them playing and laughing coming back to her. They would never meet Max, but when he was older she would tell him about his brothers, share the daydreams she had about the people they might have become.

That, though, was for another day. After the funeral they were going to travel, her, Max, James, Mum, and Dad. She had a list of places she wanted to see. Places she wanted Max to see.

Places she had told him about.

Australia. Thailand. Nepal.

London. Paris. New York.

Mountains. Lakes. Rivers.

They were going to see them *all*.

Acknowledgements

The more books I write the more I feel that the space dedicated to thanking those who have provided guidance, counsel, support and encouragement is too brief to truly acknowledge how important they are.

So, that said:

Thank you, Sarah Hodgson, for your wisdom and guidance on *Seven Days* and the other books we have worked on together. Your editorial insights have made them better than I could ever have done alone.

Thank you, Becky Ritchie. I always feel like you have my and the books' best interests at heart which – along with your advice and unfailing support – is all one can wish for in an agent.

Thank you to the team at HarperCollins, in particular Kathryn Cheshire. I appreciate all the effort and dedication you put in.

Thank you to Tahnthawan and Barbara, once more vital early readers.

And thank you to my three sons. You are an inspiration.

Read on for a sneak preview of
Alex Lake's new novel

Coming Autumn 2020

Prologue

I told them I was trouble.

I told them I would not allow them to do this to me.

I *told* them I would take revenge.

But they did not believe me. And now they will find out they made a mistake. A big mistake. A mistake which – although they did not know it at the time – changed their lives.

You will think of what I have done – what I am doing – as the worst crime imaginable. You will read about it in the news and hear about it on the radio and gossip about it with your colleagues and say how wicked and evil I must be to do such a thing.

But you will be wrong.

You will hate me, even though you will not know who I am. All you will know is that I have done this terrible thing to these lovely people.

I don't deny it.

And I would do it again.

Because they *deserve* it.

And I deserve it, too.

1

It was the smell that woke him.

Graham Dean opened his eyes. The room was dark, the curtains drawn. The small fan on his bedside table buzzed gently.

There was definitely a smell.

He sniffed.

It was the smell of smoke. He glanced at the curtains. He thought the window was closed, but it was possible they had left it open. The neighbours were younger than him and Kathryn and didn't have kids, so at the weekends they often had people over. Maybe they were having a fire in the garden.

He reached out and turned off the fan. He listened for the sound of voices. Nothing.

Which was not a surprise. When he turned off the fan he had seen the alarm clock. It was just past three in the morning; even their noisy neighbours wouldn't be up this late.

He sniffed again, smelling the air. There was *definitely* a smell of smoke. It wasn't wood smoke, or the smell of cooking food. It was harsher, more chemical. Acrid, almost. He paused, waiting for it to pass. It didn't. If anything it got stronger.

Not a fire next door, then, but a fire somewhere. Maybe

a building, or a car. He'd seen a news story about kids stealing cars and setting them alight, but that didn't happen around here.

Or it hadn't, at least to date. He got out of bed and opened the curtains, looking for a red haze or a plume of smoke.

Nothing. He opened the window and leaned out.

The night air was fresh and clean. There was no smell of fire at all. He pulled his head back inside the room. The smell was back, which meant the fire was not outside.

It was in his house. The house he and Kathryn shared with Jake, their five-year-old son.

He sprinted to the bedroom door and yanked it open.

And he saw the source of the smell. His house was *ablaze*.

2

The landing stretched in front of him. On the left were doors to two more bedrooms and a bathroom; to the right were the stairs.

And at the far end was Jake's bedroom.

Which was also where the fire was.

Jake's door – half-open – was at the heart of the fire. It glowed red, the frame a gaping mouth of flame. The heat – even at the far end of the landing – was intense. Graham waved his hand in front of his mouth and coughed, the air thick with smoke.

'Jake!' he shouted. 'Jake! Are you there?'

There was no answer, but even if there had been it was unlikely he would have heard it over the noise of the fire.

'Graham.' He heard his wife's voice from inside the bedroom. 'Why are you shouting?'

'There's a problem,' he said. 'Get out of bed.'

He stared at the heart of the fire, the skin on his face feeling tight with the heat.

And then he heard his wife scream.

'Jake!' she said. 'Where's Jake?'

Graham pointed at the fire. 'He's in there.'

'Get him!' she shouted. 'Go and get him!' She started to move towards their son's bedroom but he put his hand on her shoulder.

'I'll go,' he said. 'Get your phone and call 999. Then go outside. It's not safe.'

Kathryn nodded and ran into their bedroom. He stared at the fire, mesmerized. It was a wall of flame, and Jake was on the other side. He took a step towards it, then another, and raised his hands. It was already incredibly hot.

Wet towels, he thought. *Wrap yourself in wet towels.*

He pushed the bathroom door open and turned on the bath. He grabbed three towels and shoved them under the water, then, when they were wet, wrapped one around his head and one around his shoulders. The third was for Jake.

He ran onto the landing and turned towards Jake's room. The smoke was thicker now, and the popping and snapping noise of the fire was louder. The heat was fierce, but the cold water on the towels gave him some protection. Dimly he remembered hearing something about getting down and crawling if you were in a fire. Maybe there was more oxygen down there, the smoke rising.

He dropped to his knees and began to crawl towards his son's room.

He realized almost immediately that it was hopeless. The heat was like a physical barrier. He could feel it pushing back at him, the heat scorching his face as he inched closer.

He felt a sharp pain on his head. The water in the towel was boiling and turning to steam. He snatched the towel away and cast it aside.

He crawled forward again, deeper into the heat.

And then he realized he couldn't breathe. There was no oxygen. It was all being consumed by the fire. Even if he could have withstood the heat somehow, there was no way he could last more than a minute or so without breathing.

It was a place unfit for humans.

'Jake,' he gasped. 'Jake. Please.'

His lungs were starting to hurt; he tried to breathe, but all he felt was hot air filling his chest. He had no choice. He had to back away, find some air.

Leave his son.

There *was* no son, not anymore. There was no way he could have survived this. No way at all.

As soon as there was air he let out a cry. He heard it as though he was in some way disembodied; it was a mixture of pain and anguish and despair. His son – his firstborn – was only feet away from him but it might as well have been miles. There was nothing he could do.

He backed up further, his right hand on the base of the bannister, feeling his way to the top of the stairs.

When he reached them, he looked up at his son's bedroom.

At the space where his son's bedroom had been.

It was a scene from hell. The end of the house was gone, replaced by a gaping red maw.

On his hands and knees, he crawled down the stairs.

MORE FROM

The real nightmare starts when her daughter is returned...

A girl is missing. Five years old, taken from outside her school. She has vanished, traceless.

The police are at a loss; her parents are beyond grief. Their daughter is lost forever, perhaps dead, perhaps enslaved.

But the biggest mystery is yet to come: one week after she was abducted, their daughter is returned.

She has no memory of where she has been. And this, for her mother, is just the beginning of the nightmare.

There's a serial killer on the loose. And the victims all look like you...

A serial killer is stalking your home town.

He has a type: all his victims look the same.

And they all look like you.

Kate returns from a post break-up holiday with her girlfriends to news of a serial killer in her home town – and his victims all look like her.

It could, of course, be a simple coincidence.

Or maybe not.

She becomes convinced she is being watched, followed even. Is she next? And could her mild-mannered ex-boyfriend really be a deranged murderer?

Or is the truth something far more sinister?